"OK, you know the drill. Stay close, and don't panic. If anything goes er... *wrong*, give JC or Helen a shout right away, is that all clear? I'll be staying here 'til you come back. I've other matters I've got to deal with. Sorry to miss out on this challenge – please have some fun. See y'all later."

David Cooper's tone came across as a bit authoritarian but was understandable in the circumstances. Jason, David's son, still wasn't convinced.

Looking around at the assembled small group of guests JC, as Jason was fondly known, wondered if they could possibly get away with this one. Today was supposed to be some kind of psychodrama but all JC could see was a bunch of seriously committed cross-dressers about to go out to a really wild party in Swansea or maybe California, one or the other.

Helen Pope, the Medical Director of *The Place,* in her infinite wisdom, had announced the night before that the current batch of in situ celebrities – Tracy, Huck, Richard, Annie, Toni and Betty – would engage in some ground-breaking and innovative 'Gender-Reversal-Therapy'. This would involve each guest being dressed up by Helen as a member of the opposite sex. The entire troupe would then follow a secluded path leading from the rear exit of the gardens of *The Place,* down a private lane which lead to a discreet entrance to Hampstead Heath and then on to single-sexed bathing ponds. The challenge was for Huck, Toni and Richard to have a 'quick dip' in the ladies-only pond and Annie, Betty and Tracy to take a quick dip in the men-only pond.

It was a testament to Helen's authority – *'Le Pose'* as she called it – that no one, not for one moment, questioned the intended purpose of this exercise; it was clearly for their own good.

Huck 'the Micro-Psycho', a vertically-challenged cage fighter by day and a cross-dresser by night, was in his element. Huck looked so happy and excited; his raw enthusiasm was quite infectious. The group had assembled in the rear patio area of *The Place* usually reserved for 'The Graduation Ceremony'. It was not yet 10 a.m. on a clear, crisp spring morning and the group had been preparing for nearly two hours.

As a small but perfectly-formed trained martial artist, Huck had developed well-proportioned and alarmingly flexible kicking legs which he was quite keen to show off. Huck twirled to and fro in front of the full-length mirror, making sure that just enough leg was on show and his butt looked hot, "You're as hot as your butt" being Huck's favourite pre-evening-out war cry. The shapely and newly shaven legs were exposed up to his knees until guarded by the mid-length skirt which, combined with a tidy tight-fitting jacket, worked surprisingly well Huck thought. The late addition of the tiny purple bell-boy hat was – as all present readily confirmed – quite inspired. Huck stood sideward and studied his profile in the mirror, flicking the hair of his full length wig across his ears whilst pushing around his make-shift boobs this way and that.

"Your tits are fine, Huck – I'd swop them for mine any

day. At least they're both the same size. If you think of a drunken chef trying to fry two eggs at the same time you've got an insight into my boobs, Huck. You don't want to know what I'd do to my surgeon; I'd make you look like a pussy. Not my pussy of course, that's another story you don't want to know."

Annie – 'Botox Annie' to friends and foes alike – was determined to have a ball, pushed Huck away from the mirror with one swing of her hips and took a long gaze at the image she was bravely standing in front of.

Placing a bald head piece over Annie's thinning real hair in combination with some loose-fitting workman's overalls and heavy boots was all that was needed to give the plausible impression of a male, of sorts. Annie was taken aback as to how effective the transition worked, with so little effort. She studied her reflection and thought of a rugby-player-turned-builder she once experienced, and sighed.

Tracy Howler, looked very subdued, frightened almost. Dressed in a loose-fitting macho tracksuit and baseball cap she looked even younger than her actual age of twenty-four and was the only one who appeared terrified of Helen's challenge.

Richard Fingal Beckett, being an intellectual middle-aged bipolar manic depressive comedian, was, unsurprisingly, not convinced. "Do I really, you know, look like a woman?" The question was directed at no one in particular.

Helen decided to intervene before the conversation took a wrong turn.

"OK, ladies and gentlemen the challenge will start in a couple of minutes. Please do not engage in any conversation with anyone outside the group. We've having a quick dip then straight back the way we came. I'll be with the girls and JC will look after the boys. Betty, please stop fussing – you look *fine*."

Betty Grisse was having some difficulty in accepting that she looked fine and had serious doubts that she looked anything like a plausible member of the opposite sex, for good reason. Helen had all manner of props hidden away in the extensive wardrobes of *The Place* for such occasions but Betty had the biggest obstacle to overcome – her hippo-sized arse.

In the end Helen had a brainwave and decided that Betty should go a bit 'Arabesque' and don a full-length *Thoub* – a long sleeved, one piece garment made of light white cotton. On her head was a blue and white tea-towel which made a decent enough substitute for the more traditional *Shumagg* and a brightly-coloured headband gave a fair impression of what should have been a black *Ogal* to hold the headpiece in place.

There had been much debate about whether Betty needed a moustache to round off the full intended effect, an issue which was yet to be resolved.

"Helen, about the moustache? What do you think, really?"

"Betty, didn't we make a decision about the moustache, I mean a firm decision?" Helen, sounded slightly exasperated. "Yes, a moustache would look better but you were worried it would come off in the pond."

JC from the beginning feared this was a personal challenge too far and lost it completely, bursting out in a muffled laughter which he tried to disguise with a sort of strangled cough. It didn't work.

'OK, JC, out with it, what's so funny?" Helen knew

how to deal with this one.

"What's so funny?" JC looked around the group and let forth an uninhibited scream of laughter. 'What's so funny? Are you joking Helen?"

Helen knew JC would think quickly enough to diffuse the tension and even Tracy pursed her lips hiding a half smile.

"Look, it's not about whether Betty needs a moustache or not or it's more a question of what happens when Betty takes off that robe thingy... Betty – go on give us a preview."

Betty rolled her eyes and hesitantly lifted the enormous cotton garment to reveal the lower half of a full-length wet suit. Even Betty would have conceded that she looked a like a whale or some as-yet-to-be-discovered creature from the deep.

"And you're worried about the moustache?" JC tried to be serious for a moment. "Look Betty why don't we just draw on a small moustache with some waterproof mascara? You've got a skull cap under your head scarf. You've got goggles. Keep a towel around you once you've taken the robe off, we'll sort of surround you when you get into the water and when you come out. It'll be fine. At this time on a weekday there's likely to be only one or two men around, if any. And if there are any men, I mean real men, they'll be so old I can guarantee they won't bat an eyelid. It'll be fine, believe me. So, let's do the moustache thing and then we can get going, OK?"

"You can use mine, if you like" Huck said, dipping into a dainty wee bag now hanging on his arm.

Betty shrugged her big shoulders and nodded awkward-ly, with feigned resignation.

"OK, JC. Fine with me. I mean what can go wrong?" Betty didn't like being sarcastic, but on this occasion was ready to make an exception.

2

Simon Hall was only twenty-eight, but had been the editor-in-chief for the *Sunday News* for nearly two years. He sat behind his cluttered desk in his large disorganised office and stared firmly at the aging hack, Ralph Crossley, in front of him.

"Ethics is for suckers and philosophers, Ralph. I'm a straight enough kind of guy but it's like they're talking about some code that I haven't read."

Ralph Crossley, despite being a veteran investigative red top journalist of some experience, didn't look convinced.

"As far I understand, ethics isn't a go-to-jail-thing but isn't what we're doing like illegal, Simon? Journos were arrested and jailed for this, weren't they? Hacking people's stuff is jail-time, isn't it?"

"Listen, Ralph, I've told you before. If you haven't got the balls for this game then retrain as a plumber or something. Yeah, the heat is on but the game is still in play. The goons at the *News of the World* went too far, they lost the most important knack of all, Ralph – the art of not being caught. Speeding on the motorway at eighty miles an hour is illegal, but if you know there are cameras watching you don't do it. Simples."

"Yeah, but you don't go to jail for speeding on the motorway do you, Simon?"

Simon took another long hard look at Ralph and wondered whether it was time to contact Human Resources and get the ball rolling for another redundancy. "Ralph, get my point or get out of this job. We're not hacking into anyone's phone; this isn't phone hacking. Besides, don't you recall the fundamental lesson every hack in the world learnt after the closing of *'The News of the World'* and all the fall-out from the Leveson enquiry?

"Er, was it to respect other people's privacy... no, hold on – that was it – don't get caught."

"Well, done Ralph. Top of the class. I understand that the legal difference between accessing a phone message and accessing information held on a computer is a bit much for your generation, old boy, but our lawyers get it, so relax, OK? It's a bit late to be having a moral attack at this stage, Ralph, we're in too deep already."

Ralph took a deep heavy sigh and knew Simon was right. It was too late to turn back.

"Listen, Ralph, listen carefully. Turn up the volume on your hearing aid. Our guy out there isn't you know – hacking into phone calls or even messages. What he's doing is access-ing the computer network. I mean it's not our fault if those crooks are so dumb they don't understand that their wireless connection is so unsecure you just need to be within a hundred metres of their system, type in their wireless pass-word and hey presto – all is revealed. The Russian Trade Delegation next door aren't so stupid, are they?"

Ralph still wasn't convinced and straightened up. "But we're still you know intercepting private communications whether they're phone calls or not; isn't that go to jail stuff?"

Simon was on the verge of losing it with Ralph com-pletely but managed to control himself for another round. "Listen again Ralph, read my lips you aging dipstick. It's only

the computer systems we're having a little look at; it's completely different from phone hacking. Is the penny beginning
to drop? How our guy got their password isn't our concern.
As far as I'm concerned he's parked his car near Hampstead
Heath intending to go for a little stroll. He decides to do
some work on his laptop, types in the wrong password and
what do you know – he's suddenly in amongst the suppos-
edly secure network of a private rehab place for frigging
celebrities. Don't look so cynical, Ralph, it works for me.
Our Q.C. has said that provided we're not damaging or interfering with their system or threatening national security
we're OK jail-wise. So, just get on with it, OK? Besides,
we're not going to spill the beans on all that whacky stuff
that the celebs are paying through the nose for, or their personal problems; we know we'd have a *super* injunction up our
rear ends within an hour of asking them for a comment.
Keep focussed, Ralph, we're doing a turn on those tricksters
that run *The Place* – we've already got a bucket full of dirt
from the private investigators, that Henry guy has been a
god send. The info you're pulling together will just help us
put a bit of spice in the mix. They'll never be able to separate out what we've got from one source or another. Now,
Ralph, do you get it?"

Ralph bowed his head in resignation, as he had done
many, many years ago. He got it alright. His brief was to
expose those who were running the celebrity rehab joint
known as '*The Place*' by fair means or foul, thoroughly and
quickly.

"I get it boss. I'm on the case; I'll catch you later once
we're ready to roll."

"That's my boy, Ralph. Now get your butt out of here
and get digging. Offer Henry Stallard a few more quid and I

bet he'll come up with some more dirt. Give him a 'Judas' –
or the twenty grand consultancy fee as the accounts depart-
ment like to call it. I want to know everything about these
jokers, everything – and soon. And maybe some interesting
pictures for the photo spread. Try and stay legal. Listen
Ralph, the way I see it, we're the good guys, OK?"

3

"Well, Tracy you've had quite a day, haven't you." Helen was rarely, if truth be told, sincerely sympathetic, but at this moment, she did genuinely feel for young Tracy.

Tracy took the ever-present box of designer tissues from the coffee table and plonked them on her lap knowing they would soon be needed.

"OK, where to begin Tracy? Today was a bit of a shocker wasn't it?"

Tracy went straight for the tissues.

"I suppose I should have told you, I can see that now."

"If you're to make any progress you'll need to start being a bit more honest, don't you think, Tracy? I mean, you stated on the forms that you could swim and we asked you again when we first told you we were going to the ponds; maybe that was the time to say 'Helen, I can't actually swim' or something like that, Tracy. Don't you agree?"

Tracy nodded her head, her eyes covered by a thick layer of tissues.

"I know, I know. It's not the first time. I don't know why I can't tell people I can't swim."

"Tracy, it's not the swimming bit that matters, it's the lying. Do you get it?"

"Helen – it's not an excuse I know but… I never feel like I'm lying or telling the truth when I fill in a form. I know that sounds wrong but it doesn't feel like a lie. It's feels like… a deliberate mistake or something. I don't even know when I should have said something. I had a feeling that the ponds would be – you know – like up to my waist or something and I could pretend to swim. It's what I do on holiday – in the sea or the pool – I stay in the shallow bit and nobody notices."

"But I heard from JC that you jumped in, came to the surface, and then you started to sink like a stone. It was Annie who pulled you to the surface wasn't it? Good for her. Thank God for Annie, that's what I say."

"Helen, I'm so sorry for what happened – really, I am. It's all because I was afraid to tell the truth. Or maybe I was – am – afraid of the truth. This is hard for me Helen. Maybe the truth just… hurts. But I've learnt a lesson today, a real lesson. From now on, it's the truth. Thank you."

Tracy put down her tissues and gave Helen a good old sofa hug.

"OK, Tracy from now on we'll work on, and build on, this day, won't we?"

"We sure will Helen."

Tracy dabbed her eyes for the last time that day and smiled.

"Now, as a special treat I've ordered in some WagYu steak. I thought you'd all like something extra special. We don't always eat together, but tonight I think we should make an exception. We'll set up a table downstairs instead of you all hiding in your rooms. You know what WagYu steak is, Tracy?"

"Er, I think so. It's the best you can get, that's all I know. I've heard the name before somewhere – *Wag You*. Funny name." Tracy momentarily seemed distracted by some random thought, but then quickly came back.

"By the way, what happened to me was nothing compared to what I heard happened to your lot, Helen."

Helen smiled a rare, uninhibited, genuine and broad smile. "That's an understatement, Tracy."

***

So, Huck what was that all about? I mean we're lucky we're not all down at the police station." David looked very serious.

"Well, how the hell was I supposed to be prepared for that? I mean that pervert must have thought I was a genuine... you know... *lady*. We were all on a journey – you know an emotional journey. He was just a *perv*. Bastard. He was lucky to get away with a broken nose."

"And the rest, Huck."

"In my game bruises and squeezed knackers don't count, David. And I can't see him making a complaint to the police, can you? In fact I wouldn't be surprised if he is a policeman. Or a magistrate or an MP."

"OK, Huck, in your own words..."

"Sure, David." Huck paused, cupped his hands around his mouth and took in a long deep breath, as if he was determined the get the story absolutely right, for posterity.

"So we've had our little swim. That was great, really enjoyed it. A bit cold, but quite... energising. Anyway, I've nearly finished putting my kit back on – I was straightening my skirt if I remember right, I had a towel wrapped around my head so I couldn't hear much but I had a feeling someone was behind me – you know that feeling

David? I turn around and the guy's behind me – naked – and obviously up for it, you know what I mean?"

"Yeah, go on."

"Well, I didn't have time to work out whether he thinks or knows who – what – I am, I'd deliberately chosen a dark corner in the open changing area, but I can see he's coming closer and closer staring at me like I'm some sort of tart. I mean you don't expect that in the ladies-only swimming pond on Hampstead Heath, do you? I thought it was for ladies of a certain age, not some guy up for a bit of al fresco rumpy. What really got me David is that there was no sign of a 'may I?', you know what I mean?"

"Er, quite so, Huck. So, you decked him."

"Yeah, well, I bent over as if it was party time and then let rip with a classic high back kick, heel of my foot straight to the nose. Beauty it was. Cage fighters call it 'the donkey' you know."

"And that was it?"

"Sort of, David. I then grabbed his bits and said in my deepest voice. 'Don't try that one on me sunshine' – or words to that effect. I've never seen a guy so scared in all my life. He ran out naked. Must be somewhere in Brighton by now."

"And the blood, Huck. I was told there was a lot of blood."

"Well, there was a bit of blood but not a lot. You should have been at my last fight – now that's where you'd have seen *a lot* of blood. This was – you know – just a sort of… nose bleed. Reckon I should get a medal, don't you?"

"Know what you mean, Huck. I guess Helen was a bit freaked, that's all."

"Not surprised David, not surprised. It was quite a day,

really. The girls had some excitement as well, from what I heard."

"Just another day at *The Place*, Huck. It always seems to make sense in the end."

4

David Cooper was always wary when he saw Paul Jones at his door. An appearance by Paul Jones meant it was 'rebirthing day'. The problem David had with rebirthing was that he had such a nagging feeling that it was just so risky. He was always saying to JC: *'if there's no mark, there's no evidence'* but in his heart – and from experience – he knew that not all 'marks' are physical.

David had consistently expressed serious reservations about rebirthing, not on any ideological grounds or for therapeutic reasons – that wasn't his call – no, it simply scared the shit out of him. Every rebirthing David had ever witnessed reminded him of a small plane trying to land in high cross winds.

"Hi, Paul. You're looking great. You working out these days or are you just naturally super looking?"

"Good to see ya, David, my friend. I'm great, really great. Just back from Washington, due back in LA this weekend. Busy, busy, busy. Thanks. Who we squeezing out today? I've had a look at the profiles. Not sure I under-stand why they're all here, but I guess that will all come out in the wash. God I love this job," sighed Paul.

David's stomach churned; Paul's relaxed manner made him feel very nervous.

"Er, we got a full house but you'll need to speak with Helen about who's up for it. That's not my call. I know the

Richard guy — you now the manically depressed bipolar comedian — Richard Beckett, is a candidate, don't know about the others. Can't see how we can rebirth Big Betty without a fork lift truck — have you seen her? Annie Young's face might fall off, I wouldn't try and contain Huck — he might have a *major* freak out and from what I understand he's really earned his cage name: the 'micro-psycho'. 'T-Bone' Toni, our very own Italian stallion? Er, not sure that rebirthing's quite right for a sixty-year-old rampant sex addict. Tracy's a bit too fragile I reckon. Wait a minute, I'll buzz Helen and we can talk this one through."

***

"OK" said Helen "this is Paul Jones, he's our visiting rebirther. Now I know most of you won't know too much about rebirthing, so I'll let Paul do some explaining."

The six guests stood around Paul in the large sound-proofed basement of *The Place* referred to as 'The Encounter Area', used for all manner of activities, particularly those which involved loud noises such as shouting, screaming or crying. The entire troupe, Betty, Tracy, Huck, Richard, Annie and Toni, formed, without instruction or command, a nervous-looking half circle around Paul while Helen took a couple of un-noticed back steps towards the door.

"Hi, everyone I'm Paul, Paul Jones. My, you all look so… apprehensive, there's nothing to worry about, I promise. OK, a bit about *moi*. I am, as you all are, special in my own way. I was trained as a midwife in London — Clapham Maternity Hospital, believe it or not — but on a trip to LA, some years ago, I stumbled across a rebirthing workshop. I went along out of curiosity and, hand on heart, it changed my life."

Paul paused for effect.

"Er, but what does it involve, Paul?" Huck wasn't willing to wait for Paul's warm-up to take its course.

"Thanks, for that. You must be Huck. I was getting to that point. OK, we only rebirth volunteers. Richard, I understand you've already signed up, so you'll be first."

Richard froze to the spot as if he had just been hit with a stun gun, before the shakes kicked in.

"I've found over the years that the best way of explaining what I do is to demonstrate, rather than explain. So, before we start I need a volunteer, just to show you what we're going to do. Huck do you want to help? I thought so, thanks. Now if you wouldn't mind crouching on the floor, like this."

Paul adopted a sort of crouching foetal position; kneeling on the exquisitely smooth parquet floor he bent forward, tucked his knees tightly into his chest and placed his hands over his head as if bracing himself for some form of impact. Paul looked up to make sure everyone 'got it' and then got to his feet.

"OK, Huck if you can do the same as that, I'll explain – well you know – demonstrate what's going to happen with Richard. You OK with that, Huck?"

Huck gave a cocky shift of his broad shoulders and went for it.

"OK, Betty can you sit behind Huck's legs and wrap your arms around his body, as best you can, Betty? Try kneeling. Thanks. That's it, get the soles of his feet wedged against your knees. Now, Richard and Toni – you go on either side of Huck, by his shoulders, and also wrap your arms around him.

"Now, Annie you sit in front of Huck and form a circle with your thumbs and first fingers like a circle, OK sit in front of Huck, turn your hands around and place the circle around Huck's head. Huck, make a bit of space around your head for Annie's fingers. OK, looking good. Now who we got left? Tracy you get between Richard and Betty, yep, that's good. OK, I want you all – except you Annie – to spread your arms around Huck. Spread your *love* around Huck."

Now, ordinarily Paul would have stopped right there, very quickly, in case *it* started. Once it started it couldn't be stopped, not until the actual birth was complete. But sometimes, Paul knew it was best to do it this way, because then everyone realised how spontaneous the whole process was. He knew Huck would thank him, later.

"OK", he said to the six bodies huddled around Huck, "I want you all to hum, like this".

Paul took a deep breath and started, well, humming. His eyes were closed and he hummed and hummed some more. No one noticed Helen turning down the dimmer switch and the room went dark, not completely dark, but dark enough. From hidden speakers a wailing sound appeared, or more accurately, whale music.

Over the music Paul shouted just one word: "GO".

It was to Paul's credit that he had discovered through much trial and a great deal of error that his particular form of rebirthing required almost no practice; in fact, that it was best conducted with as little practice as possible seriously troubled him.

Huck's version of events, as recounted for some years

later, did not seem to match up to the experience of everyone else that day. What Paul witnessed was, by his standards, fairly routine. As soon as he said 'go', as was always
the case, without exception, it started. The first sign was
always very heavy breathing from the 'baby'.

More often than not a muffled sniffling could be heard
from within the assembled, tightly-knit bodies. Huck was
no exception, except his sniffling soon developed into the
loudest, eeriest cries Paul had ever heard. Huck's heavily
exaggerated breathing and loud, soulful cries disturbed
Helen who thought it best to 'hang around', now feeling
ever-so-slightly guilty at the pre-planned Huck set up.

Paul also hovered around, ready to intervene or lend a
guiding hand, as might be required.

"Stay tight, keep with him" Paul whispered, loud
enough for the group to hear, and respond. Soon the collective mass of bodies was heaving around all over the
place, groans and crying coming loud and fast from the
baby, Huck 'the micro-psycho', who was now in the throes
of being seriously reborn. Helen realised what a stroke of
genius it was to have Betty positioned at 'No. 8' as Paul
sometimes described it.

The group quickly picked up on Huck's rhythm. He
pushed a bit, struggled a bit, stopped and then started
again. All the while he cried and cried some more.
Everyone, except Paul, was surprised as to how controlled
it all was. Huck was strong enough to break free at any
time of his choosing but he seemed to exert just enough
force to enable the group to contain him. Eventually both
the group and Huck seemed to know when the time was
right.

Annie picked up on Huck's readiness and felt the time

had arrived to let him free. She let the grip around his head loosen and Huck sort of spurted out through Annie's aching arms away from the group, into a mass of a blubbering newborn babyness.

Annie spontaneously re-positioned herself and cradled Huck's head in her arms, stroking his sweating forehead. "There, there, my little sweetie, there, there."

How long did it take? About average, Paul reckoned – twenty, maybe twenty-five, minutes. To Huck, and the others, it had been an eternity; a very tiring and physically demanding eternity.

Huck held tightly onto Annie's arms as though he might disappear down some black hole if he loosened his grip, tears flowing freely and without inhibition.

"Thank you, Annie, thank you." That's all Huck could manage to say, but it was enough.

The rest of the group lay around in various states of disbelief and exhaustion; one by one they spontaneously reformed around Annie and Huck, creating a closely-knit group. Everyone was crying. No one noticed the precise point at which the background music had stopped. What they did remember was Paul's next 'announcement'.

"OK, everyone. All together – 'Happy Birthday to you' – come you all let's *hear* it – 'Happy Birthday to you, Happy Birthday, dear Hu-uck, Happy Birthday to you'." The group gamely joined in and then erupted with a very loud and spontaneous cheer. Within moments their tears had turned to laughter, as loud as belly-aching laughter gets; except for Huck, who was still sobbing quietly.

"Jesus" said Betty. "That was tougher than when I gave birth to my daughter." The thought of Betty's teenage daughter, Diane, appeared too much to Betty who collapsed again into tears.

Helen looked long and hard at Richard who was rolling around the floor, clutching his aching ribs, in the throes of uncontrolled hysterical laughter. Helen turned her steely gaze towards Paul, and whispered 'thank you'.

5

Tracy was lying wide awake, her mind swirling with all sorts of fragmented details and worrying thoughts. So many little episodes of her cosy life started, for the first time, to raise questions – why did her premier league footballer-husband Martin have so many mobiles, why did the home telephone go dead *so often* when she answered, why wasn't Martin at training when he said he was, why did a room go silent when she came in, why did her own mother change the subject when questions about Martin's fidelity were raised, why did Martin *always* head for the shower as soon as he got home? Why did the very thought of a double cheeseburger make her think of her sister, Cheryl? And of course there were the constant rumours and the frequent, frantic meetings with lawyers. Why had she remembered the phrase *super* injunction? Most of all Tracy wondered: "Why am I here? It should be Martin here, not me".

Tracy knew it was time to go. The penny had dropped, big time. She remembered overhearing – unseen – one of Martin's team mates from the far side of her enormous kitchen. The two of them were talking as if they were in a crowded bar. Tracy tried really hard to remember the detail; it was like trying to putting together two jigsaws which had got all muddled up. She remembered being about five years old, with her aunt Nessie, having the same problem. "The first thing you have to do my angel, is to separate out the different pieces", Nessie had told her.

The conversation she had overheard, for some reason, always troubled her. It started off OK, something like: 'I don't know why they don't get it, Martin. I mean humping the wife is like having the best fillet steak, ever." Tracy remembered that bit; it was quite sweet, in its own way. Then Martin had told a joke: "What did the Big Mac say to the *Wag You*?" Tracy was trying to remember the punch line.

Yes, that was it, Tracy finally separated out the pieces of the conversation she wasn't supposed to have heard, and it must have gone something like this: "You may be sweeter and more expensive, but you'll never hit the spot with a wag, you know".

It meant nothing at the time, but Tracy was now putting the pieces together. There was the final comment, from Martin's friend, who hadn't finished. After Martin's joke the friend had said… Tracy had to concentrate to remember: "Listen, Martin. What I was going to say was: 'I don't know why they don't get it. I mean humping the wife is like having the best fillet steak, ever. *But sometimes you just have to have a big, juicy, maxed-out, double cheeseburger with crap relish.*"

Tracy at the time had taken no notice of the last bit; maybe she had been distracted and was trying to concentrating on two things at once. She had simply enjoyed hearing Martin having a laugh with his mate. Now, the words began to haunt her as they began to unravel, play and replay over and over again in her mind: 'sometimes you just have to have a big, juicy, filthy, maxed-out, double cheeseburger with crap relish'. In a bizarre way those words reminded her of quite a few of her 'friends', including her own sister, Cheryl.

Tracy felt as if some invisible arrow had been ripped out of her aching heart. It felt so painful, but brought such relief at the same time. The *truth* was that Martin was at it, all the time. This much Tracy now knew, for sure. Tracy began to wonder who Martin had taken liberties with, and the answer as Tracy also knew was 'probably everyone', including her sister, Cheryl. Tracy remembered one time shouting at her: "Cheryl, I'll tell you what. If you are what you eat, you're a great, big, stinking, *well cheap* double cheeseburger".

Tracy felt a single tear trickle down the side of her face. Something had happened. It was frightening, but *OK*. Tracy began to cry and was suddenly filled with an overwhelming sense of love for her beautiful little baby daughter whom she missed with all her heart, and at that point longed for only one single thing: to cradle Tracy junior in her arms.

Tracy looked at her phone. It was 3 a.m., the name of the club where it had all started with Martin and their first heavenly encounter in the gent's toilet. Someone had once commented to Tracy that a quickie in the gent's bog was a tad on the tacky side but Tracy remembered the frenzied shag as being 'well-romantic'.

So, it was time. Tracy crept out of bed, got dressed and disappeared into the darkness not knowing how she'd find her way home but that was the only thought in her mind: to get home and have it out – with everyone, starting with her mum then her ever-so-sweet-and-innocent big wee sister, Cheryl, big time.

Tracy felt a surge of anger as her mind cleared: she was being driven crazy by everyone around her trying to cover-up Martin's uncontrolled shagging. Her loving husband had set her up to be sorted at some rehab place, well out of town, to get her out of the way and shut up her up. The truth hurt, and it was time to share the pain.

*****

"OK, David, what's the problem?"

Helen, David and JC had a few discreet codes they used on their mobile phones, just in case they were being hacked into by some overzealous journalist. One of them, a single exclamation mark, was 'code red' meaning a real and immediate big problem. It was not yet seven in the morning and JC, Helen and David were already convened in David's office.

"Well, Helen, it's like this. Tracy's gone. She arrived back home in Manchester about half an hour ago in a black cab all the way from London. I've just taken a ferocious call from the mum. Apparently Tracy stormed in like a person possessed. The mother's a wreck; Tracy's having a rant at anything that moves. Martin's been getting no end of grief from the missus. I mean, non-stop… she keeps going on about fillet steak or something. She's been threatening to drown her sister. Think we better check the emergency medicine cabinet. Tracy's apparently going to Max Griffiths later today, that's if the mum doesn't go to the lawyers first. This is going to be all over the papers tomorrow, one way or the other."

David took breath and buried his head in his hands. "I don't think *The Place* is going to come out of this one too well. The mother's take is that Tracy nearly drowned, *The Place* is full of perverts and Huck the micro-psycho has been turned into a little baby and might end up in a nuthouse. Can't get much worse. Shit, it can – just remembered – Martin's got a home derby this afternoon. He'll be lucky if he can remember who he's playing for."

Helen stood up and composed herself. "Listen. I'll talk to Tracy, and mum. Just give me a few minutes, that's all I need. I'll start with Tracy. I've got her mobile, she'll talk to me."

David and JC had total confidence that Helen knew what to do, so they left her to it. For this type of challenge they knew Helen needed to be left alone. Not more than twenty minutes had passed before both David and JC received another coded message on their mobiles, this time just two letters, 'OK', and they headed straight back to David's office.

Helen was sitting in David's chair, a serene smile clearly displaying a high degree of satisfaction.

"So, it's 'OK', Helen. How is it now 'OK'?" asked David.

"You two are both men, so you wouldn't understand."

"Try us, Helen" said David.

"It's quite simple – to a member of the superior sex. Tracy doesn't want revenge. Not really. She doesn't want to do Martin in, or her mother. The sister's a different issue... what Tracy wants is Martin. He's the father of her daughter. She wants Martin to grow up, to be a responsible and loving father and husband. Some peace and family love, that's all."

"Still don't get it, Helen. And...?" JC was a bit slow on the uptake, but David was already there. "Don't tell me Helen – there's a deal afoot."

"That's right David, a deal's afoot. When my mobile receives a text message with the letter 'y' it's a done deal'"

As if the telephone was part of the conversation it buzzed in Helen's hand. It took Helen a few seconds to access the message. Helen's broad smile was enough confirmation for David and JC.

"OK, what's the deal?" asked David.

"The deal, gentleman, is that Martin spends a few days

with us, starting this very evening. He's to head down straight after the match. Apparently he's been persuaded he needs a bit of addiction therapy at *The Place*. If he does appear and there's improvement in his behaviour, then Tracy will be happy. Max has already been told to stand down. She reckons it will at least be a start – as she puts it – to an 'honest conversation' between her and Martin, and her mother. Maybe even her sister."

David let out an exaggerated sigh of relief and looked to the heavens and said 'thank you' to no one in particular. He had just been handed a get out of jail card, and he knew it. And he was bound to have great time with one of his all time heroes.

"Who are we going to let Martin double-up with? I'm not really sure placing Martin with Huck will work, seeing as Huck's about six months old at the moment, putting Toni and Martin together would go against our policy of not mixing like with like and Richard really needs his own space right now. Maybe we'll have to juggle them around a bit." David was on to the practicalities right away.

Helen gave David one of her knowing, mischievous smiles. Perhaps it was because JC, Helen and David had been through so much together, or perhaps they had simply learnt to communicate so well with each other; whatever it was they all knew that for every problem, there was always a solution. As David liked to say: 'there are no problems; only opportunities'. It was simply a state of mind.

"I'll have a word with Toni," said Helen. "That's all there is to it. Let's talk a bit later, David."

"Helen" said David, "I'm getting worried, you know. I thought my job was the 'fixer'. You're getting better at this than me."

"Well, David. Didn't you say 'it's a poor pupil who doesn't overtake his master'?"

"Hmm. Thought that was Bruce Lee. Or wait a minute, was it Confucius? One or the other. Maybe it works both ways, Helen. I mean, if you're my pupil at fixing then I must be your pupil at this therapy lark." Helen was always going to get in the last word. "David, is there any difference?"

6

"Hi, Paul. Thanks for seeing me. I wondered if you have a moment?"

"For you, David, I've always a moment. Will this take long? I was hoping to catch a flight to LA later today. Just got a recall to Washington. Don't need that on top of everything else, but hell, I ain't complaining. It's all a bit up in the air at the moment. I can always re-schedule, if it's worth my while. My clients seem to like the fact that I'm so in demand. That was a great session by the way with Huck. Textbook stuff. What can I do for you?"

"It's like this Paul. I'm a man down on the therapy side. How's your hypnotherapy studying coming along? I mean are actually you doing it, or still – like – studying?"

"David, I'm surprised. Didn't you hear how I got Huck and the group into the session?"

"Yeah, I heard Paul. But that wasn't hypnotism – that was manipulation – wasn't it?"

Paul smiled a little evil grin. "Not much difference, really. Just a matter of control, you know, without being seen to be in control."

"OK, Paul. That's all I need. Got a challenge for you."

"Let's hear it, David."

***

Gustav Grolsh, whose past was a swirling mist of implausible stories without end, was 'multi-talented', in therapy terminology. 'Gootsy', as he liked to be called, was best known for his laughter therapy, was a pretty good *Hatha* Yoga teacher, and if truth be told a sophisticated and talented masseuse, but his speciality was Primitive Screaming Therapy.

"OK, my friends. I know Richard pretty well already. That was a real breakthrough one-on-one session the other day. You did great Richard, you really did. You'll be heading the next laughter session."

Richard went all coy, like he did at school when his maths teacher praised him for good homework in front of his peers. Richard felt, and was, well chuffed.

Gootsy excelled at 'PST' as he called it. Gootsy *loved* PST, so much so he liked to improvise or 'play' with the 'fear of fun and the fun of fear' which was about as far as the coherent explanation of his 'art' went. He knew some people thought it was a bit far out, but he believed it was only a matter of time before the naysayers would get it. He'd also learnt to avoid too much theorising before the event itself.

He accepted that getting PST recognised as mainstream was never going to be easy, partly because a feeling of release and well-being couldn't be seen under a microscope, and then there was always the practical difficulty of finding the right – sound-proofed – space. It was unfortunate that on film at least, PST always came across as pretty freaky; on that point there was no debate.

Gootsy also accepted that as an advocate of PST he did look a tad weird with his stick-like body and long, straggly, thin, grey hair – but time, he felt, was on his side. After all, he was always in demand at *The Place* – and many other rehabs all over the world.

"So, who we got here today? I know Richard. You must be Betty, then there's – wait a minute don't tell me – Annie and – of course – Toni. Now, my name is Gustav, but I like to be called Gootsy. Is that OK? Today we're going for a touch of Primitive Screaming Therapy, or 'PST' as I call it. It's my very own creation. Now, are we all here?"

No one wanted to mention Huck, and Tracy had been all but been forgotten in the blink of an eye. It was like that in *The Place*. The whole experience often seemed quite surreal to the short-stay journeymen, particularly if their faculties were impaired by the sudden deprivation of their favourite fix; guests came and went like bit players in a half-remembered dream.

To Gootsy the group was just about perfect.

"Now before we get into this, we need to be relaxed, and warmed up. So a few basic exercises just to loosen us up and we'll be right in. Just copy me. Now, on the spot – imagine you're running for the last bus home."

"Oh, Jesus," said Betty under her breath. "Can't I just wait for a taxi?"

"Now now, Betty. I heard that. Behave. Just move… up and down a bit – as best you can – we need to get everything moving and relaxed. Push those arms up and up… as if you're trying to catch a falling snowflake before it melts. Keep going. OK, we're off; I think we need some sounds."

Gootsy went over to the very discreetly hidden state-of-the-art hi-fi system and pressed a button or two on a remote control; his playlist of special effects was already loaded.

The basement room of *The Place* was another 'art form' as Helen called it. The speakers were so ultra modern and gave such a great all-round sound that it would take an expert to work out where the speakers were actually placed.

"OK, let's talk a little walk around the room. Follow me."

Gootsy started to walk, not quite in a circle, but randomly, and the group followed. He walked quicker and quicker; the small group managed their best to keep up, for a while, and then he stopped.

"OK, we're going to do that one again, but this time, imagine you're in a dark forest and you can hear a worrying sound behind you. Off you go, on your own. And mind the low-hanging branches. And the spiders – they're deadly."

Gootsy broke away from the group and twiddled with the dimmer switch. The room darkened slightly but noticeably.

"Now, stop where you are. Standing on the spot, shake your arms around, shake everything about. Close your eyes. OK, now relax. Let's all breath in. Hold it, now breathe out. Slowly. Breathe in, hold it again. Now out… slowly. Let your mind empty of all thoughts. Relax. And breathe. Relax. Breathe in… and out. Keep going. Now open your eyes – wide open – and run, run as if some *thing* is about to get you. OK, that's enough, now stop! Don't make a sound, don't move an inch."

And so it went on, only for a few minutes, but soon everyone was *very* tired but relaxed, dizzy even. The small group was told to come to a complete halt, again. "OK, eyes closed, silence, absolute total silence" instructed Gootsy in a whisper. The silence seemed to go on for a long time.

Out of the blue, and without warning, a sound filled the room like a scream from the depths of hell. The group screamed back in terror, particularly Richard, who had a totally different expectation of 'PST'.

Gootsy laughed. "Oh I love that bit. What were you

expecting – Michael Jackson?"

The room seem to get darker; the group sort of huddled together, not knowing what to expect next. Another sound come from nowhere and filled the entire room. It was the sound of waves breaking on the shore. The group huddled even closer, like the last few fish of what once was a large safe shoal of a carefree species about to be finally swallowed in one last go by the *big beast*. The waves crashed louder and louder. And then silence.

Toni was the fall guy, today. Stepping forward he wiped his brow with relief as if it was all over. The others weren't so dumb. Now the seemingly invisible speakers emitted a sort of heavy breathing which appeared to get louder and louder, closer and closer.

"What the hell is this, scare-the-shit-out-of-you therapy?" Betty's attempt at diffusing the situation was not very successful.

"Now" barked Gootsy pretending not to hear Betty. "Scream, as if your life depends on it, *scream*! Or they'll get you!"

The troupe didn't need that much encouragement. They were *ready* to scream and they didn't hold back. They screamed even louder when the heavy breathing stopped and some indescribably unearthly roar filled the room, quickly followed by all manner of B movie horror effects: a cacophony of screams, cries, moans, creaking doors, bangs, and crunching sounds.

How long this went on for was the subject of much debate. As with the rebirthing, the entire session had lasted less than half an hour, but felt like an eternity.

Suddenly the penny dropped that the room had brightened and Gootsy was clearly seen pushing another button or two on the remote control which operated the hi-fi system.

The entire group spontaneously lay down on the floor as if they had been asked to play dead. There were distinctive collective murmurings of 'oh god', 'what was that?' with a few 'it's over, please, tell me it's over'. The group gradually began to prise themselves, one by one, off their backs to sit and then gradually – with some effort – to stand upright giving the collective impression they had just finished a parents' one hundred metres race.

"Now, wasn't that fun?" asked Gootsy as if they had just come off a routine theme park ride. "Let's take a comfort break and we'll get straight into the laughter zone."

Toni looked down at his lightly coloured track suit which now had a distinctive brand new dark patch around the groin area.

"Er, I'm OK with that one, Gootsy. Already had my comfort break, thanks."

Richard and Betty both sweating profusely, were more than ready for a comfort break and headed straight for the door, passing David and the rebirther, Paul, who gingerly stepped into the room.

"Everything OK, Gustav, I mean Gootsy. You know Paul, don't you?" asked David.

Gootsy and Paul embraced like long lost brothers.

"Sure we know each other, you know that" said Paul, realising that it wasn't the right time to display his friendship with David.

"Bit unusual for you to er… interrupt the proceedings… anything the matter?" enquired Gootsy.

"No, nothing the matter," said David. "Just thought we might borrow Annie, you know, for a few minutes."

Annie, still in a state of mild-to-extreme shock, sweating

to such an extent she looked as if she had just been for a swim, looked around with some relief. The thought had crossed Annie's mind that Gootsy was actually a long-term guest who had flipped some time ago. Perhaps he had just escaped from the yet-to-be-revealed dungeon where all manner of cock-ups were hidden.

"OK, I'll tell you what" said Gootsy. "Why don't we leave you here with Annie, and we'll all catch up a bit later – say in half an hour. I'll tell Betty and Richard. I think the last session really hit the spot – they might welcome a break. That OK with you Toni?"

"Sure" said Toni, worried that he might sound as shaken as he felt. "Any chance of a fresh track suit David, this one's been seen better days. Better give it some *Vanish*, you know, round the back. Think Betty was right."

David tried to pretend he couldn't detect the odour coming from Toni and the reference to Betty went straight over his head. "Will do Toni. See you later."

"OK, Annie. Let's sit down, if that's OK. Paul's had a brilliant idea. Do you mind if he shares it with you?"

Annie sort of smirked as if she was going to be awarded a special prize. The three of them sat down on the floor in a cosy little circle.

"Now, Annie. Have you any objections to a bit of hypnotherapy?"

"Like, right now?" asked Annie.

"Yeah, that's the idea, right now."

Annie was up for anything her manager could afford. "Fine with me, let's do it, right now. That's kind of what we're here for. Shoot."

"Annie, this is all about you. So, are you up for a bit of hypnotherapy with Paul, right here, right now?"

"Sure am, David."

"OK, I'll leave you to it then. I've got work to do."

David stood up indicating that it was time for him to leave, at which point his mobile phone buzzed inside his trouser pocket.

"Fine with me" said Annie, "I'll catch you later".

David flipped his mobile phone as soon as he had stepped outside the Encounter Area and knew it was an old mate Henry Stallard on the other end.

"Listen, David. I'm not phoning about any of your guests, it's something else, something a bit more serious. Can we meet later? Maybe at the café at Kenwood House, we need somewhere real discreet."

"Sure, Henry. Is tomorrow OK, about 10 a.m.?"

"David, I mean like in half an hour, not tomorrow."

"Shit, Henry, that serious?"

"Yep, David, that serious. I'd rather not go into any detail on this line."

***

"Do you feel as bad as you look, Ralph? Don't go dying on me pal; it'll screw up our insurance premiums for the next quarter. Could even screw up my bonus." Simon was a great believer in tough love.

"I've done you proud, mate, proud." Ralph enjoyed the thought of the impending reward from his much younger boss and for some reason momentarily thought of himself as an off-coloured pack of sausages still on the shelf, despite its now-past sell-by date.

"Better be good shit, old boy otherwise you're for the knackers' yard."

Ralph smiled; he knew Simon's sweet spot. "I've got it all, every tweak and twiddle. Where do you want me to start?"

Simon moved not one muscle, stared at the old git in front of him and waited for the goods.

Ralph looked down into the floor and spoke softly. "I was sixteen when I first worked for the *Sunday News*. Sixteen. I've seen them all come and go." Ralph lifted his eyes to meet to Simon's. "What keeps it all going is… a great story; nothing more, nothing less. Would you be surprised that daddy bear – David Cooper – is a recovering alcoholic and has done time for fraud? Its gets better. He met the love of his life – mummy bear – when she was working as a prison psychologist, and – wait for it – baby bear, David's kid, Jason, was a problem child ever since his mother died in a car accident whilst being driven by the drunken daddy bear who has reinvented himself as a *Group Operations Director*, or 'god' to his friends. Couldn't make it up."

Ralph sat back as if waiting for a standing ovation, but Simon wasn't as naive as he looked.

"It's a start, I suppose. But not bad Ralph, not too bad at all; looks like you'll live another day. Sounds like Judas was worth his twenty pieces of silver, keep him talking. I guess David hasn't twigged that his best mate is on our pay roll. Get a draft up-and-running and let's see how this is sizing up. And don't forget we're light on the photos' side. Get that one sorted."

"Sure thing, boss. Will do" said Ralph.

Simon threw Ralph a tightly wrapped small chocolate sweetie from a drawer under his desk. "Good boy, Ralph, good boy."

7

"OK, Listen up Helen and JC." Both JC and Helen knew when David was in deep serious mode; something was up.

"I've just met with me old mate, Henry Stallard. We've a problem brewing and I'm not sure what we're going to do about it. According to Henry someone's on to us. I mean us personally. Seems there's someone doing a lot of digging around. They've been in contact with one of our mates from prison. From what I hear they're so into us they've even sent investigators to Tallinn, Helen."

"Tallinn? Why send someone to Tallinn? Where's Tallinn?" JC looked more confused than worried.

"Tallinn" said Helen "is where I did my doctorate in psychology. It's the capital of Estonia, JC."

JC was still confused. "Yeah, but like so what?"

David looked at Helen, as parents sometimes do when their kid is about to hear a truth known only to mummy and daddy.

"OK, JC. I've been honest with you all my life. You know my past and you know what happened to your mum."

JC looked at his dad with a sense of impending doom.

"Go on dad… and…"

"Well, I'm not sure you know all there is to know about Helen, son."

JC looked at his dad and Helen with some apprehension. "I know Helen came over from Estonia and got a job in the prison where you were er… staying, Helen was the prison psychologist and that's how you two met, right?" JC was now more worried than confused.

"Yeah, that's all true. It's just that Helen had a bit of rocky upbringing before she decided to qualify as a psychologist." David looked at Helen to finish the story.

"JC, OK, it's like this. I don't know how much you know of my past, but it's not all good." Helen sighed, deeply. "My father was a well known psychologist in Estonia; his reputation was built on the studies of families – disturbed, disrupted families – and how it affected the children."

JC look at Helen as if was about to hear something shocking. "I know about that, but like I said, so what?"

"Well, my dad seemed to spend all of his time with other families. It made me really rebellious and jealous JC. I mean by the time I was thirteen, going on thirty, I was… well, a bit wild – nothing outrageous by today's standards. You know JC, the usual." Helen lowered her head half hoping that might be enough for JC.

"The usual, Helen? Like drinking vodka, smoking weed… fooling around?"

"Er, yeah, just about, JC." Helen paused knowing that if there was a time for a quality confession, then this was the moment.

"Look, JC. If there's someone digging around who's about to come out with all my glorious past, I may as well tell you right now. Here's the worst of it. When I was about fifteen or sixteen I became aware that men – older men – found me very attractive, sexually attractive. It felt like a way of getting revenge on my dad. And, you know these older men seemed to have a lot of money, and my dad was always mean in that respect. I never felt that I was doing anything *wrong*, JC."

JC's jaw dropped. "Helen, I get it. Holy shit. And now there's someone who we think knows all about this – dad's stuff included, like why you ended up doing time, dad. All that con man business. You've told me everything, right? Jesus, put that altogether and that sounds like quite a story to me. I suppose they intend to just print and be damned. I had always thought – naively – that they had no right to drag all that stuff up. So, we're screwed, that's what you're saying. It's like the end scene from *Oliver!*, right? I mean we pack our bags and head off into the sunset and start again. Is that it?"

David placed an arm over his troubled son's shoulders. "Listen JC, I've been through tougher times than this. No, we're not doing a Fagin, far from it. Listen, it's business as usual, I'll work something out, trust me. In the meantime let's be careful about what telephone messages we leave for each other, OK?"

***

David was beside himself with anticipation. Martin Howler was about to arrive, one of David's all time favourite players for his life-long favourite football team. He really couldn't wait.

"David, could you… calm down a bit. Remember where you are, who we are – you're expected to be… you know, calm, collected, professional. Stop pacing around. Remember what I've always said… "

"Yeah, yeah Helen I know," said David, "'a celebrity's just a big kid with attention-seeking issues'. How do you want to play it with Martin? I mean this isn't the usual scenario is it? He's not coming because he wants to or feels he has to do. This is one of those press gang type appearances. We'll have to be very careful; we don't – you know – want to push him off the edge. Can't have Martin Howler doing a runner, can we?"

Helen, as ever, looked very composed, serene even.

"Let's be clear how long we've got. Two, maybe three days? He has to attend training on Wednesday at the latest, we know that much. So, nothing too heavy. We've got to make sure Tracy feels Martin has learnt something. We should start straight away with Tim and Tamara."

David's mobile buzzed. Martin was about one minute away from walking through the door.

David looked at JC. "First off, JC why don't you show Martin around? Not *everywhere*, but enough for Martin to feel he knows *The Place*. Show Martin his room, settle him down a bit. Try and talk football. Don't know how you're going to deal with the match earlier, that's your challenge son. Just give us enough time to brief T 'n' T."

David's door opened and in strolled, tall and cocky, the celebrated premier league striker, Martin Howler, looking every inch the nouveau rich and carefree womaniser he was known to be.

David practically jumped over to Martin and introduced his son, JC, and then Helen who took swift control.

"Hi, Martin. Hope the journey wasn't too bad. I heard your agent drove you down."

"Yeah, wasn't too bad. He's a great agent but a crap chauffeur. Thinks 'Sat-Nav' is an adult television channel."

Helen maintained her professional but friendly look. "My Martin, you do look a lot bigger – and younger – than you appear on television." Helen looked up into Martin's deep blue mischievous eyes. "You must be... what... six foot three, six four?"

Funny you should say that, I get that a lot." Martin wasn't too much interested in or good at small talk either. He was, after all, sacrificing a Saturday night – against his will as he saw it – just to *keep the peace with the wife*. The threat to a very lucrative sponsorship deal was also preying on his mind; these new sponsors were getting quite touchy about *bad behaviour*, after all Martin was a much-loved family man.

"Yeah… OK. I mean what happens now? You gonna hypnotise me or something?" Martin was clearly very nervous, which made Helen feel even more relaxed.

"No, no Martin. Well not right away. Only joking. We're going to iron out your schedule – still got a bit of work to do there. How about in the meantime JC shows you around, it'll make you feel more… at home. You'll be back up North well before next big week's big training session, promise."

Martin visibly relaxed. "Come on Martin, I'll give you the guided tour, this way."

"OK. I suppose I'll see you both later then."

Martin felt a bit awkward as JC ushered him out of David's office. They were the first people he had met that day who hadn't mentioned the match earlier. It had been a great game, for the other side. Losing one nil against your arch rivals when you've missed two penalties was about as bad as it could get for a star striker. 'A bad day at the office' was how the BBC commentator had described Martin's performance. The home fans weren't so diplomatic. Martin was grateful for a good excuse to lay low for a couple of days. He could always redeem himself in the next match.

As JC lead Martin on a guided tour of *The Place*, Martin was engulfed with a sickness to his stomach which reminded him of two very specific occasions, the first was the feeling he had some years ago, when he was making his name in the reserves. The other time was when he took his wedding vows.

Martin Howler was for the first time in a long time totally out of his comfort zone.

***

"You ready for this, Richard?"

"I'm not sure, Helen, don't really know what a 'Kaleidoscope Review' involves, so to be frank, I don't know whether I'm ready or not. Do we just jump in or do I get to know what it is before we start?"

"'KR' is very simple but very effective, Richard. It doesn't involve anything else other than honesty and concentration."

"Like a marriage, then?"

Helen smiled and stared deep into Richard's eyes, which were a lot less weary looking since his arrival at *The Place*.

"OK, this is all it involves. I've got a specially designed timer here. It's quite neat, isn't it? Look I can set a number – let's take your age. Fifty-one, yes? Right, what happens is that I set the number on the display. I can then set the display to count down from fifty-one to zero in intervals of, say, one minute at a time."

Helen pushed a few small buttons on the back of the compact little device which looked like a digital travel alarm clock. On the screen, brightly displayed in red lights was the number '51'.

"OK, Helen, very nice. Looks like an expensive detonator. What are we going to do with it?"

"As I said, Richard, it's very simple. You're going to keep one eye on the number, as displayed. Starting with the

number fifty-one and working right back until zero. You're
going to talk about your birthday according to the number
displayed. Get it? It's best if you just talk without thinking –
I know that's difficult for you Richard because you are a
thinker. You've told me already Richard that every year, as
your birthday approaches, you feel more and more
depressed, suicidal even. By the time you leave *The Place* I
want you to be looking forward to your next birthday. Is that
so ambitious for such a successful, handsome man like you?
So, we're going to start off with your last birthday. Tell me
anything you want – for a minute – about your last birthday.
For example, where you are, who you are with, any presents
you can remember, any specific incidents that come to mind.
Most important of all is to try and remember – on balance
– whether you were happy, or not. Does that all make sense?
It's just a game. Shall we have a go? I'll be making some
notes as we go along, so just keep talking – you enjoy talking,
don't you, Richard?"

Helen pressed a button and the game started.

8

The basement room of *The Place* had been the subject of great debate in the early design stages. Helen always had the last word on the matter, not least because it was her money that paid for it. The room had to be adaptable for several purposes: as a dance studio, a theatre-like room for psychodramas, a dining room and a space that could be adapted for all manner of group activities. Group therapy sessions took many forms, but Helen had understood from the beginning that most of the guests, at one time or another, would have experienced or be familiar with old-fashioned confessional-type encounters, favoured from Alcoholics Anonymous to slimming clubs. It was called 'The Encounter Area' for good reason.

On one wall was a row of mirrors which were great for the dance and exercise sessions. When a more intimate atmosphere was needed, a discreet curtain could be pulled across the mirrors making the room feel far smaller and quite intimate, particularly when the carefully controlled lighting was used to full effect.

For a group therapy session with Tim and Tamara it worked well to start with the curtains drawn. If the session progressed to an exercise session, the curtains would be pulled across the mirrors.

Behind one of the wooden panels on the wall facing the mirrors was a storage area which housed a variety of props.

All that was needed today was six lightweight armless but sturdy folding chairs, enough for Tim, Tamara, Martin, Annie, Betty and Toni.

Tamara had already placed the six chairs to form a generously-sized circle. By the time the guests had arrived both Tim and Tamara had already taken their seats directly opposite one another, Tamara's back deliberately facing the door through which the guests would arrive.

Neither Tim nor Tamara stood up when Martin, Annie, Betty and Toni walked into the Encounter Area; instead they waited, silently, for the group to decide where they would sit. This process of settling down always taught Tamara a great deal about each and every member of the group.

Martin appeared confused. Initially he could only see the back of Tamara's head. Thinking that the lady was quite young he had decided to sit next to her, but when he had seen enough to realise that Tamara was on the wrong side of fifty, he ignored her and sat next to Tim.

The others took their places, Betty appearing reluctant to place her full weight on what appeared to be a lightweight chair that might collapse under the strain of her weight.

Tim and Tamara waited until everyone was seated; the absence of any 'meet and greet' small talk created an immediate and growing sense of anticipation.

Tamara was ready to break the ice.

"OK. Hi, everyone. I'm Tamara, over there is Tim."

Tim sort of waved to the group with an inane grin, looking as he intended: cool and groovy as if on his way to a 70s disco party. True to form, Tim was dressed in tight floral-patterned trousers and a loose-fitting, light mauve coloured, frilly, open-necked shirt matched by his soft suede moccasin shoes.

"Now, I've already met Toni and I recognise one or two of you," said Tamara knowing she would be safe with that line.

"I'm not sure exactly what Helen or JC may have told you about me and Tim – we're known as 'T 'n' T' by the way – but our *thing* is dealing with – well – *addressing* – issues of addiction, mostly addiction to *sex*, but addiction takes many forms, you know."

Betty tried not to move one little bit in case her precarious perch collapsed, but decided she could get away with putting her hand up. Betty had wanted to say 'what in god's name has sex addiction got to do with me' but the penny dropped, a bit late, that this T 'n' T double act had her covered.

"Yes, Betty... what do you want to share?"

"Er, nothing really, right now. I was... er... wondering if I could have a bigger seat... you know I'm feeling a bit vulnerable on top of being a bit big."

Tim had an idea. "I know, I'll get some cushions and stuff and we can all sort of sit around, instead of being on chairs."

"Oh, Tim" said Tamara, "you're just so sweet and thoughtful. Don't you think so everyone?"

Within a few minutes the group had reconvened having selected various cushions, bean bags and even an exercise ball which Martin tried to lean on until he gave up and lounged on the floor.

"Now, are we all comfy?" asked Tamara looking at Betty who was implausibly sitting on a few scattered cushions, looking far from comfortable.

"OK, now let's introduce ourselves, properly, one by one. I'll start with myself."

Betty squelched around a bit trying to find a comfortable position, wondering how this could get any worse.

Tamara was off. "I'm sixty-five years old. *Sixty-five*." Tamara let the number hang in the air until everyone present expressed some degree of disbelief. "I didn't find happiness in my life until I was well over forty. In a way I can see now that my happiness started when men no longer wanted me just for sex." Tamara paused and looked over at Tim as if that was his cue.

"Tamara's a wonderful person, absolutely wonderful. She's endured all manner of hardships and pain but still her beautiful soul shines bright, clear for all to see."

Tim sighed and took a deep breath before embarking upon his number.

"I'll tell you my story in a nutshell. I always was so *horny*, from a very early age. No reason, you know it was just me. I must have been playing with myself in the womb. I was just, if I have to say so myself, pretty damn good at doing the business. I was probably the only young guy where I lived who took his time with the ladies. 'Adonis' gets it. You know what I mean? The word spread, I guess. To cut a long story short, I got myself a job from a very young age in adult movies. Anyway after years of being a well paid stud, one day at work I just couldn't you know… do it. I mean in front of me was this delicious and beautiful lady in all her naked-ness, and I just couldn't. It had never happened to me before, ever. I saw a beautiful person in the whole, not just a beautiful hole in a person."

Tim paused as if for dramatic effect.

"And that's how me and Tamara first met. It was quite romantic, don't you think? Pure Karma."

Tim's mini-speech stunned the group into silence. No-one dared make a sound or give any suggestion they wanted to, or could, follow the T 'n' T story; it was by any standards a difficult act to follow. Betty was terrified she was about to gag, or, preferably, faint. The bar had been set a tad too high for this group, except for Toni who felt he was among very dear and old friends. The need to share was overwhelming.

"My name's Toni, I guess you all know me as an aging rocker but the fact is I've sacrificed everything for sex. It's been my life, now I'm paying the price. I've no wife, no children, no family left at all. I'm… frightened."

Toni paused as the tears welled up in his eyes. "I don't want to die a sad and lonely sex addict. There, I've said it: I'm a sex addict." Tim and Tamara clapped and with almost one voice said, "Well, done, Toni, good for you."

Toni hadn't intended to disintegrate so quickly; in fact he hadn't seen his mini-breakdown coming at all. Making such an unguarded admission, so quickly, took him by surprise. Toni burst into tears, placed his head in his hands and sobbed.

Tim leaned over and gave Toni a cuddle, and whispered "well done, Toni" and then returned to his space on the floor.

"OK" said Tamara. "Toni's already made such progress, that so wonderful. Take your time, Toni, there's no rush. Anyone want to say anything to Toni?"

Betty though it was best to get in there before the others.

"My name's Betty. I haven't had a good shag for frigging years."

Martin couldn't quite contain a giggle and pretended to stifle a cough. "Sorry about that guys, it was just the way it came out. Honestly, Betty, I wasn't being rude or anything."

"That's OK," said Betty, "I suppose you wouldn't understand any of this stuff. I mean you probably have to fight off girls all the time. Maybe it's just an age thing."

"It's a respect-thing Betty" added Annie caustically.

No one had quite noticed exactly when it was that the deceptively diminutive figure of Huck appeared in the Encounter Area but there he was, loud and proud.

"Hey guys. I must appear pretty rude just barging in on... this. Helen said I could join in when I was ready, and to tell you what, I really feel *ready*, so here I am. Hey, Toni, you OK? Hope I haven't screwed anything up."

"Pull up a cushion, Huck. I'm Tim. You're more than welcome, really – come on, join in. We're just getting going. I think we'd just touched on the issue of respect. That's right isn't it Martin?"

Huck had developed a habit of clocking the 'big guy' whenever he entered a potentially confrontational situation; it was part his training. Huck recognised immediately who the 'big guy' was, but kept his reaction in check. He was after all a trained fighter. He had heard all the rumours about the celebrated Martin Howler.

Huck pulled up a cushion and sat opposite Martin.

"So, you were talking about respect. Now that's a subject close to my heart." Huck sounded strong and confident, almost a touch too macho.

For the second time that day Martin felt quite sick. It wasn't just that he was outside his own comfort zone, but realised that he was deep inside someone else's. Everyone, apart from Martin, seemed enormously pleased to see Huck who was beaming from ear to ear, clearly *very* happy and raring to go in any direction.

9

'Are you sure this is a secure line, Henry? Talking over the 'phone makes me feel very uneasy, I mean I know how easy it is to access calls; but hell I guess I'm talking to the market leader in hacking so just tell me we're ok. I mean that's how it all went tits up the last time when the hackers were hacked."

"Listen Ralph, we're ok. Believe me. I've told you one hundred times that it's better to talk over the 'phone and not leave messages or send texts. I know Simon will have your guts for garters if I don't deliver the goods. I promised you I'd find some photographs you might add in, as I recall. Are you listening? Ok, here it is and I'll be quick. I've got some pictures which will add some spice. The great thing is that the lawyers aren't going to give you grief over this. I've pictures of the Gootsy guy when he was a young guy. They're hilarious; he looks like a twenty year old mad professor. And some photos of Helen when she was a teenager have popped up on Facebook. They're priceless, she looks so frigging hot for a thirteen year old. And wait for it – I've a snap of God, David I mean, looking like a member of a chain gang. That took some digging I can tell you. When he was on the inside he had a sort of day out helping in the community. The old lady whose garden he was clearing up took some snaps. Can't see any privacy issues with that one. You gotta see it, there he is in the front garden with a rack looking like he's an extra from Porridge. Don't ask me how I got that one, you don't want to know. And I ain't finished yet, got one or two more tricks up my sleeve."

Ralph sighed with relief. "Look, don't send anything in the post for god's sake. Let's meet and you can give me a USB stick with digitised images. Is that do-able? Great, and thanks. You're doing a grand job, Henry."

***

"OK, Richard" Helen looked at what she called the 'score sheet'. "Do you realise that of the fifty-one birthdays you've had in your life the score looks like this: there are fourteen, *fourteen* Richard you can't remember; there are seven you appear to have enjoyed as you put it 'to some extent'. Then there are thirty that you can remember and 'positively loathed.' What does that tell you, Richard?"

Richard was too tired to say anything. He had thought this exercise would last less than one hour. That thought was now over two hours old, due to the number of times Richard had to stop 'the game' and collect himself. He had been to hell and back and to hell again.

"Richard, you looked a bit tired. Do you want to call it a day, or carry on?"

"What would you recommend, Helen?"

Helen studied the score sheet once again, and sighed.

"I recommend that we start again. This time we're going to start from the other end, at year zero Richard, and work upwards. I know in the early days you can't remember much. That's not the point. Tell me where you think you are living, who you are living with, something about your mum, your dad and your brother. Tell me how you felt. You know what

I'm asking for, Richard. OK, we'll spend one minute on each birthday, starting with the day you were born. Are you up for this, Richard?"

Richard took a deep breath, took off his glasses and rubbed his weary eyes.

"Guess this is why I'm here, Helen. Sure, I'm up for it."

***

Martin was beginning to feel increasingly nauseous in the Encounter Area. Tim and Tamara seemed to have not one ounce of inhibition between them. Toni was coming back to some kind of stability and was now difficult to stop, once he got going. Betty had been through the tears and had confessed to her 'bigness' being a useful barrier to avoid sexual situations. Tamara was impressed; this group was making progress in leaps and bounds.

Annie was still cagey. But, as Tim remarked later, it had become clear that Annie wanted to keep back her contribution as if she waiting to deliver the great finale. The last to blow often blew loudest; T 'n' T knew that from experience.

Huck had kept unusually quiet following his grand entrance. He knew this wasn't a Huck day; it was a Martin day.

Huck had decided that direct confrontation wasn't the correct form, in these particular circumstances. How could he come out with the fact that he hated Martin's team, as Huck's dad and his dad had before him? Looking at Martin he could hear the below-the-belt chants from Martin's yobboy bully-boy supporters. Huck had no chance of an honest encounter with Martin Howler. Besides, there were very specific and clear conditions attached to staying at *The Place*. The most important of which, as David had said from the beginning, was the fundamental 'Darcy Rule', or the concept of 'DRC': discretion, respect, confidentiality. The guests of course were expected, encouraged even, to share and discuss experiences together while at *The Place*, but that was the 'first amendment' to the otherwise strict Darcy Rule. The fundamental principle came down to this: 'what goes on in *The Place*, stays in *The Place*'.

Huck looked at Martin once more and thought of little Tracy before they split off for the ponds. He remembered what had happened and, for some reason, unfairly or fairly, blamed the 'Martin the scum-bag two-timer' for all of Tracy's woes.

Huck wasn't going to let a delicate situation get between him and Martin; this opportunity might never, ever come again.

"I'll tell you what Tamara" said Huck at the first opening he had. "A man who screws around is a slag. He's not really a man; he's a tart, a male tart. If he's married or you know committed, he's also a man without honour, a scum-bag and a coward. That's what I think."

Martin lowered his head; this was fighting talk coming from a freshed-up, reborn, cage fighter.

Annie however had no fear of Huck and could smell the fun to be had.

"But Huck, isn't that a bit rich coming from a guy who wears woman's clothing? I mean who's the tart in this room?"

Martin tried very hard to hide a snigger.

Huck was on a roll. "OK, I'll tell you what, dressing up as a woman is a matter of respect. It takes courage to be who you want yourself to be. It's not about being right or wrong. It's about having the balls to express yourself. I mean I bet Martin here doesn't have the balls to dress up as anything other than a school boy."

Huck stared at Martin for the first time. "Isn't that right, Martin, you just don't have the balls to put a dress on, do you? It's about *fear*."

Tamara was beginning to feel that the session was taking a bit of a wrong turn.

"Huck, maybe we've had enough for one day. I don't feel we're making constructive progress any more. Perhaps we should warm down with a few exercises and move on. How does the group feel?"

Before the group could respond, Martin not unexpectedly, decided to swallow the bait.

"I ain't afraid of nothing." Martin jumped to his feet and suddenly sounded – and looked – like a giant ten year old. "I'll tell you what, get me the kit – any kit – and I'll show you I can strut it like the best of you lot. Let's do it."

Martin betrayed more than he wanted with the use of the word 'lot' which caused Huck to smile broadly; in fact Huck was back to where he was when he first came into the Encounter Area.

"Oh god" said Betty. "If you think I'm getting back into that whale suit under that tent thing, you've got another thing coming. Any chance I can skip forward to the Movie Therapy, maybe even a nice cup of hot chocolate? I've been looking forward to that one. Maybe even a chocolate hobnob. Oh god I'd do *anything* for a chocolate hobnob."

Toni put his hands over his ears and muttered 'tmi', tmi'.

"Fine, Betty, off you go. Tim, would you mind escorting Betty and sorting this out with JC? You're a sweetie,

Tim, thanks." Tamara felt Betty deserved a break, and a chocolate hobnob.

Tamara surveyed the group and reckoned everyone present was OK with the next challenge, late as it was. "Now, looks like we're heading into the role-reversal zone a bit sooner than we thought. OK, Tim let's get the kits out, looks like it's going to be a long night; I feel some serious role playing coming on. Sisterly love, here we come."

***

"Today is such a very special and happy day. This doesn't always happen. We – David, JC and I – would like it to happen far more often and if we had our way, we'd make it compulsory. Only joking, everyone. It doesn't always work out like this, but when it does it's a real joy. Now, in accordance with our Darcy Rule, I've discussed this with Richard who knows what to expect, don't you Richard?"

Helen looked over to Richard who was positively beaming. Standing besides Richard was Martin, Huck, Toni, Annie, Betty, and a nervous looking new arrival, Davy Crocket. Everyone had been asked to wear fancy dress clothes from the store room and their collective appearance in the conservatory overlooking the garden on such an unexpected warm and sunny day was a sight to lift the spirits.

"Today", Helen continued "is Richard's 'Graduation Day'." The group spontaneously applauded and lifted their champagne flutes, filled with chilled organic grenadine, in Richard's direction.

"And as a little token of our appreciation and in recognition of your very special journey at *The Place*, we would like you to have this."

Helen handed Richard a pretty little package, all wrapped up in gold coloured paper with a little silver bow which Richard immediately but very carefully took off, and with equal care unwrapped the box like a child with the very last, special Christmas present.

Inside was a little box and inside the little box was the digital counter Helen had used for Richard's Kaleidoscope Review session.

Richard kissed and thanked Helen.

"Look on the back, Richard."

Richard turned the timer around and on the back was inscribed the letters: 'MCMLXXXI' which Richard, with some pride, read out aloud.

Richard took a moment and then burst out laughing. "OK, very good; I get it, I like it. 1981, the year I had my twenty-first birthday. Yep, that was the happiest day of my life. Why thank you Helen. It sounds almost embarrassing to admit that I was getting more and more afraid of not being able to face another birthday. Before I came in here I was convinced I was destined to be unhappy forever and I felt there was only one way I could deal with that. Couldn't even get that right."

Richard paused and smiled as if to reassurance his audience that he was ok.

"Every day I'm waiting for the rain to fall. Even when it's sunny, I'm waiting for the rain. I guess when all's said and done, I am bipolar. But you know what? I'm quite happy with that. If you take time to look back at your life and remember the highs and the lows, it's quite obvious, really. I'm mean what the hell – we're all a bit bipolar when it comes to it. Praise be, I don't really give a shit. I mean I know it might rain later, but right now, I mean right now at this very precise moment, it's such a beautiful day. I just feel so happy. Thank you Helen, thank you all."

As speeches go, it wasn't an Oscar-winning performance. But that didn't matter. It was from the heart and brief with it. There were no embarrassing moments and no tears.

Except for Helen's, who discreetly wiped away a tear or two with the back of her fingers and opened a new box of tissues.

10

Martin had been awake for some time; in fact he couldn't remember sleeping at all, not for one second. In the previous twenty-four hours the glitzy veneer of his glory-filled life had just seemed to fade into dust. He felt strangely exposed and vulnerable; his bravado had, for the moment at least, simply disappeared.

For hours he had been thinking of the moment before he took his first penalty in front of the very hostile and extremely vocal away crowd. As a seasoned professional he was used to the hand gestures, the jeers, and the verbal abuse. But yesterday, for some reason was different. The hostile crowd had somehow come up with a spontaneous new chant, and it hurt; as if it was designed to hurt. To the melody of 'glory, glory, hallelujah' he could hear, loud and clear: 'who's yer daddy Tracy junior, who's yer daddy Tracy junior?'

As Martin had placed the ball down to take his first penalty, the chant became louder and clearer, as if the whole crowd somehow knew of the open secret that he screwed around at will, and also knew that Tracy now knew. The lyrics seemed strangely cruel but shouted with real feeling as if there was a hidden message.

Martin knew these were not the right type of thoughts to be having just before taking a penalty; he felt very self-conscious. As he ran up to take the penalty something was wrong, badly wrong. When the ball flew widely high into the baying, jeering mob, and the deafening cheer and laughing had died down, the words of the chant changed: 'it ain't that dickhead Martin Howler, it ain't that dickhead Martin Howler'. Some of the crowd pretended to howl, wolf-like, just for the fun of it.

The second penalty was even worse. It was the dying moments of extra time and his side was losing one nil. If he scored this time, he could partly at least make up for the first catastrophe; if he missed this one even his own supporters, his team mates and The Boss, would give him quality grief until he won back their respect, all over again.

The rabble behind the goal had seemed to morph into a well-conducted three part choir, one side starting with 'who's yer daddy Tracy junior, who's yer daddy Tracy junior?' and sort of cocking an ear to the other side of the crowd who responded with 'it ain't that dickhead Martin Howler'. In the meantime, an undefined element of the mob seemed content simply to howl; it was a quite a performance.

As Martin had approached the ball, the net seemed to get smaller and smaller. At the very last moment he changed his mind as to where to place his kick and whacked it straight into the arms of the goalkeeper. He had never seen a crowd react with such passion and joy; the immediate and all-engulfing feeling of sheer unadulterated failure and humiliation was a first for Martin who had slumped to the ground in abject shame.

Not one of his team mates had approached him to console him in his obvious despair, not one. Martin imagined an iconic picture of himself, on his knees, head bowed, blown up on the back pages of all the newspapers. Every cruel school boy nickname he could remember flashed through his mind in big, bold letters.

Before the match Martin had managed to fight off Tracy's demand that he head straight to *The Place*. At that moment he couldn't wait for his agent to whisk him away and head south, quickly.

To wake up on a Sunday morning with a clear head and an even clearer recollection of the night before was a rare event for the young man who was used to being the centre of unbridled adulation during the hours that followed each glorious victory.

Martin was becoming quite familiar with the small twin bedded room and looked across at the other bed in which Huck was resting, also wide awake.

"No hard feelings about last night, Martin?" Huck spoke in a clear, confident voice staring straight ahead as if he'd been waiting for the right moment to clear the air.

Martin paused only for a moment, relieved that Huck had broken the ice.

"Huck, I guess I had it coming. Strange twist for Tamara to ask us to role play sisters, bit weird, really. I was a bit surprised at how quickly you kinda got into it, took me by surprise, that's all."

In between the painful, immediate memories of the match, Martin had been playing over in his mind all the things which Huck had said to him the night before. They were spot on, really.

By any standards, Huck had launched into a sustained and vicious verbal attack. Huck, in his role-playing Martin's-sister persona, had stood right in front of Martin, his head raised high to meet Martin's glaze, demanding to know how he could betray 'sisterly love' by sleeping with Huck's 'husband', ranting all the while that everyone knew what Martin was doing.

The final coup-de-grace, delivered as a wild, high-octane tirade was that Martin was the lowest of the low, a complete cow and an evil bitch. Eventually Martin had thrown away the wig and broken down in a flood of tears before Tamara wisely decided that the 'game' had been played out to its conclusion and should come to an immediate halt.

What had surprised everyone was that Martin and Huck ended up in a long, heart-felt embrace, as fighters sometimes do after a life-defining physical encounter. Tamara had suggested that Martin and Huck share the same room for the night, a calculated gamble that Helen had agreed was worth the risk. Huck lifted himself up a bit and placed his hands behind his head.

"We all knew about the match, Martin."

"I reckoned the whole world knew about the match, Huck. I'll come back, you'll see."

Huck raised himself upright up in his bed and looked over at Martin. "Listen kid, I've nothing against you, really. You know when you put on an England shirt we're all behind you. We'll torment and abuse you if you wear one shirt, and cheer you when you wear another. It's just a game. But what you've been doing to Tracy mate is just, you know, out of order; it's not the right way to go about life, to destroy someone who loves you so much Martin. You know what I mean? That isn't a game, Martin, that's real life. You're treating your wife as if you hate her, as if you want to humiliate her. Why would you do that to a woman? You're doing her head in. It doesn't make sense unless you're so... so... unable to understand how she feels. If that's all it's about then maybe you can change things, Martin."

Martin let the words sink in. There were few people in the world he listened to, really listened to, and Huck was now one of them.

"I guess you're right, Huck. I felt as if I had the shit kicked out me yesterday. It's not that I really enjoy the screwing around that much any more, I just get a kick out of doing it. Maybe I'll just stick to the WagYu steak and give up the crap double cheeseburgers."

"That's a good way of putting it, Martin. Maybe try spending some quality time with your daughter before it's too late. These days will come and go in the blink of an eye Martin, but your family will last forever. What's the point of being a hero to your fans and a complete shit to your family? I don't get it."

"You're right Huck; I know that, I do."

"So, you just going to head off, or what?"

"I guess I will, soon enough. I've some catching up to do, time to face the music all round. I mean everyone wants to lay it on me, Huck. Everyone. But that Helen lady said I should stick around maybe for just a bit, just for one last session. Straighten me up before I head north."

***

"Alrighty, I'm ready for some serious side-splitting laughter therapy. No mercy, no prisoners. Who's with me on this one?" Gootsy just looked so happy.

Betty looked apprehensively towards Toni who failed to return any sign of reassurance, being somewhat pre-occupied with scratching his arse, a bit too intensely.

Sometimes these sessions were a bit of a challenge to Gootsy. Not that he couldn't hack it as and when required;

it was just that sometimes he felt pretty low himself given his age, but today Gootsy felt nothing short of perfect. Today was going to be a great day, he could feel it.

Gootsy surveyed the faces in front of him: Huck, Betty, Toni, Annie, Davy and Martin.

"I must be blessed, you know, to be so lucky to have you lot with me today. OK, here's how we're going to start. Each of you will stand in front of the group and simply say: 'I'm so-and-so, and I'm a 'whatever' you do, or even what you shouldn't do. Get it? We can start with you, Martin. You can say: 'My name's Martin and I score goals.' OK, maybe not."

In times past Martin might have taken immediate and serious umbrage with such a comment. But he was the first to let loose a little self-effacing snigger, as if to confirm that he was OK with Gootsy's risqué comment.

"So, Betty, off you go."

Betty gingerly stepped forward and faced the group.

"Hi, I'm Betty and I like chocolate hobnobs." Betty's one-liner caused instant and prolonged whooping and cheering.

Next up was Toni. "OK, I'm Toni and I like *ladies*." Mock boos followed.

"My name's Huck, and I'm a fighter." An awkward silence ensued.

"More like a tart with a heart" responded Annie provocatively, a comment which generated ringside-like hoots and applause.

"I'm Annie, I may look like a Zombie but I sing like an angel." Annie seemed taken aback with the prolonged laughter and spirited whooping.

"I'm Davy Crocket, the Last King of Disco." The new boy, Davy, immediately hit the spot with this crowd, judging by the whistles and cheers.

"OK", said Gootsy. "I want you all to lie down on this beautiful floor, on your backs, feet facing outwards, heads in a tight circle. Lie still with your arms by your side and close your eyes."

Gootsy waited until the group was still. "Now, think of the last time you laughed – really laughed – try to remember what it was that got to you. But don't – I said – don't *start*; hold it back for as long as you can."

Maybe it was just Gootsy's light touch but the group one by one started to hold back stifled giggles until eventually Toni blurted out an uncontrollable loud outward wheeze of a laugh which became instantly infectious. Betty was next to blow; her contribution was unbelievably raucous, an old-fashioned filthy laugh from somewhere very deep inside. Soon they were without exception in the throes of conspiratorial laughter and child-like giggles, all in their own particular and peculiar ways. Betty's contribution was just so *loud*. An unattributed fart from one of their number gave new life to the session.

After a couple of minutes Gootsy ordered everyone up and asked them to stand in a circle facing each other. "Now, you all know how to pull a funny face – one at a time into the circle and pull your best funny face, back into the circle and let someone else have a go."

Annie was first in and simply tried to put on the straightest po-faced look she could manage, which not only brought about hoots of laughter but a spontaneous round of applause, prolonged when she dramatically pulled off her wig revealing a tight-fitting hair net and then threw the wig with gay abandon into a far corner of the room.

Davy surprised everyone with his award-winning gurney

best, and Huck's 'little girl lost' look took everyone by surprise.

Martin was now in full flow of the game and pretended to take a kick at a ball and then pulled a face of horrified disappointment.

Gootsy was taken aback; even by his own standards this session seemed to have a life of its own and he let the group take turn after turn pulling faces and acting out improvised mini-scenes that come from nowhere.

When he felt that the session was nearing the end of its natural life he realised he had reached the very satisfying point where no verbal commands or instructions were required. Whatever he did, the group simply imitated. He started by peering deep into Annie's eyes, nose-to-nose, then moving on. He ran about the room flapping his arms, shaking his head with his tongue wagging wildly from his mouth. He did a pretty good impression of a staggering drunk, followed quickly with some spontaneous silly walks.

It did help that Gootsy had a notoriously infectious manner, which for the most part did not consist of actually laughing, but his theatrical attempts at trying to stop laughing.

Finally Gootsy dramatically fell to the floor as if he had been shot in the heart and lay still. The group immediately copied Gootsy, one by one, feigning their best dying moments until they were all completely and utterly still with exhaustion.

Huck was the first to come round, back to some sense of normality. The whole process had left him feeling dizzy, and he felt real pain in his sides from the laughter.

"OK, Gootsy, are we done? That was really – I mean really – great."

The small group quickly picked up that Gootsy was not playing any more; in fact Gootsy wasn't even moving.

Huck sort of crawled over to Gootsy's still body.

"Oh shit. I think Gootsy's had it. Still breathing – maybe. Er, can someone can get Helen? Quickly!"

Huck placed two fingers on Gootsy's nose and opened the thin-lipped mouth with his other hand, in preparation for mouth-to-mouth resuscitation. As Huck's wide, opened mouth lowered Gootsy's eyes suddenly sprang open. "Fooled ya!" Gootsy shouted, his face turning rapidly bright red clearly trying to hold in one almighty splutter of a laugh which seemed to try and escape through the sides of his tightly clenched mouth.

Huck's reaction was not unreasonable, in the circumstances – screaming like a young girl and jumping back if he'd been repelled by an invisible force. The group fell back into another round of tear-filled laughter while Huck and Gootsy enjoyed a prolonged giggle-infused bear hug.

Toni placed his hand on the back of his new track suit. "Oh shit. I mean, oh *shit*."

11

David and Helen were in their favourite chairs, facing Martin Howler in David's office. Martin looked a lot less cocksure than when he had first arrived, that much was obvious. Helen even detected a sense of loss, a new maturity even. She had seen it many times before; it wasn't uncommon for such a transformation to happen in less than twenty-four hours. Martin had been in *The Place* for a couple of nights, and the time was right to review how long his stay would last.

"I had a call from Tracy this morning Martin" said Helen. "She sounded a lot better, more relaxed, much calmer all round. Tracy said she'd spoken with you in the middle of the night. Did she call you?"

"No, Helen" said Martin looking down at his feet like a school boy in front of a very serious Headmistress. "I sent text after text and then I called. It wasn't easy. I've only been here a couple of nights but it seems like a lifetime."

Helen looked very concerned and adopted what David called her 'headmistress pose'.

"Martin, I'm not telling you off or anything like that. But we have explained that in this day and age you have to be very careful about sending texts."

Martin cast his eyes to the floor like a naughty school boy. "Sorry, yes I should have remembered. Sorry, Helen."

"Ok Martin. Just be more alert, please. What's done is

done. Let's move on. How do you feel? I mean towards Tracy."

Martin picked his fingers, shook his head, dug deep and eventually found the courage to look Helen in the eye.

"Look, Helen, David, it's like this. I've been doing what the hell I want for years. I've been screwing everything that moves – behind Tracy's back, since day one. Even on our honeymoon. Even with her big, I mean little, sister, Cheryl."

Martin placed his heads in his hands as if he couldn't believe what was he was saying.

"That Huck guy, the one I've been sharing with? He said it all Helen. I get it now, I really do. Something happened. Maybe I wanted to get caught. I wanted it to end. I wanted an end to the crap, the lies… the pain I was causing. It was like a kind of joke with Tracy. You know everyone knew what was going on, the mum included, even the punters – everyone, except Tracy. When Tracy came back from here it was like she knew everything. I've never seen so much hurt in someone's eyes. I could see it was cracking her up. Huck said to me: 'why do you treat Tracy as if you hate her so much. Like, what has she done to you? And Tracy junior'… Oh god… why, why?"

David was quicker to the tissues than Helen and passed the box over the Martin who manfully wiped his face with the back of his sleeve and declined the offer.

"Look, I'm OK, I'm OK. I'm probably just as upset about the game if I'm honest. You know with me mates, the fans, and The Boss. I've had a look at myself, and it's not a pretty picture. Yes, I phoned Tracy. I told her I'm sorry, I'll change, I'll make things right. I told her I love her, and I meant it. And I miss my little baby girl, I really do."

"You're ready to leave, Martin. Don't you think so, David?"

David nodded, stood up and gave Martin a healthy pat on the back. "Come on Martin, you're agent's been hanging about nearby for a call, he can be here in twenty minutes. Time to go, my friend, time to hit the road."

Martin looked up, relieved there was agreement, and smiled.

"Give my regards to that Gootsy guy. What a laugh I had. And to Betty, Toni and Huck. Mind if I take a few minutes to say thanks to Huck? I owe him."

"Sure, Martin, take all the time you need. Anything else we can do?"

Martin paused and thought for a moment.

"Yeah, there is, come to think about it."

Helen could sense some mischief in the air. "Come out with it, Martin, what have you got in mind?"

"Well, I was just thinking… perhaps you need another… guest here. Tracy's been, I've been, maybe…"

David was ahead of this game. "I know, Martin, perhaps Tracy's sister – Cheryl – maybe she could do with some time here? Not for long, but for long enough."

"Yeah, that's what I was kind of thinking. It wasn't right me sending Tracy here." Martin placed his hands over his face in disgrace. "Jesus. We all saw it unfold in front of our eyes. Tracy trusted me so much she felt she was going crazy with all the signals and vibes that I was screwing anything that moved. I guess it was just about right Tracy getting me to come down. But if anyone needs a bit of therapy or whatever it is you do here, it's that Cheryl."

"OK, Martin, don't you worry about it. Not right now, not today, but soon, very soon."

Helen looked over at David with a look he'd seen a thousand times before.

Martin suddenly appeared a bit more composed. "Thanks, guys. I know it's not Cheryl's fault, like I'm not blaming her. But, you know, if Cheryl can get half of what I've learnt then things might start to get better all round, you know, for Tracy."

Helen sounded her solemn best. "Don't worry Martin. We know. Now, say your thanks to Huck and get back home safely – share your love Martin, not your lust. And score some great goals."

"Er, not too many, Martin" said David with a smile.

***

Helen had decided that it was time to appraise Annie.

"OK, Annie, how do you feel? I mean do you think you're making progress?"

Annie certainly looked different. Having abandoned the wig, her thin grey hair and the absence of any make-up made her look several years older but in some way better.

"Well, look at me, Helen. I guess I feel different. More real, I suppose. Haven't had Botox for days. Jeez, haven't had anything for days. But you know what? I feel better, yes that's it – *better*. I looked in the mirror this morning and thought, well that's who you are, really. I've no choice about it; it's take it, or leave it."

David who had been sitting quietly decided the direct approach was in order.

"Annie, what I want to know – you know, really want to know – is whether your feelings of despair are lifting? Seriously, Annie, the question you raised when you first arrived was whether your life was worth living – or not. Have you come any closer to an answer?"

Annie stared at David with a very solemn look. "I'm getting there David. I feel as if I've been through you know – so much in the last few days. I just feel a lot more positive about life. What with that escapade to the ponds, and that whole episode with Tracy, then there was the first session with Gootsy – that was really weird but you know in a funny way. Not as funny as the laughing session, that was a joy. He's a card, that Gootsy. You should have heard Huck scream, it was priceless."

Helen was slightly apprehensive. "Do you remember the session with Paul, you know Paul Jones the hypnotherapist?"

Annie had to pause, and think. "I remember the beginning, Helen. It was just after the freak-out session or whatever you call it with Gootsy. I was already sort of beaten up, emotionally, when Paul came in. It's a bit of a blur, quite frankly."

Helen and David had to consciously avoid looking at one another.

"Listen, Annie. I think you've come a long, long way. But you're not quite ready to leave, yet. Nearly, but not quite. I think it's time for another session or two, and then see how you feel. We always say that our guests know in their hearts when they're ready to leave *The Place* and it seems to me you don't really want to leave right now. Is that fair enough?"

"I guess it is, Helen. What have got in line for me next? Something special, I hope."

David smiled. "We sure do, Annie. Wait till you meet Aaron, now he is special."

There was a polite knock on David's office door.

"Look, Annie we'll catch up with you later. We need a few

minutes with a new guest, you'll like her, Annie. You'll be sharing with her in fact, hope you don't mind. Maybe you've heard of her? Does the name Mandy Haddock ring any bells?"

Annie's face lit up as if she had just heard some amazing news. "Mandy Haddock? Really? How interesting."

David stood up and opened his door, letting Annie pass by Mandy, exchanging a brief 'hi' to each other.

"Mandy, please sit down, anywhere on the sofa. We've a lot to discuss. Great to see you."

Mandy Haddock looked every inch the brassy, lippy, cockney soap star that she had become associated with in the public's mind. The journey to television fame had left many a deep scar on Mandy's psyche whose chiselled features betrayed just too much unwanted history.

"Cut the crap, David. We all know why I'm here. It was either this *place* or Holloway prison. This looks marginally better. Just give me a good report; I'll make sure your bills are paid. But none of this therapy crap, OK?"

Helen seemed to gain an inch or two when she straightened up and placed her hands on her lap.

"Mandy, you're here by choice. You've already made an important decision. We understand the dilemma you were faced with. I've seen the transcript of the judge's comments. You're back to be sentenced in a few days. I recall he said, what was it? Oh yes: 'As far as I'm concerned, all options are open. You may be a celebrity in your world but you're a common thief in mine', something like that, wasn't it Mandy? I guess you wouldn't be in so much trouble if it wasn't for that suspended sentence hanging over you."

Helen stood up looking rather miffed, but dignified.

"I'm going to leave you with David to sort out some

details. In the meantime, Mandy, remember that you're on a knife edge. You've made one choice, but over the next few days there'll be other decisions to make. The first is this: treat all of us who are responsible for *The Place*, and all the guests and therapists here, with the same respect as you expect from us. David will explain what we mean by our 'Darcy Rule'. And you can put those cigarettes away, there's no smoking in this office. David will also explain the drugs policy. Now Mandy, is there anything I've said that you want to challenge? You are perfectly free to walk back out the door, no one is going to try and stop you. Or, you can agree to show a bit of respect and for a short time abide by our rules. Which is it, Mandy?"

Mandy reluctantly placed the cigarette back into the packet and gave Helen a steely gaze. "I get you, Helen. OK. You win. Happy?"

Mandy turned to David, fluttered her false eye lashes and placed her hand on his knee.

"Now, David, what do you want me to do?"

12

Aaron Westernson was by any accounts a strange looking guy. It wasn't just because he was on the portly side, that wouldn't be fair. It was more to do with his shock of white brillo-style hair which stuck out from the sides, but not the top, of his otherwise bald, shiny head. The thick-rimmed, black-framed glasses gave him the air of an absent-minded professor, or perhaps a long-term inmate from some institution, it was difficult to call.

"Now, Annie you're familiar with this room, I understand."

Annie picked up a faint trace of an eastern European accent in the rather high-pitched voice that came out of the ambiguous figure in front of her.

"Yeah, I feel I've been here many times," said Annie cautiously.

"Really? Oh that's very good, very good indeed. Now my name is Aaron, Doctor Aaron Westernson. Have you heard of me? OK, maybe not. You know Annie what I do is very special. I am a trained Jungian analyst but I've been told I have a gift for what is sometimes called 'Regression Therapy'."

Annie was getting the point that all of these therapies, in their own way, were special. Annie had taken a quick look at her 'Special Programme' but barely registered the words 'Regression Therapy' before heading down to the

Encounter Area. Annie had no idea, at all, what this might mean and even less idea as to what relevance was supposed to be attached to the description 'Jungian analyst'.

Annie looked around and was surprised as to how much the atmosphere of the room could change with so little effort, rather like the stage of a small theatre. Today the curtains were drawn over the mirrors and the lights were on the low side, but not to a disturbing degree.

Unusually, there was just a rug on the floor in the centre of the room and on this rug were two comfy armchairs facing each other, and that was it. Annie was now embedded in one chair, facing the Hobbit-like Aaron Westernson in the other, equally comfortable armchair opposite.

"Now, Annie. Have you been hypnotised before?"

Annie had a passing thought of being a bit cheeky and saying 'how would I know' but decided quickly against the flippant approach. This guy was really serious.

"Er, yeah, the other day, right here actually, well more or less. That nice guy, Paul. He asked to hypnotise me, but I was a bit flaked out at the time – you know with the Gootsy fella and all that screaming. It's funny you should ask because I can't say if Paul hypnotised me or not. I don't know, it didn't feel right."

Annie realised she was only talking out of nerves and tried, unsuccessfully to shut up.

"OK, Aaron, what's the form – you know – what do I have to do? Have you got a swinging watch thingy or something? I can't even remember what Paul asked me to do, exactly."

"No, Annie, I don't have – or need – a 'swinging watch thingy'. Just listen to my voice. Tell me a bit about yourself, Annie. Do you ever have feelings of déjà vu? Have you ever felt some *connection* with a figure in a past life? Helen told me you were once the most popular person on *Planet Celebrity*. The last person to hold that title was probably Helen of Troy, Cleopatra, or... the Queen of Shebah, Boudicca, Queen Elizabeth the First... Marie Antoinette – ring any bells?"

Annie sighed and for a moment felt quite hopeless. This was going to be an A1 disaster she thought. Aaron however was not giving up on Annie, not by a long shot.

"Now, let's start with the real you. This 'Annie Young' name is a prop is it not? Your real name is Fannie Tucker? Do you mind if I call you Fannie, Annie?"

Annie closed her eyes. This was going to be a long session.

"OK, you can call me Fannie. So, like... let's go, Aaron. You know, when I think of it, there was one person I read about some time ago and I did feel some sort of 'connection' as you put it." Annie took a deep breath and closed her eyes. Aaron's presence was somehow reassuring; she felt safe and secure despite some reservations about what on earth was going to happen next.

"That's good, very good. Tell me more, there's no rush, take your time, we've a long journey ahead of us Fannie, a long, long journey back into a time and space where there are only thoughts, intuition, memories... feelings. A long, long time ago... "

Annie closed her eyes, took another deep breath, dug deep and tried not to think of Fanny Craddock.

***

Mandy was lying on her bed, wondering what Annie Young

was really like. Mandy had been encouraged to have a light meal brought to her room and get to sleep early. She had heard Annie creep into her bed in the middle of the night and decided to leave her alone. Even in the semi-darkness it was obvious that she was exhausted and ready for bed.

But curiosity and impatience got the better of Mandy and she looked over to see if there were any signs of life coming from her roommate.

"Hi, Annie. Annie. It's me, Mandy. We met yesterday when I arrived? You awake? Do you want to talk?"

Annie turned over to face Mandy, her head still resting on a pillow.

Mandy and Annie took a long hard look at each other, out of mutual curiosity. Mandy recalled seeing Annie perform on television in a Christmas edition of *Songs of Praise* years ago, but the image in front of her bore little resemblance to that Annie. But despite there being no wig and no make-up Annie looked surprisingly content and relaxed, happy even.

Annie, likewise, sized up Mandy whose wild and reckless real life competed constantly with her soap star character, Sharon. The tabloids never seem to let her be, partly because there was such fun to be had comparing Mandy's real life with the life of her on-screen character. The dividing line often seemed so blurred that it was difficult to keep track. Even Mandy's current real life predicament, facing a possible jail sentence for repeated shoplifting, mirrored a story line from the soap opera. The producers had become so concerned that Mandy in some bizarre manner was being overtaken by her on-screen character they had delayed killing her off in case Mandy committed suicide. They were working on a happy ending for Mandy, but that was proving quite a challenge. The whole point about the Sharon character was that she was there to suffer, in biblical proportions.

"So, Annie what's it like in here? I mean, really."

Annie smiled and took her time. "It's what you want it to be, I guess. I've had some really weird experiences Mandy but, you know, worthwhile. And to be fair some real laughs, I can tell you. But last night was really, really weird."

Mandy was intrigued. "Well, go on, what happened?"

Annie tried hard to focus and put together the sequence of events. "There's a lot of therapies that go on here, Mandy. They – you know Helen and David and David's boy, JC – call them activities – that's true enough. Last night I was with this nutty professor-looking guy called Aaron something. He's into regression therapy."

"What the hell is that – do you like howl at the moon or what?"

"No, Mandy the howling and screaming stuff is something else, I'll tell you about that later. No this is like finding your past life."

"Your what?"

"You know, your past life. Everyone is born with memories, Mandy. Think about it. Somewhere in your head is a chest of memories going back… forever, back to… to… cosmic dust." Annie paused for a moment and looked over at Mandy who had a concerned look on her face. "Don't worry Mandy, I know I probably sound a bit like this Aaron guy, but you have to go through it, to get it."

"Annie, listen. You don't suppose they've just hypnotised you into believing all this? I mean who do you think you are, right now?"

"Mandy, no, you don't get it. I know who I am. I'm Fannie Tucker."

"Fannie Tucker? Bastards. Jeez, couldn't they have given you Cleopatra or something a bit more exotic than Fannie Tucker! I mean what did this Fannie do? No, don't tell me. Bastards." Mandy sounded pretty angry.

"Mandy, listen. My real name *is* Fannie Tucker. My manager got me to change it years ago. When I started off there was only one Fanny, and that was Fanny Craddock."

"Who the hell is Fanny Craddock?" Mandy was completely lost.

"Look, Mandy that's not the point. My mum spelt the end of my name with 'ie', not 'y', you know so I wouldn't be confused with Fanny Craddock. Anyway, after I sort of came around, last night, with this Aaron guy, I remembered a whole life. It was so real. You know like one of those dreams that just seem as real as real life."

Mandy felt she was beginning to understand. "Yeah, OK. I mean was your dress undone or anything?"

Annie laughed. "No, nothing like that. No I remembered living in ancient Greece, it was so real."

Mandy shook her head. "Oh gawd, so they did go for Cleopatra. I could have told yer."

"No, Mandy not Cleopatra, she lived in Egypt, you know like Cleopatra *of the Nile*. My name was… was Aspasia, that's it… Aspasia."

Mandy leant back on her bed. "Aspasia. Could have been worse. You know like a frigging witch being fried alive on the stake; a sort *Barbeque of the Bitches: Live and Exclusive at The Place,* sort of night." Mandy shivered at the thought. "They better not ask me to go through that shit, I can tell you. So, you gonna tell me about *Aspasia*? I mean you must know a lot about her, if you know what I mean, Fannie, I mean Annie."

"Yeah, I will, later. I'm so hungry Mandy."

"Come to think of it, so am I. What do they do about feeding you here? For the money they take I'd expect a five star service 24/7."

"Just pick up the phone and ask for what you want, Mandy that's all there is to it."

"What, anything you want, and like it just arrives?"

Annie laughed. "You ever done your shopping online? What you ask for and what you get isn't always the same. I mean the other day I asked for chocolate cereal and was given some muesli. Ask for beer and they'll give you alcohol free organic ginger beer. It's a bit of a game. If Helen feels a special occasion is in order we eat together in the Encounter Area which doubles-up as a dining room. Doubles-up as a lot of things that Encounter Area, come to think about it."

"Right," said Mandy, "I know what I want" and picked up the phone and shouted her demands as she did when on holiday, sounding ever more like her soap opera character Sharon, than Mandy Haddock.

Mandy held the phone out at arm's length and turned to Annie.

"Regression therapy? Jesus. What next?" Mandy asked.

"What next, Mandy? On my 'Special Programme' looks like we've got something called 'Pap Therapy' coming up, God knows what that involves."

13

Deep inside the offices of the *Sunday News*, Simon Hall read the on-screen draft of Ralph's expose on his Mac computer with some interest, giggling and smirking throughout.

"Oh, I like this Ralph. Oh yes. Great strap line: '*The Wisdom of the Unholy Trinity': why JC, God and the Pope can cure your woes — at a price, of course'.*"

Simon licked his lips and carried on. '*Today we expose the three stooges who run one of the best kept secrets of our celebrity age. When we see our favourite celebrities break down, freak out, crash — spectacularly — under our noses, in front of our very eyes, we often wonder where they wake up the next day. Today we tell you. It's not always the local police station or their best mate's sofa or a park bench in Brighton. No, they're just as likely to open their weary eyes at the rehab joint called 'The Place,' a discreetly-placed, modern-looking building next to Hampstead Heath in north London. From the outside the magnolia-coloured sandstone building looks serene and quiet, inside it's another story.*'

Simon read on silently pausing only occasionally to let rip another exaggerated roar of laughter until he came to the end.

"And the photo spread is fucking ace by the way, well done to Judas I mean Henry. Priceless."

Simon's smile disappeared in an instant, to be replaced with the scowl of the bastard he had become.

"OK, Ralph, it's squeaky bum time. It's best if I deal with

them, I'll start with God, as one should, and see if I can get any more out of him once they're given an opportunity to respond. Forty-eight hours seems reasonable in the circumstances, don't you think, old boy?

"Very reasonable, in the circumstances, Simon, very reasonable."

***

Helen was particularly keen on encounter therapies. She liked the unpredictability and creativeness, the spontaneity and above all, the fun. Moreover these sessions actually worked. Helen wasn't entirely sure exactly how or even why they worked, but work they did, every time, without exception. It was also, as Helen knew, something to do with the way she defined success.

Today the Encounter Area had been subtly adapted for one of Helen's favourites which she insisted in conducting personally, 'Pap Therapy'.

All guests were present and accounted for: Annie, Huck, Toni, Betty, Davy and Mandy.

"OK, this morning we're having some 'Pap Therapy'. Have a look around."

In the centre of the room was a door, well what looked like a real door. As to how it managed to stay standing was a moot point but no one cared about that. It looked pretty shaky but it was a definitely a door. David and JC were dressed up looking like spivs from a 1950s musical; it was surprising what a fancy coloured waistcoat, shiny shoes and a fedora could do for a man.

"OK" said Helen excitedly, "here's the game. Each of you – I'll give you a running order in a moment – will go behind the door, wait for the signal from me, then come through the door and be 'papped' by the waiting paparazzi. Sounds easy, doesn't it?" Helen smiled, betraying deliberately the possibility that there was slightly more to this 'challenge' than at first appeared. "Now, if you're not being papped, or a member of the paparazzi, you're a fan, OK. Not difficult this one."

Mandy's initial cynicism was overtaken with the excitement of it all, and waved her hand in the air like an excited school girl who was keen to show the class that she knew the right answer.

"Me, me, me… can I go first, please Helen?"

Helen paused as if she wasn't sure whether to agree to Mandy's request.

"Er, OK. Mandy's first up. Go behind the door and wait for my signal. Can the others come with me?"

Helen took Annie, Huck, Toni, Davy and Betty to the far side of the room to brief them out of earshot of the waiting Mandy. David and JC knew what to do. After a few moments, Helen turned the lights down low, except for a single well-aimed spotlight which shone from the ceiling onto the door. "OK, Mandy, come through the door, *now*."

Mandy gingerly opened the makeshift door and stepped forwards with a sort of 'here am I' pose, head flung back, arms outstretched, waiting for an explosion of flashing lights and wild cheers.

Instead, there was silence. All of those present, including David and JC, stood looking at Mandy and then one by one starting murmuring to each other, and gesturing as if to say, "Who is this? Nah, let's wait for the next one." One by one they turned their backs on Mandy. Toni who felt the urge to surpass his brief instructions, muttered a bit too loudly:

"Couldn't shift a signed photo of that one on eBay for one penny; post and package included."

Helen waited another moment or two and then said. "OK, Betty your turn."

Mandy looked around in disbelief but quickly got the point, gave everyone a filthy look, especially Toni, and promptly burst into tears, retreating to a corner of the room.

The group reconvened and this time Betty emerged to a cacophony of positivity, David and JC's large old-fashioned theatrical cameras sending out flashing lights and puffs of smoke. Toni approached Betty pretending to present an autograph book. Huck was whooping and shouting as if Betty was some megastar while David and JC poised on either side of Betty shouting 'One more, Betty, This way. That's great, really great. Love it darling, love it."

Eventually the group quietened down as Betty walked through the gauntlet-style group, emerging at the end with a huge beam of a smile, theatrically wiping her brow.

"OK, Annie, you go" said Helen.

Annie surprised even herself with her immediate reaction. "No, thanks, Helen. I... er don't feel – you know – dressed for the occasion."

Helen moved on quickly. "OK, Huck, let's see what you're made of."

Huck practically ran behind the door; Helen followed discreetly.

Huck burst through the door and immediately gave it his over-the-top theatrical best, moving quickly from one pose to another, pushing out his rear, hands on hips, tongue licking round his lips all tart-like and generally hamming it up in girly fashion one moment and then by way of deliberate contrast throwing some very masculine, macho, martial-arty stances the next. Huck's antics were played out to an exaggerated cacophony of whoops, cheers, flashing lights and smoke. Even Helen let rip with a two-handed, four finger wolf whistle at one point.

Huck suddenly straightened up and started blowing kisses towards his fans. Without warning he shouted out: "No, please – you shouldn't… why thank you, thank you so much. Please, I wouldn't be here without the real star of the show… the great Annie Young!"

Huck gestured wildly for Annie to join him. The group spontaneously pushed and shoved Annie towards Huck despite her protestations. Once Annie was on the other side of the lights her persona seemed to change, completely. Tears trickled down her cheeks as the fans shouted her name while the cameras of the enthusiastic paparazzi papped and smoked away.

To say Annie milked her moment was an understatement. Despite being reluctant to face the spotlight initially, once on the other side it seemed she couldn't get enough. After what seemed an eternity Helen signalled to David and JC to slow down and stop the antics with the camera. The crowd, such as it was, continued defiantly with a prolonged and genuine applause which Helen was content to let continue without interruption. Helen eventually turned up the lights but the applause continued.

Huck took Annie in his arms while Annie sobbed uncontrollably. Betty and Toni turned Huck's embrace into a small group hug while Davy sat next to the still-distraught Mandy and placed his arm around her.

"OK" said Helen. "Time for a little breather; let's take fifteen and then we'll restart with Mandy. And this time Mandy we'll do it right, OK?"

The group, as one, looked at Mandy half-expecting a full-bloodied, spite-filled verbal attack directed towards Helen and anyone else who might be caught in Mandy's firing line. Everyone was expecting Sharon, Mandy's alter ego, to make an appearance. But Mandy meekly wiped away her tears and replied sheepishly as if she had just been a taught a painful but fair lesson. "OK, Helen, thanks. I'd… appreciate that, I really would."

***

"You look great, Annie." David had learnt the art of faking sincerity a long time ago, but this time he didn't have to; Annie really did look great. Her hair was dyed a dark-grey but natural looking, nonetheless. Helen thought that the stylists who were paid – generously – to 'turn out' guests, on special occasions, were the best therapists of all. With a new hairstyle, some flamboyant clothing and professionally applied make-up, absolute wonders could be achieved with most ladies of any age. But the shine and sparkle in Annie's eyes was all to do with her experiences at *The Place*, a fact which she was more than ready to acknowledge.

"I can second that" said Helen before Annie had time to respond. "My, what a big day, Annie. We've organised a formal send off for you – a real special Graduation Ceremony. But I know you wanted a little chat with me and David before we go outside. Now, I'm intrigued, Annie. It's not often we're asked to have a 'guest of a guest' attend the Graduation Ceremony. This chap, 'Bill', he's your manager, the one you first described if I recall correctly as a scumbag?"

Annie looked a bit sheepish, coy almost. "Yes, he's my

manager. Well, Bill's more than a manager; I expect you've already worked that one out. I have a surprise for Bill. I'm going to ask for us to get married. Well, what I mean is that he had asked me before I came in here that if, when I was ready to leave – and ready to live – really enjoy life, he'd like us to get married, so I'm really just saying 'yes' to his proposal rather than actually asking him. I mean, there is a difference. And I'm going to sing him a song, a cappella, one of his favourites. You know I really feel like singing. I can't wait."

"So, are you ready now Annie?" asked David.

"Yeah, I'm ready." Annie closed her eyes as if savouring every breath she took. "What a time I've had. I'll never forget Gootsy... Huck... Betty... Toni... and Tracy, how could I ever forget Tracy."

Helen leaned forward and placed her hand on Annie's shoulder. "You saved her life, Annie."

"And you saved mine, Helen. OK, come on, let's do this, I'm so excited."

"OK, Annie do you mind going ahead, we'll join you in a minute. It will make it more special if you go ahead. Be one of the crowd, we'll call you up when we arrive."

"Sure," said Annie "it'll give me time to decide what to sing to my Bill."

David and Helen waited for Annie's footsteps to fade down the corridor.

"Phew" said David. "That was a close one."

"All your fault, David. I thought we agreed to leave the therapy decisions to me."

"I'll have to plead guilty to that one, Helen. Look, I wasn't sure from the start whether the hypnotherapy stuff would, you know, do any real good. I should have left that to you if I'm honest about it; you're right on that score."

David sighed as if he'd learnt something about himself and continued. "All's well that end's well. We were just lucky to find Aaron on such short notice; I mean that guy's got genuine talent. You know he told me what I suspected all along. Annie's not going to make any real progress with traditional hypnosis; that was a wrong call of mine. It's a quick fix but only a temporary solution. Annie needed something deeper and longer lasting, otherwise she might have stayed trapped inside her mindset forever. It's not Paul's inexperience that was the problem, it was mine. It wasn't about hypnotising her to believe she was beautiful; I should have known that was too easy a solution."

David looked chuffed with himself as if he had just worked out a difficult puzzle. "Mind you, no words can solve the problem of her lop-sided tits; guess she'll need a surgeon with a steady hand to sort that one out."

Helen looked at David with an air of resignation. David still didn't 'get it' as far as Helen was concerned, but as long as he thought he'd got it, that was good enough. In that sense David was in the same position as most of the guests of *The Place*. It was all a bit ironic to Helen, who knew that Annie needed to feel some good old-fashioned love, for and from her bloke, and something romantic, that made her feel special. It wasn't difficult, as far as Helen was concerned.

"Well, we're OK now, David. Annie will always see the beauty inside of her, as long as someone loves her. Hopefully that will all be taken care of by Bill."

"Amen, to that Helen."

As they left David's office and headed towards to the patio, Helen picked up a beautifully wrapped present which would soon be ceremoniously handed to Annie. Wrapped up, it looked as if it might be small statute, an Oscar even. But inside the golden wrapping paper was not an Oscar but a similar sized miniature statute of a gold leaf plated figurine which could have been mistaken for a Greek Goddess were it not for the inscription on the base which read: Aspasia.

14

David and Huck were sharing a quiet moment on the patio, seated opposite each other, sharing an ice-filled jug of home-made lemonade and enjoying the soft warm breeze of an early evening.

"So, how do you think it's going Huck?" David was content to wait for as long as it took before Huck decided to respond.

"Hell, if I could afford it, I think I'd just sort of move in, David. It's funny but I don't want to leave because in a way I know I'm ready to leave. Does that make sense, David?"

"Sure does, Huck. You're not the first one to feel like that. Can't say it happens too often, but I guess there comes a point when you're over the fear, you've faced your demons and then it feels like a breeze, almost like a holiday."

David and Huck took a synchronised sip of their ice-filled glasses of lemonade and let their eyes rest on the country-like view of the back garden to *The Place*.

"Those trees could do with a bit of attention, David. If you cut them back a bit might let in a bit more sunlight in the evening. That would be nice, don't you think? I mean it wouldn't affect the feeling of privacy, would it? You could do some activities in the fresh air – maybe some martial arts training – even some light sparring – controlled of course."

David was intuitive enough to know that the conversation had taken a different turning and was quite willing to go with the flow.

"You remember when we first met in my office, Huck? You said something like 'just after a fight you're most at risk'. Tell me Huck, what are you most 'at risk' of?"

Huck understood David's question to be seriously loaded and felt as if there was a lot at stake.

"I guess what I meant was that just after a fight I'm most at risk of jacking it in. I don't mean doing myself in, David – don't get me wrong, I'm not that type. I mean giving up the fighting, the training – you know all that side of my life. Problem is I'm not quite sure what I'd do next. And there's the dressing-up side. I really enjoy that. That's why I booked myself in here David. I guess a lot of your guests have a sort of breakdown and they end up here instead of the local A&E. I wasn't like that. I knew that after my last fight I'd need some real good space to sort my head out and decide what to do – who I am, even." Huck looked at David who returned a wry smile. "OK, it's complicated. I know that David."

David let Huck's words hang in the air.

"I'll tell you what Huck. Maybe I could have a chat with Helen and JC. Maybe there's a deal to be done here, Huck. I mean perhaps if you were… how can I put it? If you wanted to contribute to *The Place*, I can think of stuff – I mean activities – we could get you involved in."

Huck smiled and took another sip from his glass. "I'd be more than happy to sing for my supper, David. Not literally, of course. But I could get into this. I felt with Martin that I did – you know – help."

David looked at his watch. "Oh shit, didn't realise that

was the time. I'd better get back inside; I've got a meeting to attend to. But listen, Huck, seriously, I'll tell you what, I'll have a little chat with Helen and JC, see how they feel. No promises."

David sat back with a sense of smugness, feeling quite chuffed with how he had dealt with Huck, and felt the familiar buzz of his mobile phone go off inside his trouser pocket. David flipped the phone and realised at once it was a number his phone didn't recognise.

David turned away from Huck and half-whispered into the phone. "Yeah, who's this?"

"Hello, Mr Cooper. I am speaking to Mr Cooper, am I not? Maybe I should call you God. OK, listen up Mr Cooper, my name is Simon Hall, senior editor at the *Sunday News*. We need to talk. Is this is a good time?"

David could sense Huck's interest in the call and for some reason felt physically sick. "Er not right now, I'll call you back in a few minutes." David flipped the phone back, placed it into his pocket and looked at Huck.

"Everything OK, David?" asked Huck who had detected a sudden change in David's mood.

"Everything is fine, Huck, absolutely fine."

***

Helen and David were already seated in their favourite seats in David's office when Davy Crockett arrived. "Hi, Davy, come on in, sit down, please. This isn't an interview – you've been through that already, just a little catch-up chat. You've had time to settle in and we just wanted to make sure you're ready for the next stage," said Helen, sounding friendly, but intentionally formal.

"I'm cool, Helen," replied Davy Crockett looking every inch the aging soul singer that he was.

"I heard that you described yourself as 'The Last King of Disco' at the Gootsy session. Is that how you feel, like some sort of surviving relic from a bygone age?" asked David.

"Listen brother, I'm still alive. It's not that I'm from a 'bygone' age, it's just that in my world there's always a King – sometimes even a Queen – and since our brother Michael and sister Donna passed on, hell I'm OK claiming the crown. Point is, I'm the only the black Davy Crockett there's ever been or likely to be. For sure, I mean it's been a while since me and the boys were on *'Top of the Pops'* but our revival tours are always packed out, I mean we're big in Brighton, brother. They know every word to every song we ever laid down, better than I do. If I forget the lyrics I point the mike in their direction and they fill in for me. It touches my soul, and that's the truth…" Davy sounded OK, but David and Helen knew better.

Helen had picked on Davy Crockett's problems from the first screening. In many ways Davy was what *The Place* was all about. Davy Crockett was, after thirty years, still the lead singer of *The Dreamers* which in its day was up there with the best of the disco bands of the 80s. Times had moved on, but Davy hadn't, and there was the problem.

Davy Crockett's management team had decided that a few days in *The Place* was a worthwhile investment for the group and the whole entourage that now followed and managed *The Dreamers*, one of the most successful revival groups on the lucrative retro scene. But there was a legal problem. They could only use the name *The Dreamers* provided at least one of the original group was in the line-up, and Davy Crockett was the sole survivor.

If Davy Crockett failed to appear – for any reason – on stage with *The Dreamers*, then a contractual clause flushed out after years of legal wrangling would kick in. The game would be up: the right to use their stage and recording name would be automatically transferred to another, rival management company.

Keeping Davy Crockett on his feet, alive enough to perform, was the name of the game, not that anyone had thought it necessary to tell Davy Crockett, who had never read or understood a contract in his life; in fact anything remotely concerned with contracts or finances had, over the years, flown over Davy Crockett's head completely. Davy thought he was in *The Place* for a quality chill-out before the tour started, like a sort of pre-tour reward.

David and Helen had promised the management team that under no circumstances would they let the cat out of the bag. That was the deal. The 'brief' was simple: get Davy Crockett straightened up as best as could be done before the tour started. Quite simple, really.

Davy realised that David and Helen were looking for a few words of comfort, that everything was OK. "I'm loving it here, really. That girl – what's her name – the one who was given a bit of rough ride in the last session. I felt real sorry for her. What's her name again?"

David stepped in. "You mean Mandy, Mandy Haddock."

"Yeah, wild Mandy. Man, she's got problems that one. I mean who is she? Boy, you must get used to all sorts in this place."

"Er, we sure do Davy" said David trying not to sound sarcastic or betraying any hint of irony.

Davy Crockett began to relax, and it showed. "Any problems with me skinning up? I was told you guys were like –

cool about that sort of thing."

Helen and David were ahead of Davy on this score, but Davy wasn't to know that.

"Listen, Davy. We've got a ton of rules and regulations we have to live with. We have a drug policy which is stated clearly in our house rules." Davy looked confused.

"You remember there were some papers on your bed, you know like a 'Welcome Pack'." Davy shook his head as if David was talking another language.

Helen decided to have a go. "Listen carefully, Davy. We don't condone any drug use at all, and that includes all forms of alcohol, tobacco and any type of dope, grass, gear, stuff or any type of un-prescribed drug."

"You're shitting me guys, come on, tell me you're shitting me. Hell, I can't go cold turkey on my smoke after… after fifty years. You trying to kill me? No way, brothers. I've got to have my smoke. Got to."

Helen and David had been here before; David preferred Helen to do the talking on this one.

"OK, Davy. Here's the deal. We have to confiscate your… your gear. We can then say hand on heart we acted above the law." Helen produced a couple of bits of paper and turned the first page over, indicating a dotted line.

"You need to sign this piece of paper which confirms that we've taken your stuff. Don't panic, I haven't finished yet. We can't stop you finding your stuff and having a discreet smoke outside in the patio area. We do try to dissuade our guests from smoking – anything – but we do accept that some addictions are so deeply rooted that we can't expect to detach our guests from real physical addictions over a few days."

"Yeah, OK, but what's the deal, lady?" Davy looked

very concerned, and confused.

"I prefer Helen, Davy. The deal is that after the next session, when you go back to your room you might just find that your stuff has found its way under your pillow. You mustn't smoke in your room. But we're not going to stop you from smoking – as I said – outside in the patio area. So, all you have to do is believe in the tooth fairy."

Davy looked considerably more relaxed. "OK, Helen, that's cool. I like that. I'm OK, you're OK. Why hell, we're all OK."

"OK," said David "now we're all OK, let's head down to the Encounter Area and we can get going on the next session."

"The Encounter Area, like that's what you call that dungeon downstairs. I'm OK with that. I'm into encounters David, my whole goddamn life has been one long encounter, that's for sure. I'll wait for the tooth fairy to deliver. Man, I *believe* in the tooth fairy. Where do you want to me to sign?"

***

The guests arrived more or less at the precisely allocated time to take their very carefully arranged seats for what they understood to be a 'routine' group therapy session. But each of them, Davy, Huck, Betty, Toni, Mandy and the newest guest, Cheryl Smith, had a worrying feeling that nothing was routine about *The Place*.

Helen had decided that she would conduct this session on her own; it was something she enjoyed, immensely. Helen's passion was to ensure that every session had some form of lasting impact on those who took part. It wasn't enough to have people sitting around simply having a chat. That was too easy. To make the encounter special, some other ingredient had to be added and Helen had come up with the idea of the 'Spotlight Zone'.

The group took their seats in nervous anticipation. There appeared to be no props, music or sounds on this occasion but the wry smile on Helen's face betrayed something.

"Please, I want each of you, first of all, to relax." Helen enjoyed her opening line as it always had the opposite effect which was part of the fun.

"My, that didn't work did it? You are all so tensed up; it's like looking across at a wall made of stress and anxiety. Now, we're going to try again. This time close your eyes, breathe in through your nose and hold it for a few seconds. Now breathe out, slowly through your mouth. Now can we just try that a couple of times. Try placing your hands on your knees and keep your back straight otherwise you'll get distracted by being uncomfortable."

Helen waited until the feeling of palpable tension had been reduced. "Now I want you all to tense up as much as you can. Clench those fists; make your body rigid – that's it. I can see none of you have any problems with this one. Now, hold it, hold it. OK, now relax, and breathe. Imagine there's a pencil attached to the end of your nose. Draw a great big circle with that pencil, that's it – great big circles, feel those neck muscles working. Do it one way, then the other, wider circles each time, that's it. Good, very good. Now, open your eyes."

Helen looked round at the group and as expected, everyone was smiling and looking a great deal less stressed than a few minutes ago. Now they were ready.

"OK," said Helen "here's how this session works. I've

conducted countless group therapy sessions and most of them were a complete waste of time. The problem is that there are too many distractions."

Helen reached beneath her chair and held up a small remote control. "We've been thinking how to make this work, and this is what we came up with. Watch this."

Helen pressed a couple of buttons and for a moment the room went pitch black until Helen spoke again.

"You see," said Helen, as a strong spotlight focussed on her face highlighting quite dramatically her features against a background of almost total blackness, "when I speak a sensor on one of the spotlights on the ceiling picks up my voice. Each of you has a light directed towards you, and it will shine in your direction when you speak or make any noise. It's quite neat isn't it? The technology's been around a long time mainly for security purposes but it will work great for this setting, believe me. When I stop speaking, the light fades out. Watch."

True enough a moment or two after Helen had stopped speaking the room plunged back into total darkness.

Helen continued and the light appeared on her face again. "Now, everyone in turn, just to check all is in order, simply say your name. Wait until the light has gone out before you say anything. Let's go round the circle starting with you, Cheryl."

As soon as Helen stopped speaking, the spotlight dimmed and the room went dark.

"Oh yes, and before we start I just want you to say, after you've said your name, one of two things. You can either say: 'I shall not be totally honest with this group' or 'I shall be totally honest with this group'. It's your decision, it really is."

Everyone waited for Cheryl to say something, anything. The time passed as slowly as if in a dentist's chair and still no word from Cheryl. After what seemed like an eternity, a spotlight focussed on Cheryl not because of any words she had spoken, but as a result of her distinct sobbing.

Helen was content to let this continue; it was a bizarre and very intense scene as Cheryl's tears continued unabated. It was too much for Huck who knew he was supposed to wait his turn.

"My name is Huck, and I intend to tell the truth, the whole truth, and nothing but the truth." Huck's interpretation of Helen's opening statement came across as if Huck was giving evidence in a courtroom, which Toni seemed to find funny. Toni's giggles came to an abrupt end when a light shone on him.

Toni looked somewhat startled and embarrassed. "Oh, shit. Hey, I'm sorry guys. Just nerves you know. Feel like Gootsy's about to appear and say 'we have ways of making you scream'."

Nobody responded, not even Toni's ally Betty and the room went dark again.

"My name's Betty and I'm going to be totally honest with you all."

The room once more descended into darkness and Davy Crockett was now prepared. "My name is Davy Crockett. Man, this is *heavy* shit. I'm cool, no bullshit from me."

"I'm Mandy, and I'll be truthful, I promise." Mandy looked and sounded like a naughty school girl; there was a clear sexiness in her voice.

The room went dark again; there was a group anticipation of Cheryl finding the courage to actually speak, but instead she hung her head as if in shame and tried very hard and very successfully to make no noise at all.

Helen liked this part, the bit where nobody knew what to do. It was the interesting stage and started a new challenge, like a see-who-blinks-first type of game; a Mexican stand-off in complete silence. Helen closed her eyes and breathed consciously and lightly, content to wait for as long as it took for someone to crack.

After what seemed like an eternity, Cheryl lifted her head and said "My name… my name is Cheryl Smith. I promise I will try and tell the truth."

"What kinda shit is that sister? Like I will *try* and tell the truth? I mean come out with it lady, say it how it is, say you gonna tell the truth or like you ain't gonna tell the truth. I mean is you, or ain't you, gonna tell the truth Cheryl?"

Davy leaned back and let the light fade, feeling immediately quite smug until Cheryl's sobbing started to continue.

Davy, perhaps feeling guilty over his outburst or perhaps just wanting to lighten the mood, couldn't resist the opportunity and quite spontaneously sang, slowly and softly, the opening bars of a reggae version of '*Somewhere Over the Rainbow*' that always brought the house down. Davy took a breath and continued, this time upping the tempo and giving the song his soulful best.

This was too much for Toni who felt he had no choice but to support Davy with a backing vocal and some serious-looking air guitar movements.

And so Toni and Davy carried the song through until even Betty and Huck were clapping hands and singing along until the final crescendo which resulted in a loud and spontaneous applause from everyone, except Cheryl, who remained defiantly silent and then burst forth like a breaking dam.

"OK, OK. This is my first day. Maybe you've all been sort of broken in already, I haven't. I'm only here because of the pressure from my family. It's a big family. We were all shit poor until my sister got properly hitched up with Martin. Oh god, I've been a bitch, I really have. A right fat bitch. Is that what you wanted to hear? OK, you've heard it. That's the truth. Can I go now?"

Cheryl burst into tears and headed for the door, but it was Davy who got to her first and placed an arm around her and led her back to her seat. Helen discreetly pressed a button on the remote control and the room lit up.

Davy stayed with Cheryl, his arm placed protectively around her shoulder, while the others tried hard not to stare too consciously in Cheryl's direction.

Helen decided it was time to resume control.

"OK, this time we can keep the lights on. Let's start again. Cheryl, over to you." Davy looked at Helen quite intensely as if to say 'are you sure' and returned to his seat but Helen all the while kept her gaze on Cheryl who composed herself with surprising speed.

"Right, my name is Cheryl Smith, Tracy's sister, and I'm going to tell you all the truth."

15

Helen, David and JC sat in their familiar seats in David's office. The atmosphere was intense, even by the high standards of *The Place*.

"OK, Helen, JC this is what's going on. I had a chat with Simon Hall and I wanted to have a little think before I shared this with you. Simon is the senior hatchet man at the *Sunday News*, a right little bastard. Simon told me they're gonna run with a story about *The Place*. He seemed to emphasise – a lot – the fact that the piece wasn't about our guests. It will be about us, '*the unholy Trinity*' as they're going to headline us. He said 'as was the usual practice' – what was it – oh yes, that 'in accordance with the highest standards of professional journalism' he of course would like our views and comments on the piece including the photos – jeez what has he found – before it's published. He said that we could have forty-eight hours and then they'll go to print."

David's head sunk as if in defeat, but then he picked himself up, quickly.

"That's what he said. What I told him was that he couldn't expect this to go to print without a fight. There's got to be all sort of legal issues here. I said, 'For sure, send me what you've got to say, we've got nothing to hide, or worry about.' I was dead cool. Anyway, the entire text will be with us later today, tomorrow latest. I'm sure it will be very entertaining."

"Oh shit," said JC, "we're done for, surely. Helen, why are you still smiling? Shouldn't we be in tears, in a state? It's time to panic and run, isn't it?" JC wasn't sure if he was joking or not. It was just that he couldn't understand why Helen and his dad seemed so in control and unperturbed.

"Listen, JC. When I met your dad he was different from all the others. First of all I'd never come across someone with such inner confidence and ambition. OK, he's pretty good looking too."

"And," continued Helen, "your dad is the coolest person I've ever met when confronted with a crisis. I'm sure he's told you the stories. Anyway, I always had complete faith in David and I still do. David, how was it left with Simon?"

"It was left on the basis that I needed to review the entire material, the text and the photographs. I said it sounded like a gross invasion of not just our rights but the rights of our guests. I said if he published without us having a fair opportunity to review the material, take advice and respond then he would be out of his job without question."

"Yeah, OK dad, and what did he say to that?"

"He said, JC, that he'd give us seven days instead of the forty-eight hours he originally had in mind, and that he'd send me a copy of the material by email. Funnily enough he didn't ask me for my personal email address; he seemed to know that already."

"So, we've got a week to find an answer to this one, dad?"

"Not quite, JC, more like five days."

"Five days," said Helen calmly, "more than enough time

to sort this one out even if we do have to put it high on the list of Cosmic Ordering."

JC looked at Helen and his dad, still puzzled as to why they weren't having a major meltdown.

***

Helen sat opposite Huck in David's office. Huck knew this wasn't routine simply because he wasn't sitting on the sofa but in a chair opposite Helen.

"OK, Huck. I've heard the story from David. He's coming to join us in a few moments with JC. I understand that there's an idea afoot to give you a sort of trial at being part of *The Place*, is that right? I mean, how do you see it?"

Huck rubbed his chin with his hand and looked Helen hard into her eyes.

"In my line of work there's no room for bullshit, Helen. When you get in the cage you've given the other guy an invitation to hurt you, I mean really hurt you, physically... emotionally... totally."

Huck paused as if he was trying hard not to repeat some pre-rehearsed speech but to speak spontaneously, from the heart.

"What I like about *The Place* Helen is that it's the exact opposite of what I do in the cage. Here, you try and put people together, I like that. I can see also that you need to help them fall apart a bit and then help put the pieces back together. I felt I did that with Martin, it was just instinctive. I didn't feel like I was giving him therapy or anything like that. It was just honest advice. I'm not saying I'm a born-again therapist but I reckon I can help, you know, put people back together."

At that point David and JC came through the door, obviously a bit taken aback at seeing Huck in one of the comfy chairs and not, where all guests were expected to sit, on the sofa.

Huck stood up and shook David and JC by the hand in turn.

"Am I sitting in someone's seat? I feel like Goldilocks." If Huck had intended to diffuse the obvious tension it didn't work.

David immediately sat in the chair Huck had been sitting in; it was after all David's chair.

Huck sat down again, this time where he felt he should be, on the sofa, while Helen, David and JC resumed their familiar places, all facing Huck.

"OK, this feels more comfortable, I know my place. I'm not trying to, you know, take someone else's seat." Huck looked at JC with some concern. "JC, you know what's being discussed. Are you OK with me getting a bit more involved? I don't want you to feel I'm stepping on any toes or anything like that."

"I like you Huck, I do. I guess it's a big step, that's all, to have someone else on board." JC felt jealous, threatened even, and it showed.

"I know," said Helen in an unusually matriarchal tone. "Huck, why don't you spell out in a bit more detail what you've got in mind and we can have a chat as to whether we think it will work, or not."

JC nodded in agreement.

"What I've got in mind is that you let me take a class – activity – and see how it goes. If I'm staying here then it might be useful, if you let with me share with someone who might be difficult. I don't mean to set myself as a sort of double-agent… but you know it might just be helpful."

David was warming to the idea. "I like it, Huck. What do you think, JC?"

"Well, yeah, I can see it. What sort of activities did you have in mind Huck?"

Huck smiled, as he felt they all knew the answer.

"I'll tell you what I'd like to do. I want to introduce some martial arts training as a part of your programme. Nothing too heavy, I know when to stop. I've been trained in several martial arts from Tae Kwon Do, Kung Fu, Krav Maga, Karate, Judo of course, to Ju-Jitsu, Aikido... it's been my life since ever I can remember. The great thing is that the training is great exercise and it helps people face fears – it all seems to fit in with what *The Place* is all about, don't you think?"

"OK," said Helen. "We'll talk it through and we'll pick up later on. In the meantime Huck what you'll need to learn is patience. Earlier, you know in the Spotlight session, you took over Cheryl's turn. I'm not saying that was wrong, but it's not what I'd expect you to do if you were on the inside. Do you accept that, Huck?"

"Helen, I'm really glad you mentioned that one. As soon as I opened my big mouth I felt I was out of order. I've got a lot to learn for sure, I accept that one hundred per cent. I'm willing to learn, and I'd love to teach; point taken, Helen."

Helen smiled at Huck and gave a slight nod of her head to signal it was time for him to leave the unholy Trinity alone to discuss.

***

"Listen Aaron, I promised myself I'd never ever be put through any shit like this, so I just want to get that straight from the start, just so you know where I stand. And by the way I've three pairs of tights on under these very tight jeans, and right on the inside – where it matters – is a thick wedge of layers of cotton wool which I call my 'Fannie pad', so any fumbling won't be worth the hassle, you know what I mean?"

Aaron Westernson stared at Mandy Haddock as if he was looking at an alien from outer space. He had dealt with tougher; they were always the most rewarding.

"What do you think this session is all about, Mandy?"

"I think it's about you, for a start. I heard from Annie, I mean Fannie – hell what was her real name – that's it – Aspasia. Nice one, Aaron."

Aaron studied Mandy's pretty but hardened features for some time.

"And what's your name. I mean your real name?"

"OK, here we go. My real name is Matilda Haddock. I never liked the name Matilda. We did Roald Dahl at primary school; it wasn't fun for me. One of my friends used to call me Mandy and it sort of stuck. I liked it, so I always told people my name was Mandy. When I got to senior school everyone knew me as Mandy, so that was OK."

"You're a well-known actress, Mandy. Tell me who you're playing, right now." Aaron looked deadly serious but Mandy wasn't sure how much Aaron was holding back.

Mandy smiled in a relaxed, off-guard manner forgetting for a moment how much she actually enjoyed talking about her work, and besides she was beginning to trust Aaron Westernson.

"Mandy, can you see that lever on the side of your chair? If you pull it up the footrest will pull out and the back of the chair moves to a more comfortable position."

Mandy pulled the lever and the chair smoothly changed

shape into more of a lounging position.

"Is that better, Mandy?"

Mandy leaned back and heaved a very heavy sigh. "That feels a lot better, Aaron it does, really. Now, where were we? Oh, yes I play Sharon, Sharon Beecham; she's kind of like me, this Sharon."

"OK, Matilda – it's important I call you by your real name, the name you were born to, otherwise we might get a bit confused. Is that OK? Now please try and relax, I'm sure you've been taught how to do that. It's all about breathing, isn't it? Now breathe in and out, slowly, consciously, and close your eyes."

Mandy closed her eyes and didn't notice the subtle dimming of the lights as Aaron continued to talk.

"Matilda, that's a beautiful name. Maybe one day you'll decide to return to Matilda. You see, once you decide to be called by another name then it's easy to forget who you are. Sometimes you're neither Matilda nor Mandy, you're Sharon Beecham. It must be very confusing for you, Matilda."

Mandy talked as if she was half asleep; there was something so peaceful and reassuring about Aaron's voice.

"Oh, it's OK, I mean they're the same really, so there's no confusion. We're just the same."

Aaron, unusually for him, was worried this was just too easy. "Really, just the same? But one is real and one is a fictional character – not real at all."

"No, you don't understand, they're both real. Actually, Sharon is more real. Nobody knows Mandy Haddock, nobody, really. Millions of people know Sharon, millions and millions, they make her real. You know, like God, and magic, and stuff like that. Like me, really."

Aaron paused for some time while Mandy seemed to fall

into a deep but semi-conscious sleep.

"Listen to me, listen very carefully. Sharon is not real; Sharon is a character in a television programme, nothing more. Matilda you decided a long time ago to forget about, you've made her *nonexistent*. Mandy is a pet name given to you by a friend when you were a little girl. What I want you to do is to let your mind drift, drift way, way back, back before Sharon, before Mandy, before Matilda – you'll find your true self, believe me."

Aaron let Mandy drift even further off into what felt to her like a deep sleep and looked at his watch and scratched his head.

"Does Joan of Arc ring any bells, Mandy?" Aaron Westernson knew how to hit the spot.

***

Cheryl Smith and Betty sat upright on their single beds settling in ready to watch a film together. David had always thought the idea of 'Movie Night' to be a fine example of Helen's concept of *The Place* as 'a work of art in economic form'; it involved no real expenditure and kept the guests occupied for a couple of hours. It also provided an opportunity for the guests to watch a film with specific instructions to learn from the experience.

David and Helen had thought carefully as to which guests should pair up with whom. Each of the six twin rooms in *The Place* had a state of the art, high-definition, plasma television, and every screen was controlled by the unholy Trinity, from the security of David's office.

Helen had come to understand that for the 'Movie Night' to be effective, it was important that the experience be discussed soon afterwards, preferably early the next morning over breakfast. This provided a subtle forum for what was always an intense group therapy session and the guests inevitably debated whether any real, lasting emotional impact had been made as a result of watching the film, or not. The choice of the film was to Helen an art.

Betty and Cheryl had been instructed to watch a film of the choosing of *The Place*. Betty was quite certain they'd had chosen *Shallow Hal* because it was the only feel good film she could bring to mind that would feel relevant to her and Cheryl, and would keep quiet two emotionally drained guests who were suffering from real withdrawal symptoms for too many reasons to think about.

The television came on automatically at precisely 8 p.m. The film was preceded by a very smart-looking Helen talking straight to the camera.

"Good evening, Betty and Cheryl. It's a special treat tonight. You're going to watch a movie which we have decided is just right for you two. Tomorrow morning we can discuss whether you got anything out of it and whether you thought it was a good choice. But please do sit back and enjoy."

"Bet it's *Shallow Hal*, Cheryl."

"I reckon it's going to be… a Santa Clause movie – that's about the only time *the fat one* is portrayed as the good guy and not a loser."

Betty and Cheryl waited patiently for the film to start, and it did.

"They're havin' a laugh, Betty. 'Walt Disney Presents… *Dumbo*!' *Dumbo*? Do you think they've pressed the wrong button or something? Bastards."

Betty seemed quite pleased with the choice. "I love

Dumbo, Cheryl. I haven't seen it for years. Could have been worse."

"Could have been worse? Worse than *Dumbo*? Like *The Texas Chainsaw Massacre* or *The Sound of Music*?" Cheryl was clearly disappointed but quickly realised that she had no choice and it was *Dumbo* or nothing at all.

As the opening credits began to roll, Cheryl was silenced by the familiar music and settled back out of curiosity, not sure whether she had actually watched the entire film. Cheryl took a deep breath and thought it a good moment to get feedback from Betty about the events earlier in the day.

"I guess it makes sense to put us together, Betty."

"Have you ever watched *Dumbo*? I mean really watched it? It's a great film, Cheryl, you know for people like us."

"Like us?" Cheryl sneered.

"Yeah, big elephants like us." Betty laughed out loud but a discrete knock on the door instantly silenced her.

"It's OK, it's just David. I've got something for you."

Betty moved from her bed as quickly to the door as she could. David was holding four small boxes of what looked like exquisite chocolates, the very expensive individually-wrapped-in-shiny-paper types which made chocolate hobnobs look like stale, crusty droppings of a small wild animal with serious health issues.

David quickly explained that the challenge was for Cheryl and Betty to watch the film from beginning to end without taking one nibble, however small, of any one of the chocolates. All they had to do was to wait until the film was over, then they could eat all they wanted. David left the boxes in Betty's hands and made a quick exit.

"Cruel bastards, don't you think, Betty? I mean it would be like leaving a paid-for hooker in Toni's room with the instructions 'don't open till Christmas'."

Betty looked longingly at the enticing package of up-market chocolates. "Perhaps we should put them away somewhere, just to help us resist temptation. You know we only have to wait until the film is over."

"What, like under your bed? Or maybe under your pillow, Betty?"

"Under my bed is a good idea, Cheryl."

"Or under my bed, Betty."

Betty and Cheryl looked at each other mischievously. "What about half under your bed, and the other half under mine, Cheryl?"

"Well, you can't say fairer than that, Betty – OK you choose which two you want to hide, and then we can settle down to the film. Oh look; the storks – I remember this bit, it's great. Do you mind if we turn the lights off?"

Cheryl pretended to watch the film while she took out her state-of-the-art tablet device and started to find out what she could about *The Place* and her fellow inmates. The chocolates would help her concentration, she reckoned.

***

"Hope you don't mind me sharing with you Davy, I guess they know what they're doing," said Huck staring at the television waiting for the film to begin.

"Hell, I'm cool, Huck. You ain't going to give me no trouble, I can tell that. I mean you're a fighter, a dog – you know what I mean? I like that Toni guy but I guess he could swing both ways, depending on what's cooking. I'm OK with you, tough guy. What's this movie therapy shit? I mean we watch a movie and that cures us. I'm already cured, Huck,

I'm as cured as a big chunk of meat. Is there any way we can choose what we want or do we have to watch what they decide is good for us? I know what's good for me. Maybe they'll put on the 'hot young babes channel'. I bet they've got a *hot* channel, don't you Huck? Maybe we should check out Toni, I bet they've given him like *Deep Throat with Herpes* or something."

The television came to life and there was Helen, looking at Davy and Huck.

"Good evening Davy and Huck. We've chosen a film for the two of you to watch, together. Tomorrow morning we can discuss whether you got anything out of it and whether you thought it was a good choice. But please do sit back and enjoy."

"Oh man, give me some *loving…*" Davy knew what he wanted to see, which was anything involving naked ladies.

"I'd be happy with *Seven Samurai*," said Huck.

"You mean *Seven Dogs for Seven Bitches* – you ever seen that one brother? I mean like *class*."

Both Davy and Huck stared in disbelief as the credits rolled.

"What's this? 'A Walt Disney Production… *Snow White and the Seven Dwarves*.'"

"Hey brother I was close," said Huck giving a good imitation of Davy Crockett.

Davy jumped up and started ranting wildly at the television. "Oh man. *Snow White*, no, no this is shit man, shit." Davy's growing rants were interrupted by a firm knock on the door.

"I'll get it," insisted Huck, asserting his physical authority.

JC stood at the door with a big grin, holding a six-pack of

very low alcohol beers, but the gesture was enough. "They're for both of you, but only to be opened after the film, is that fair enough?"

Davy looked at the film as it began its journey and looked at the beers.

"Shit, man. That's a tough deal," said Davy.

"But we'll take it, thanks," said Huck, in case JC decided to change his mind.

No sooner had JC shut the door than Davy pulled out a joint and lit up.

Huck looked over to Davy. "Are you sure you should be doing that? I thought the rule was that you could only smoke in the patio area. And that smells like wacky-backy to me, brother. Do you think that's *cool*?"

Davy took a long drag on the reefer. "Listen brother, this joint was given to me by them. They took away my stash and even rolled these joints for me. Can you believe it? I mean, like that's *cool*?"

Huck was a bit confused but decided to let it go. "You're a grown man, Davy, it's your choice."

"That's right, brother. It's my choice. You wanna blow?"

"I'm OK, Davy. On yer own."

***

"Well, this is nice, I must say." Helen looked around, obviously very pleased with herself. The Encounter Area was set up to imitate a five star breakfast area with the emphasis on abundance.

Sitting around the carefully laid breakfast table was Toni, Betty, Cheryl, Mandy, Huck, Davy, David and Helen, who was clearly in charge of everything.

"Now, before you gorge yourselves with all this wonderful food, there is one little catch." Helen smiled and looked around the worried faces.

"Everything you eat or drink this morning has a value. By value I mean a distance, in metres."

The group still looked slightly confused.

"OK, I'll spell it out. Everything on the counter over there has a pile of casino chips in a bowl beside each food item. Each different coloured chip represents a number which is displayed on the bowl. A little mini chocolate croissant will cost you a chip which is valued at fifty. That means fifty metres. Next to the cereal is the number twenty; that means twenty metres for each bowl. Now for the little pots of jam and honey there's another number – seventy-five – if I recall, and so on. The cooked food is very expensive, I warn you. Every sausage is worth one hundred points, every slice of bacon another one hundred points. The black pudding is two hundred metres a slice. You'll notice the fresh fruit is quite cheap – twenty for a satsuma, the same for a slice of melon. Every time you take something to eat you must collect a chip and place it next to your cutlery. At the end of this little feast, we'll have counted up your total score and then, later this morning, we'll all be going for a little jog over Hampstead Heath and you will complete a course of a length in metres equal to the number of points you've accumulated. There will be nothing more to eat until that distance has been covered, on your knees if that's how you want to do it. Does that all make sense? OK, have everything and anything you want, anything. Of course if you'd rather not have anything to eat, that's OK. The only thing that has no chips is the water; otherwise it's chips with everything."

Everyone looked at the array of food spread over the long self-serving area and collectively sighed, apart from Huck, who was straight in amongst the priciest items without a moment's hesitation.

"This is fantastic, now that's what I call a win-win. Love this game, love it." And with obvious abandon Huck stacked his plate high, collected his chips and sat down a happy man. "I'll add it up later – I hope it comes in at thousands and thousands – I'll happily jog round the Heath all day. Great idea, Helen, love it, thanks."

Slowly each guest approached the counter area and weighed up the odds. Betty and Mandy took their time thinking through the consequences of having what they wanted, which if truth be told was everything, in no particular order.

After some time, everyone settled down and Helen clinked her little china cup which was filled with a small amount of lemon tea, to bring the session to order.

"Now, I want to talk about last night." Helen deliberately stared at Davy who immediately lowered his head, like a naughty school boy.

"Last night was 'Movie Night', we don't call it 'Movie Therapy' because whether it was therapeutic or not was up to you. Same with the books we give you to read. Toni, tell us about last night."

"Er, David brought around a big pizza and we watched *West Side Story*. I had forgotten what a great film it is, I mean the dancing, choreography, singing – it was brilliant." Toni sort of dried up as if he was expected to come out with something profound but couldn't find the words. Toni looked around and realised that he wasn't going to get away with such a brief resume, so he continued.

"OK, I get the vibes. Was it therapeutic? Er, I don't know. I mean I don't know what therapeutic really means to be honest. I'm here for a specific reason, can't say *West Side Story* helped with that one."

Helen didn't look surprised or disappointed but simply smiled at Toni. "That's a good start, Toni. You see the point is that your response was honest, not... contrived or..."

"You didn't get it," interrupted Betty who in all fairness was on edge. "*West Side Story* is a love story, you know, based on *Romeo and Juliet*. I guess the point was that the story is a lesson in unconditional love, true love. That's why you didn't get it, Toni."

Toni continued slowly cutting up his one bacon and one sausage as if the conversation was all flying over his head.

"Better than *Dumbo*, though. I would have swopped *West Side Story* for that one, I can tell you." Cheryl was still upset at the choice of movie, but Betty was having none of it.

"Oh, Cheryl, you're being a bit unfair. I saw a tear in your eye when 'Baby of Mine' came on, admit it, that got you, didn't it?"

"It's just a sad little song, that's all," said Cheryl a little too quickly.

"But, it's about the love for his suffering mother, isn't it, Cheryl, that's why it's so sad. You know the scenario – helpless child watching mother suffer. All *Dumbo* wanted was for things to be as they were, as they had been when he and his mother were happy, together."

Helen could tell Cheryl was hiding something, in fact everyone could tell that Cheryl was hiding something, and Helen had decided a little provocation was in order.

"I guess so, Helen. Yeah it was sad." Cheryl had to fight hard to hold back a flood of tears which was good enough for Helen.

"And, you two – Davy and Huck, you saw *Snow White and the Seven Dwarves*, did that get to you, at all?"

Cheryl burst out laughing, as did Betty.

"Oh boy, you two had that coming; I mean *Snow White and the Seven Dwarves*. I bet that hit the spot for you Davy." Cheryl thought she had found a way to disguise her tears and was on a roll, but no one responded.

Davy looked apprehensively at Huck as if he knew that if he didn't say something, Huck would say it for him. Davy looked up and took a good look at every face around the table as if to signal that he was about to say something very sincere and potentially very *heavy*.

"OK, OK. Helen, it was a great choice. I mean I didn't get it at first. But man, I gotta tell you I haven't cried so much in years."

Cheryl looked confused. "You cried like a baby watching *Snow White and the Seven Dwarves*, how did that happen, Davy? I mean anything specific or just the whole story?"

Huck couldn't resist the moment. "Best death scene, ever; you either haven't seen it or you've got a heart of stone Cheryl. Don't you remember the bit where they all think that Snow White is dead, after she's had a bite from the big red poisoned apple? I mean why did she do that? Anyway, all the dwarves are inside sobbing and the animals are outside, heads bowed in sorrow. Grumpy's crying just kills you. Absolute classic."

"Classic, brother, classic." said Davy, happy to echo Huck.

"Oh yes, I remember," chipped in Betty, "and the rain… and the music."

The recollection was too much for Davy who was off again, tears pouring down his face. "Don't rub it in brothers; it was bad enough the first time. Man, it was just so sad. Didn't see no black little fellas though; guess that would have been a step too far. Come to think of it you don't see that many black dwarves, ever." Davy's moistened eyes gazed into the distance.

"You do in space," said Toni as if he was trying to be helpful.

David had been quiet but felt it was his turn to speak up. "And what about you, Mandy?"

To tell the truth I wanted to watch *Mama Mia* but I guess *Shirley Valentine* was a good choice, for me. Made me laugh – I mean really laugh, but I can't say it got to me in any – you know – real way. Was there some sort of hidden lesson in there for me, Helen?"

"I thought it might get to you, Mandy. Maybe not right away, but over time." Helen looked at Mandy whose face was still blank.

"It's about a woman who is trying to find herself, Mandy, against all the pressures of her friends and family, that's all it's about really. It's just a story about a woman trying to find happiness; genuine, deep happiness which she can only find if she discovers herself. And it's *funny*." Helen looked over to Mandy as if a response would be forthcoming.

Mandy looked as if a penny had just dropped and thought for a moment about her session with Aaron Westernson. "Ah, OK, Helen. I think I'm getting it, sort of."

Helen continued. "Look the thing about 'Movie Night' is that it's not supposed to hit you in the face, at least not right away. But over time, it will mean something, I promise you, if you let it. Now, why don't you all help yourself to another round of this lovely food? That bacon smells so good, might just have some myself. Those chips are building up very nicely. Talking of which, I've few penalties chips to add."

"Penalty chips? What do you mean, Helen?" Toni felt an immediate sense of impending injustice.

"No, not for you Toni. But for Davy – he knows why, and Betty and Cheryl they also know why. I think a thousand points each is about fair. Referee's decision is final. You've got one hour and then it's the Heath. You'll have to run around the Heath a few times to pay that lot off."

"Helen, I've got an idea." Huck wolfed down the enormous plate of food and headed to the counter, for seconds.

16

"Perfect," said Helen as she looked southwards over the vast expanse of rolling green fields and woodland that lay in front of her. What was perfect to Helen was not just the magnificent view but that the light rain and slight chill in the air had the effect of discouraging nearly all day-visitors, dog walkers, joggers and tourists, giving the impression of an empty, almost eerie landscape which Helen's group could enjoy on their own.

Helen wasn't too concerned that the group might attract some unwanted attention. Dressed in their light coloured pastel tracksuits and smart new trainers they collectively resembled at worst a bunch of American tourists on a special visit to Hampstead in search of self-discovery, or an early afternoon outdoor exercise club for middle-aged locals, without dogs or children.

A couple of Japanese tourists took a photograph; maybe it was just an intended picture of the house behind them but the sight of a camera pointing in their general direction caused the whole group to smile and show their white, television teeth and hit a pose.

Helen had decided to convene the group consisting of Huck, Betty, Cheryl, Toni, Mandy and Davy in front of Kenwood House, a splendid state-owned neo-Georgian mansion, situated on the very crown of Hampstead Heath and often used as the backdrop for period costume dramas and the venue for many a celebrity bash of one kind or another, from weddings to Bar Mitzvahs.

"OK, here are the scores," said Helen. "Huck you accumulated one thousand eight hundred and fifty metres. Now that's a big breakfast, Huck."

Huck smiled as if he had just won some sort of prize and clasped his hands in the air in mock triumph.

"Toni, you ate your way through six hundred and eighty metres, and Davy your total was two thousand and fifty – which includes your one thousand penalty points."

Davy shook his head in shame.

"Ladies, may I have your attention?" asked Helen throwing a stern look in the direction of Betty, Cheryl and Mandy. Helen unfolded a piece of paper with the numbers written down.

"Betty, your score – including your penalty – comes to three thousand one hundred metres."

Betty clasped her hands over her mouth in genuine shock. "That can't be right, Helen. I mean, I only had a couple of croissants, a few bits of toast and pastries, OK there was the jam… and the bacon, and the eggs and the sausages and the coffee and the yoghourt and the black pudding… oh shit… I'll just shut up. Three thousand metres, how far is that?"

"Mandy," Helen continued, "not too bad, your score including the penalty is one thousand nine hundred and fifty". Mandy looked genuinely relieved.

"OK, Cheryl. You score in total is… four thousand seven hundred metres." The group collectively gasped in disbelief.

"I can't have got that much, Helen. That's not fair. I couldn't have eaten more than Huck, and I'm sure Betty ate more than I did. That can't be right, Helen." Cheryl was almost too shocked to be angry.

Helen approached the Cheryl, placed an arm around her shoulder, walked her away from the others and whispered in her ear. "Cheryl, this is only between us unless you want me to share with the group. One part of the game at breakfast I didn't explain was that if anyone tried to cheat and not take a chip when they were supposed to, or took a chip at the wrong value, then whatever score they had would be doubled. Now, Cheryl, do want to accept the score I've given you or shall we discuss with the group?" Helen looked deep into Cheryl's worried and guilty eyes.

"OK, Helen you win. I'll do my score as you put it. But then it's back home for me. I promised my mum I'd do some time at *The Place*. It was a shitty move to pull on Tracy and a punishment for Martin and it feels like a punishment for me. The consequences of not coming down here were just… not on. Tell me what I need to do, and I'll get this over with and then I'm off."

Helen, though she tried not to betray the fact, liked Cheryl a lot. "That's fine, Cheryl. Let's do this and then you can go if you want to, with my blessing. I'm not some sort of probation officer, you know. I'm a therapist, and believe me, this is all therapy for you, OK."

"OK, Helen. I know. I'm not a prisoner. I promised Tracy that I'd come here to straighten things out between us. Let's do it."

Helen and Cheryl rejoined the group to find JC holding court with Huck, Davy, Mandy, Betty and Toni. JC certainly looked dressed for the part in his obviously well-worn training shoes and wearing some seriously tight-fitting trousers and a top which could have been designed for a swimmer or long distance runner or cyclist, perhaps all three. Helen hadn't realised until that moment how much JC had turned into such a physically fit-looking young man.

"JC, good to see you. Right on cue, thank you." Helen and JC had worked this session out beforehand to give it the best chance of success. There was a lot that could go wrong but they knew this one had the potential to be life changing for someone.

Helen stood in front of the group and explained that JC knew Hampstead Heath like the back of his hand – every nook and cranny. JC was showing off a state-of-the-art digital watch which clearly had an enormous array of sophisticated functions, one of which was to monitor the distance travelled by the wearer.

"Listen everyone," said JC as if was he talking to a group of children at the beginning of a sports day, "I've worked out the best way to do this. You see those woods over there, on the other side of the pond? From here, going to our right, along this path and then across those fields and over that bridge through the woods, turning left and back up that hill on our left over there and to return to this point is just under seven hundred metres. That's one circuit. I've set my watch to each of your scores and when I give you a signal you can stop jogging and walk back here. And see that fountain over there, you can take a drink from there each time you complete one circuit." JC looked around the group as if to make sure they were all listening, and had understood.

"What that means, roughly, is that Toni will complete one circuit, Huck, Mandy and Davy about three circuits, Betty about four and a half and Cheryl just under seven. I will – I promise – let you know when you can drop out. Is that clear, everyone?"

Huck took a pace nearer towards JC. "JC, do you have to

drop out? I mean, can I stay with you until we all finish, is that OK?"

JC turned around and looked at Helen who gestured that to JC that it was his decision.

"OK, here's the deal, Huck. Your score is the minimum requirement. Anyone can keep going with me for as long as they want. If you want to stay until Cheryl finishes or Betty or just for as long as you want after you've done your number, then that's OK."

"That's great, thanks JC." Huck smiled as if to congratulate JC on a good decision.

JC quickly resumed control of the group. "OK, everyone, before we head off we'll do some warm up stretches. Just watch and copy what I do." Without any apparent effort JC outstretched his left arm, lifted up his right leg backwards and held his foot with his right hand behind his back and stood statuesque while Helen took a seat on a nearby bench, next to the drinking fountain that JC had pointed out, and watched patiently.

The group initially stared at JC in disbelief and then, one by one, attempted to emulate JC's stance. Toni and Davy managed to lift their legs backwards but couldn't quite keep their balance. Betty and Cheryl looked at each other as if they had been asked to recite the Chinese alphabet backwards. In fact the only person who managed the task was Huck.

"OK, I get it." JC realised that he would have to lower his expectations, immediately. "Let's try this one." JC placed his left arm across his face and placed his right arm on his elbow, pulling his left arm across towards him.

This time Huck, Toni, Mandy and Davy at least looked as if they knew what to do, but Betty and Cheryl couldn't even pretend to have a proper go.

"Right, try the other arm." JC knew that the actual jogging bit was going to be tough but he had underestimated that the warm up would be so problematic.

"Can you just sort of bend over and try and touch your toes?" JC asked. Davy, Toni, Huck and Mandy had a decent enough go at this one, but Betty and Cheryl didn't stand a chance.

"Right, all of you, just jump and down on the spot, like this."

It was soon very apparent that Betty and Cheryl were in some discomfort trying to jump a couple of inches off the ground. Even David felt shocked at the sight of Betty and Cheryl trying to heave their bodies up and down with any sense of dignity, as if in all reality they had forgotten how to jump up and down; in fact they resembled to JC two large jellies being shaken around on a kiddie's birthday party table during a mild earthquake.

JC knew this was not going to get any better and decided to cut his losses after one last go. "OK, put your hands on your hips, and spread your legs a bit, like this." Despite a promising start, Betty nearly fell over backwards like an unbalanced rolling doll, but was caught by Cheryl who was involuntarily flapping around as if miming a slow motion fall forwards, but somehow Betty and Cheryl became entangled and managed to stabilise each other, like two novice ice skaters left to get on with it. JC reassessed the situation.

"I'll tell you what, let's head off at a walking pace. We'll pick up the pace as we go along. I'll head the group with Betty and Cheryl. Huck could you please stay at the back and make sure we don't lose anyone? Thanks, Huck."

JC formed an awkward threesome in between Betty and Cheryl and started walking at a slow pace intending to speed things up as soon as he felt he could get away with it. After about ten metres, next to the bench on which Helen was sitting, Betty had to stop.

"Oh, god. I'm knackered. Can I just sit down with Helen for a minute? My body's thinking 'just had a big breakfast; must be time for big sleep', and that warm up just about finished me off."

Betty was quite serious, but it was Cheryl who surprised everyone.

"Betty, come off it. You can't be that much bigger than I am. OK, you're a bit older, no offence, but Jesus Betty we'll be here for years if you don't keep going. Come on, just put one bleeding foot in front of the other and let's get this over with, please."

Betty made what was clearly a real effort and struggled on, out of Helen's sight, along the path, down the grassy slope, across the fields and across the bridge and into the woods. Helen and JC had discussed this challenge before they had set off. JC had calculated it would take the slowest member, at most, twenty minutes to complete one circuit but of course something might go *wrong*, a possibility which needed to be considered.

Helen looked at her watch and realised half an hour had passed and there was no sight of the group coming up the hill towards Kenwood House. Ten minutes later, she noticed a troupe of three, which was obviously Betty, Cheryl and JC looking like a slowly moving animated bronze statute of three wounded war heroes, returning from the trenches. Eventually the group reached Helen, a full hour after they had first set off.

"Oh God," said Betty, "are we done? Please tell me we're done."

JC looked at his space age watch and stated quite matter of fact: "We've completed less than seven hundred metres and it's taken us an hour, Betty. You've three more circuits to do. Toni has completed his task. Huck, Mandy and Davy have at least another couple of circuits to go and Cheryl another five and a bit. If we keep going we should finish before dark."

Helen remained silent and aloof, but was keeping a very close eye on this particularly challenge. It was JC's first time in charge of a session, and that was because Huck had suggested to Helen that JC should be given an opportunity to shine. What Helen knew would happen, and did happen, was the development of a group concern for Betty.

"I don't want to drop out, JC," said Toni heroically. "I'll stay with Betty, for as long as it takes."

"So will I," said Davy. "Me too," said Mandy. "I'm not going anywhere," said Huck. "Hell, I'm in," was Davy's response. Everyone looked at Cheryl.

"Well, I'm going to finish last anyway, so I'm with you Betty. Put your arm around me Betty and let's do this." Cheryl looked and sounded almost like a different, much older person.

Helen wiped away a tear; it was just so good, this one. She even clapped her hands excitedly and shouted, "Go on, let's see you do this. Come on, I know you can do this."

And with that little bit of encouragement the group disappeared off down the path and across the fields and over the bridge and through the woods and back up the hill, past Helen for the second time, and then the third. Each time they looked even more bonded and exhausted, taking turns to shoulder the burden that was Betty, and to stop momentarily for a drink from the fountain. By the end of circuit four, Betty had the determined look of an unfit marathon runner who had caught cramp after ten miles but was going to finish come what may.

But the episode that stayed with Helen more than any other that day was not the genuine and spontaneous support for Betty, but what happened after David announced that Betty had completed her course.

"OK, Betty you're done. Congratulations; I mean really, really well done." JC looked at his watch and read out the distance covered. We've covered three thousand two hundred and fifty metres. Wow. We'll put you down for the marathon, shall we?"

Betty was being held up, literally, by Huck and Davy and looked as if she had been to hell and back but still had a bucket load of spirit to show off. "We're not finished yet, guys. You've stayed with me and I'm staying with Cheryl, until the end, the very end. JC, how far has Cheryl to go, I mean from here?"

JC looked at his watch and looked at Cheryl who was still on her feet but looking as if she was about to collapse.

"We've got another couple of circuits to do, then we're done," said JC having abandoned some time ago any sense of precision.

"OK, Cheryl, come here." Betty placed her arm around Cheryl and signalled to Huck and Davy. The four of them formed a line: Huck, Betty, Cheryl and Davy holding each other up as if they were a four man team completing the last hundred metres of a three month race to the North Pole.

"OK," said Betty, "twice more round this little circuit and then we're done. OK Cheryl?"

Cheryl looked over to Betty with tears in her eyes. "Thanks, Betty. Yep, twice more round this little circuit, and I'm finished, over and out."

***

"Now, pay attention everyone. This is another great day in the annals of *The Place*. Cheryl Smith has been with us for a very short period of time, but I have to say Cheryl has proven to be one of our great success stories." Helen looked around at the smiling faces of the small group who only the day before had completed a very demanding and physical task.

"We've seen Cheryl change in front of our own eyes. Everyone who comes here does so for very different reasons. I know the *real* reason Cheryl came here was to rediscover her good side; her loving and caring side. This she has achieved with flying colours. Cheryl, please come forward and accept your leaving gift. A special former guest of *The Place* has come a long way to present this to you, Cheryl."

As Cheryl came forward, from inside the French windows which led to the patio area of *The Place* appeared Tracy, looking very relaxed and happy, holding a large, heavily wrapped present.

Tracy stood beside Helen and spoke clearly, and with affection. "Cheryl, I've heard about your stay here, within the boundaries of the 'Darcy Rule', I should add." Tracy looked over to Cheryl and smiled, as if Cheryl and Tracy now had a new, shared language.

Tracy held out the large present. "Cheryl, Helen has agreed I can give this to you."

Cheryl stepped up and took the present from Tracy and carefully took off the wrapping paper to reveal a large, cuddly toy – a beautiful pink baby elephant with big ears, wide eyes and a great smile.

"That looks a lot like *Dumbo* to me, Tracy," said Cheryl as the group clapped and cheered.

Cheryl turned towards Tracy and spoke just loud enough for the group to hear what she had to say. "Tracy, I'm so sorry for what I've done in the past. I can't tell you how sorry I am, Tracy, I really am."

"Oh, Cheryl, it's me who should apologise to you. I can't tell you how sorry I am. I don't want to hurt you, Cheryl, you're my little sister and always will be."

Cheryl and Tracy hugged, as sisters, like they used to, many years ago, and sobbed gently on each other's shoulders. The little crowd *loved* that bit.

"Can we start over, Tracy? I mean can we be friends again? You know, *sisters* again?"

Tracy held Cheryl's hands and looked into her sister's eyes.

"We'll always be sisters, Cheryl. Nothing's going to come between us. I know we've always competed for the same guy, always. I guess in the past it didn't matter. We both knew what the score was. With Martin it was different. I knew I shouldn't have stolen him from you; it was so wrong, so deliberate. But it would kill me to have to choose between two people I love so much. If Martin can stop playing away and we can stay friends, I'd be the happiest WAG in the world. I do love you so much Cheryl."

Cheryl gave Tracy an awkward smile who laughed, wiping a tear away.

Tracy turned to the group. "I know where my love lives

and it's with my family, my sister, Cheryl, my mum and my little daughter, and my husband. Helen, I can't thank you enough. I've seen my life so much clearer since I've been here. Thank you. Thank all of you."

Cheryl held her sister tight and whispered in her ear. "Tracy, I'm so glad we've made up. Dad would have been so proud of us, Tracy, so proud."

17

David, Helen and JC sat in their favourite seats in David's office for a moment of reflection. A normal business might have called it a board meeting, but *The Place* was no ordinary business.

"Are we sure we're not going to be disturbed?" David wanted to be one hundred per cent sure that it was safe to open his laptop and display the six screens each showing the guests in their rooms under strict orders or 'guidance' as Helen called it to study one of a number of books the guests had each been required to read. They knew it would-n't last for more than an hour or so.

Each guest had been given a newly released e-book reader that could hold hundreds of titles and had access to many thousands more. Each room was wired up to be a wi-fi 'hot spot' but that facility could be turned off as and when the unholy Trinity considered access to the internet to be an unnecessary distraction. For a couple of hours every so often the guests would be required to sit quietly in their rooms having access only to the material already stored on the device and were expected to read an agreed title without any interruption.

David checked and checked again that each guest was holding the device, at least pretending to read the text on the small screen.

David kept open the laptop but looked up at Helen and

JC. "I think we're OK. Now, let's get this Huck issue cleared up. JC, it's worrying me son that you're not really OK with Huck. Am I right, or what?"

JC looked and sounded quite relaxed. "Yeah, I'm OK with the 'Huck thing'. I can see that he can add something. I guess there are a lot of guys – or ladies – out there who are equally capable of providing what Huck can provide, so I'm not too excited about it. I'm not as intuitive as Helen; I can't really fathom him, to be honest. I don't know where he's coming from and I sure as hell don't know where he's going. Most of our guests end up here following a crisis that has already happened – like with Richard's cry for help. But Huck booked himself in some time in advance. I don't know whether that's a good thing or not. And I didn't really like him persuading Helen to get me to take the jogging session – I thought you'd take that one, dad. It seemed a bit manipulative to me. Why didn't he talk to me first? The session did teach me a couple of things I suppose. I just don't know whether Huck really wanted me to succeed or fail – you know what I mean?"

Helen and David knew there was a lot at stake here and it had always been agreed that come what may, the unity of the Trinity would never be jeopardised by a guest.

"OK," said David. "Let's give Huck a test. My feeling is that he's a good guy, really. But I suppose you're right that we should test out that theory. We're good at that sort of thing aren't we? I mean that's what we do, isn't it?"

"A test?" asked Helen. "What sort of test did you have in mind, David?"

"Well, I'm not entirely sure. I mean it's got to be something that JC feels – you know – comfortable with. What do you think JC?"

David turned around JC's laptop and took a long look at Huck sitting on his bed next to Davy, both of them apparently engrossed in reading from their e-book readers.

"I'll think of something, dad. You know there's a lot of really good, talented martial arts teachers out there." JC paused as if a wicked thought had just entered his mind and then changed the subject, quickly.

"What is that Davy guy reading by the way? I mean he looks so into it, totally engrossed. I wouldn't have imagined Davy reading anything too heavy."

Helen smiled one of her knowing, mischievous smiles. "You know, shortly after Davy first arrived he and I had a chat about books, literature and what he used to read. I wasn't going to get him to read anything heavy – like Shakespeare or Dickens, anything like that. He had to pick up from where he left off, and progress from there. I asked him what book he could remember reading, no matter how long ago, that he actually enjoyed."

"And what was that, Helen pray tell?" David had one or two books he would have bet on.

"JC, do you want to have a guess what Davy Crockett is so avidly reading, right now?"

"Haven't got a clue Helen. Not a clue."

"OK, I'll tell you. *Aesop's Fables*. His teacher in Jamaica used to read it to his class when he was a little boy. He told me he could remember enjoying the stories and loved to hear his teacher read. But he couldn't remember any one of the stories, not one."

Helen turned the laptop towards her. "Now, look at the face of that man. He's as happy as a seven year old on a Friday afternoon being read a story by his favourite teacher just before he heads off to play and sing. That's a picture of happiness, of innocence. Now that's what I call therapy. A work of art, in economic form."

Helen positioned the laptop so all three of them could see the small screen. "Can you turn the sound up, just from that one screen, thanks?" asked David.

"Sure, JC listen." David, JC and Helen strained their ears to hear the soundtrack being played in the room. "What is that again, Helen, it sounds sort of familiar?"

"It's that big Hawaiian guy, Helen, Israel what's-his-name singing 'Somewhere Over the Rainbow' isn't that great?" said David.

Helen remembered the Spotlight session when Davy had sang his band's own reggae version of 'Somewhere Over the Rainbow' and smiled. "His name," said Helen in a slightly exaggerated authoritarian manner, "was Israel Kamakawiwo'ole, he was only thirty-eight when died. He was over six feet in height but he weighed over fifty stones. I find it so sad, so... avoidable."

"Maybe it's just the song that kills them," said David, thinking out loud. "Think about it, Israel Kawa... Kawa... you know, Eva Cassidy, Judy Garland... Doris Day..."

"Doris Day? What are you on, dad?" JC appeared genuinely concerned for his dad and looked closely at his dad's ever-thinning grey hair.

Helen was just about to place the lid down on the laptop but stopped. It was JC who managed to speak first. "What's Davy doing now? Look he's lighting up a joint. Bit cheeky." Helen and David had not told JC that they were ahead of him on that one.

"Don't worry, JC," said Helen, "I gave him those; four a day he's allowed, left under his pillow during the day at some strategic moment. The tooth fairy cometh, brother, oh yes. Our Mr. Crockett hasn't even noticed that he's smoking some harmless stuff that smells like London skunk but has no – you know – *active* ingredient. He may as well be smoking grass from the garden outside. It's nothing more than a placebo and he can't tell the difference. Pretty neat, eh?"

"Helen," said JC, "you never cease to surprise me."

"Absolute classic, brother," said David. "Classic."

JC suddenly had a thought, a very disturbing thought.

"Er, dad, if we can access this as we are doing now, how secure is it?"

"How do you mean, JC?"

"I mean, what do you need to do to have access to these images? Don't tell me it's like just a matter of knowing our security code for the wireless connection?"

David paused for a moment, as if the same thought that had entered JC's mind had been transferred to David.

"I get it, JC," said David going bright red.

"So do I," said Helen.

***

"Today, we've organised for you a very special session with a very special guest." David stood beside a disarmingly beautiful and athletic, swishy ponytailed young lady who nobody recognised but nonetheless seemed vaguely familiar.

The group didn't quite know what to expect but the fact that the Encounter Area resembled a keep fit class with padded mats placed in the middle of the floor indicated that some form of exercise was on the cards.

"This lovely lady is Metti Wati, a highly skilled martial

artist and a professional stunt lady who often acts as a double for movie and television stars."

Young Metti stepped in the centre of the mats and without warning completed a worryingly high back flip and landed in a fighting stance, followed by a wry smile and a group "Hi, everyone".

Betty held Toni's hand as if she was about to fall over, whilst Toni tried to stop himself from scratching his arse. On this occasion Betty decided it might be best to make no comment or snide remark, none whatsoever. Metti was hot, by all standards. Maybe she was Malaysian, or from Brazil or even Peckham, it didn't matter; Metti was gorgeous in any language.

Mandy and Davy both stood rooted to the spot as if they had been turned to stone, while Huck stepped forward and bowed to Metti, his hands pressed firmly against each other as if in prayer and then Huck took a step back and adopted a martial arts 'ready stance', fists clenched pointing towards each other in front of his groin, his legs slightly apart.

Metti nodded to Huck and smiled as if they already had shared a secret. JC continued. "Metti will be staying just for a day or two, that's right isn't it, Metti?"

Metti surveyed the startled faces and smiled serenely, pretending not to notice JC's school boy oogling at Metti's perfect form.

"Now," said David, "let me explain. Metti, as with you all, is on her own special journey and has asked to take a session. It's not the usual course for us to take at *The Place* but Metti is no ordinary guest. I mean not that any of you are ordinary, but you know what I mean. OK? What I'm trying to say is that if you've ever seen a high octane fight fest in any one of the big movies in the last couple of years, it's probably Metti you've seen doing all the really dangerous stunts."

"Wow," said Toni a bit too loudly, thinking of one of many steamy sex scenes that were coming into his mind at a rate of knots.

David looked at Huck. "We've been thinking about introducing some basic martial arts into *The Place* for some time now, so this is as good as an excuse as any to get started. I'll stay for a few minutes until you get going and then I'll be back later, towards the end of the session to see how you all get on."

Metti gestured to the group to sit in a wide circle while she stood in the middle and without introduction started what looked to Betty, Mandy and Toni like an elaborate ballet dance of some description, but Huck and even Davy recognised Metti's movements as a sophisticated series of extremely precise interwoven martial art moves.

After a couple of minutes, Metti came to a very deliberate halt in the precise pose in which she had started, which brought about instantaneous applause from the group.

Metti spoke very softly. "Thank you, that's very kind of you. Well, I guess I'm not going to turn you all into martial artists in one session but we could go through some moves and maybe have some fun while were at it. How does that sound?"

The group nodded with apparent enthusiasm with the exception of Betty who feared the worst.

"It's OK, Betty. I can see you're worried as if this is not quite your thing. I was a big girl when I was younger. In fact it was martial arts training that made me lose weight.

So, don't you worry, Betty. I know where you're coming from. Will you trust me?"

Betty didn't quite look convinced but was flattered and impressed that Metti spoke to her so personally.

Metti looked around the group. "OK, Toni. I'm a great admirer of your music Toni. I really am."

Toni felt himself blush but was already dreading the next line which he knew was coming.

"OK, Toni. Lie on your back. I'm going to hold you down and you're going to try and get free. Is that OK?"

Toni considered his options for about a second, and was suddenly on his back in the middle of the floor. Metti spread herself without any inhibition over Toni, her groin dangerously close to his face and her arms wrapped around his legs.

"OK, get out of this," instructed Metti.

Toni looked ahead at the groin in front of him and lay still.

"When you're ready, Toni," said Metti politely.

"Er, I'm OK, really." Toni had suddenly found himself in a heavenly space and couldn't think of any reason to change the situation.

"Try and get out of the hold, Toni," said Metti with a trace of impatience.

"Er, I'm thinking about my options, Metti. I'm thinking *hard.*"

Betty and Mandy tried to hold back a giggle, and Davy was practically bursting with impatience to have a go. "Hell brother if you ain't going make a move, I'll have a go." Davy was practically drooling with the prospect of Metti's legs wrapped around his face.

Metti stood up and pulled Toni up by his arm. "OK, Toni.

My goodness, you're a very naughty boy. I guess I know why you're in here." Metti playfully pushed Toni back to the others.

"OK, Davy, Davy Crockett. I have partied to your sounds till dawn; you're one of my family's all time favourites. Now come over here." Metti had quickly taken stock of this group.

"Now stand still, Davy. Just put your arms by your side. I'm going to come at you from behind." Metti waited until Davy and Toni shared a little school boy snigger between them. "I'm going to put you in a hold and you're going to try and get free. That's not going to be difficult for a big strong man like you Davy Crockett, is it?"

Metti wrapped her arms around Davy who struggled gamely with some genuine effort to free himself but couldn't.

"OK, now you do the same to me." Metti turned around and waited for Davy's arms to wrap around her, which they did, a bit too slowly and loosely, like a friendly hug.

"Davy, I mean as tight as you can, as if you're really not going to let me go."

"OK sugar, if that's how you want it." Davy squeezed real tight, expecting Metti to squeak but within a very brief moment it was Davy who was squealing like a pig. All Metti had done was grab a bit of flesh inside Davy's leg with her thumb and forefinger and squeezed, hard. Davy couldn't let go quick enough.

"Now Huck. Huck the 'micro-psycho', I saw your last fight you know. It was awesome in a brutal way. OK, Huck can you just lie on the floor, put your arms by your side, face down."

Huck jumped to it as if he had been given orders in a military school.

Metti went over to the group and had a quiet word with them.

"OK, Huck. Just a little game. Lie still."

What happened next was not what Huck was expecting. As instructed, Betty lay on top of Huck, back on back. Toni, Davy and Mandy then lay on top of Betty. Huck groaned.

"OK, Huck, all you have to do is get up. Come on."

Huck puffed and pushed and panted some more but he couldn't budge this lot; they were here for the duration. Metti was sizing up the situation and deciding when or if to call it a day, but was taken completely by surprise with the light sobbing that came from inside the heap.

Metti immediately signalled everyone to get up, and Betty instinctively cradled Huck in her arms, stroking his head. "It's OK my baby, you're with me now, it's OK."

Betty looked up at Metti and tried to whisper as if only Metti could hear. "It's the rebirthing thing, I think. This is what happened a few days ago. Must be some kind of flashback sort of thing. I wouldn't worry about it. He'll be OK. Just needs a little cuddle, don't you my little sweetie?"

Davy looked a bit startled. "The *rebirthing* thing? Hell, that must have been before my time. Maybe JC should come and have a look at this. Ain't seen that for a long time."

Nobody had noticed the door of the Encounter Area opening and closing as David approached the heap on the floor that was Betty and Huck.

David sort of peered into the intimate mother baby scene going on between Betty and Huck and turned to Metti.

"He'll be fine, Metti. Right as rain. Just needs a good

sleep and lots of cuddles."

Metti looked suspiciously at JC. "You didn't see this coming did you JC?"

"See this coming, Metti? Not in a million years. Maybe we can try again later, what do you think? You know, when Huck has grown up a bit."

18

Huck and David were sitting in David's office. It was quite early in the morning and Huck looked as if he had something important to say to David.

"OK, Huck what's up?" David could tell Huck had something on his mind.

"Well, it's like this David. I think *The Place* has been great for me, I really do."

"But... I can tell you're about to come out with a 'but', Huck," said David.

"Yeah, there is a 'but' David, and it's this. Like I said, it has been great for me; I feel like I've been through so much. It's not about yesterday; that was just a sort of flashback experience. I've had worse I can tell you. I feel like I've been here for years. There was the rebirthing... now that was an experience, there was that whole episode in the ponds with that guy... the scene with Martin Howler... Gootsy... the 'pap' session, and the rest. Even the movie night with Davy was a lesson, of sorts, David. It's been wild, great – but I think I'd rather cut out now, to be honest. I don't think I'm ready for anything more, you know, involved, right now."

"Are you sure, Huck?"

"I'm real sure, David."

David was genuinely concerned for Huck. "Look why don't you hang around till tomorrow – I know Helen has got something real special lined up for later. A Gootsy special.

We could arrange a proper send off for you in the morning, how about that?"

Huck leaned forward as if in deep thought and then smiled. "A Gootsy special? I'll pass on that one, David. I mean for now. I'll tell you what I'd prefer, David. I'd prefer to come back some day soon, have a session or two – I know you and Helen would cook something up real good – and then I'd like a proper leaving do – you know a Graduation Day like Annie and Richard had. I don't feel like I've graduated, David. Not yet. I will and then it will be right. Does that make sense, David?"

"Sure it does. A lot of sense; and a wise decision if I may say so. Look I understand. It's all about timing, Huck. What I do want to know is whether you've answered the question that was in your mind when you first arrived. You remember, Huck. You wanted to come here when you felt most at risk, you know as you said later most at risk of giving up the fighting and cross-dressing. Have you answered that one, Huck?"

Huck paused for a moment and then stood up. "I think so, David. I'm going to train for one last time, have a great fight and go out in style, win, lose or draw, and then I'll consider my options."

"And what about all the cross-dressing side, Huck? I mean it that over?"

Huck smiled a big manly smile. "Hell no, David. I'm not giving that up. I didn't come here to be cured of anything. I don't really believe in being cured. There's nothing wrong with me David, as far as I'm concerned. I believe in understanding yourself better and making more… more informed decisions. After all I've been through here my head's a lot clearer, it really is."

David stood up and shook Huck's hand and they embraced in a brief, manly hug.

"Listen David, I make decisions, that's all. Perhaps I just need to meet someone who is willing to accept me for what I am, I mean for what I choose to be. I guess what it comes down to is that having spent some time here, now I know why I do it, that's all."

"Well," said David, "that's what I call progress."

"And David, would you mind giving these little thank you notes to Helen, JC, Betty, Toni and Davy? It's maybe not the best way of leaving but it's how I want to do it. As Arnie said, David – 'I'll be back'."

"Thanks," said David taking the little notes from Huck. "Will do, take care of yourself. Till the next one, Huck."

"Till the next one, David."

And on that note Huck turned his back and saluted David as he walked out of David's office.

***

David, Helen and JC quickly convened in David's office to screen an unexpected would-be guest who had just been dropped off from a chauffeur-driven Bentley. With Huck leaving the timing was perfect. The would-be guest was one of the most recognisable lead singers known to man, but the unholy Trinity, if truth be told, was totally unfazed. None of them really liked head-banging rock music. It wasn't their scene.

"Hi, Mark. It's a pleasure, really is. I'm David, this is Dr. Helen Pope the Medical Director, and my son, JC. Welcome. I hope you don't mind this sort of formality, Mark but it's important that we know a bit about your reasons for wanting to stay here, and for how long."

David took a hard look at the world famous rock star as if to check whether his ego was out of control. If it was, he would have no hesitation in turning him away.

"First off Mark – and I have to say this to you – I say it to everyone – we have what we call a 'Darcy Rule' here which means discretion, respect and confidentiality. You're free to discuss your feelings and experiences with other guests while are here, but what goes on in *The Place*, stays in *The Place*. OK? No matter who you are we ask everyone to sign our standard documentation. And, no matter what you sign, we need to trust you. We also have a very strict drug policy which is set out in the Welcome Pack but we'll talk you through that stuff in a bit more detail later, if we get that far. OK, that's my little intro, why don't you tell why you're here?"

Mark Bolland looked every inch the rock star that he was. His craggy features told the entire story of his life, every day of it.

"Why am I here? Like why are any of us here, man?" Mark had become accustomed to his acolytes hanging on every word he uttered, but he could see straight away from the three blank faces in front of him that he was cutting no ice.

Helen assumed control and straightened her back. "Mark, we all know who you are. We have been hearing your songs for years and years. You're part of our culture, an icon, a world figure, we all know your music but here in *The Place* you're a guest, one of several. We provide a very special service to those who come here, at a price. We only take people on board if we feel we can really help them in some fundamental way, otherwise you may as well sit in a hotel room for a few days and you know, chill out."

"OK, Helen lady. OK. I'm here because Toni called and said he was having a great time, I mean a weird time but a great time. He's been my bass man for over twenty years. What Toni says, goes. I love Toni, I'd trust him with my wife, sorry, I mean my life. Why am I here? Here's the truth. If Toni says I need some of this, then that's all I need to hear. Look at me. I'm over sixty and look about a hundred. I've been told that if I touch one more drop of alcohol my liver, pancreas and spleen will go on strike, immediately and forever. I take a puff every now and again but hey – who doesn't? If you knew who I'd shared a spliff with, man it would blow your mind, really."

David interrupted Mark before he dug himself too far into a hole. "Mark, that's what we don't want to hear. I'm sure you've shared the peace pipe with everyone from the Dalai Lama to Bill Clinton and Mother Theresa but we don't want to know. I'm not sure I get it, Mark."

JC's strength was that celebrities of any type just didn't cut it with him. Maybe if they could run a marathon in good time he'd be impressed but an aging rock star, no matter how famous, didn't faze JC in the slightest.

"Mark, hi, I'm JC." JC leaned over to shake Mark's hand which was disarmingly sweaty.

"I guess what you're saying is that you'd rather be here, with Toni, than anywhere else." JC looked at David and Helen. "That sounds like as good a reason as any to be here."

David tried to ignore the figures going through his head and size of the bill that would be heading Mark's way. Mark sat back and looked around at David, Helen and JC and suddenly adopted a more confident, almost arrogant pose.

"OK guys. Here it is. I can see where you're at. I like it. I like your 'Darcy rule', suits me, I can tell you. Maybe it's not for me to say but I'm relying on you guys keeping what's said here under wraps; privacy is as important to me as it is to you. We've both a lot to lose on that score. But listen, I'm here because I want to be here. I wouldn't be here if I didn't trust you, so let's just trust each other, ok? Now, let me tell you something."

Mark leaned forward as if he was going to come out with a tightly-held secret. "I've nearly died more times than I can remember. One time, on stage right, I thought I'd actually died and was singing at my own funeral, really man I'm serious. Sometimes I wake up and wonder if my life is actually a dream. You know the feeling? What I'm saying is that every day – and I mean every day – feels like a bonus. Hell, I don't know if I'm living on borrowed time or what. Maybe I'm a dead man walking, should have gone a long time ago. But I'm here. I want to enjoy myself, that's as close as I can get to explaining why I'm here. I ain't here for a holiday or to get whacked. I'm here for the experience, as recommended by my bass man, Toni. I guess I always need more energy, like you know creative energy. Inspiration maybe. That's it, that's all I got – I've laid it on the line."

Helen, David and JC looked at each other approvingly. There was no need for any further discussions or meetings, they knew each other too well for that and the answer was obvious.

Helen assumed authority. "Mark, that's good enough for us. We have a great line in inspiration therapy, I can vouch for that. JC, would you mind showing Mark around a bit, take him through the paperwork?"

"My pleasure," said JC.

"And Mark, we'll kit you out in something more comfortable than the clothes you're wearing. Your first session later today is going to be what we call a 'Gootsy Special', JC will explain."

Mark Bolland clasped his hands in a thank you gesture. "Can I double-up with Toni?"

Helen paused. "Not tonight, Mark, no. Maybe tomorrow, but I'll want to see how Toni feels about that and see how you get on today. Is that fair enough?"

"Sure is Helen. You're a real lady you know."

Helen smiled mischievously at Mark and replied without missing a beat, "Yeah, I know that."

***

JC knew that Gootsy would be busy in the Encounter Area preparing for his next session and had gambled that Gootsy wouldn't mind if he was interrupted for a minute or two.

"Er, Gootsy. Hope you don't mind. I know you're busy. This is Mark Bolland, he's a friend of Toni, you know like in the same band. He'll be staying at *The Place* for a few days."

Gootsy didn't even turn around to say 'Hello', obviously preoccupied with whatever he was up to. Gootsy had an earpiece in one ear and was fiddling intensely with a remote control which he was busy with in one hand, looking all the while at a stop watch in his other hand, counting out seconds and muttering to himself "Yes, yes, hmm, yeah, good, yes that's it."

Gootsy eventually took out the single earpiece and approached Mark closer and closer until he was nose to nose with Mark.

"I know you, don't I?" Gootsy asked innocently.

Mark was nonplussed at Gootsy's behaviour, he had seen worse, and stranger. "You might, I don't know. Does anyone know me, really?" Mark was trying to be both funny and polite but it didn't quite work.

Gootsy withdrew a little and squinted at Mark. "I do think I know you. We'll find out later, I guess. Now, don't mean to be rude, young JC, but I've still got things to do." Gootsy then headed to a corner of the Encounter Area, towards a couple of unpacked boxes.

"Not at all, Gootsy. Just showing Mark around. See you later."

JC closed the door and pointed Mark in the direction towards the room where Toni was staying.

"You'll want to say hi to Toni, I expect. I'll sort your room out and then come back and get you by which time Gootsy should be ready for us."

"Can't wait, JC. Should be fun from what I've heard."

***

"Welcome, welcome my friends. Please, come in, come in." Gootsy gestured in the group which had assembled outside the Encounter Area until Gootsy was ready.

In walked Toni Whippett, Betty Grisse, Davy Crockett, Mandy Haddock, Metti Wati and Mark Bolland.

The room looked ominous. It wasn't the sight of the carefully laid mats in the centre of the room with a generous spray of cushions and bean bags scattered around, but the single candle in a small candle holder which signified something different about this session.

"Please do sit down. Sit, go on all of you, sit, please, make yourselves comfortable." Gootsy appeared to be brimming with excitement.

The group, one by one, found themselves a space and settled in as best they could. Betty and Mark sat as close to Toni as they could which prompted Gootsy to rearrange them in a group of more or less even spacing. Eventually Gootsy sat amongst them forming a circle of seven, sitting around the lit candle.

"OK, now that we're ready. Let me explain this... this session." As Gootsy stopped talking the lights seem to dim of their own accord engulfing the room into darkness, apart from the flickering light from the small candle.

"The candle," explained Gootsy, "will last for about twenty minutes. When it goes out we will be in total darkness." The group remained very quiet, not knowing what to expect next.

"During those twenty minutes or so, I want each of you to think of who – or what – you love most, but isn't... with us any more."

Betty tried to catch Toni's attention to exchange some form of knowing and a friendly glance however brief, but Toni had his eyes firmly closed is if he dared not even look around.

"Now," Gootsy continued, "I've told you before, it's important to breathe and relax, so we'll just try some breathing exercises shall we? Oh, and one more thing. When the candle dies out you'll hear noises which I've set up to come out of the speakers which you won't be able to see. So, please there's no need for alarm. Enjoy."

The group seemed to let out a collective sigh of relief, but Gootsy wasn't finished.

"However, I can tell you now that not all the sounds you'll hear will be mine. Some sounds you will hear alone –

coming from your own inner voice, but please don't be alarmed… it's natural."

Toni tried to squelch his bottom even closer to the floor, while Mandy sort of sniffed as if she was not impressed by this one. In fact it was a close call as to whether Mandy would let fly with a comment or two of her own, but she decided to keep quiet. It would be over soon.

Gootsy closed his eyes, inhaled loudly through his nostrils, held his breath for a few seconds and then breathed out slowly from his mouth in an exaggerated blowing motion. The group didn't need any further instructions and quickly copied Gootsy.

"Now, you don't need to say anything. Nothing at all. I just want you to think about what I said earlier. Think of someone, someone or maybe some *thing* that you really loved, still love, with all your heart. But they're no longer with us. Ask them to join us. Don't be afraid."

The few minutes it took for the candle to flicker out seemed to last an eternity but eventually the light totally departed from the candle and the room descended into total darkness, so dark that it was difficult for Mark to tell whether his eyes were open, or not.

As the darkness and the silence continued, a slow creaking noise was heard from one side of the room. Not near the door but from a ceiling corner. Nobody could see Mark smile as he reckoned, rightly, that this was coming from a speaker inside the room. The creaking sound was followed by the sound of a door closing. The distinct clip-clopping of a horse was heard, moving from one side of the room to the other, to another door which seemed to creak open and then close, quietly. Mark's smile broadened; his bet was that Gootsy was about to play Pink Floyd's *Dark Side of the Moon*.

But then something happened, the deployment of a little trick which Gootsy loved. Gootsy had set up a little condenser which had been programmed, silently, and at a very precise time, to emit just a tiny spray of cold, moistened air in the direction of the group. For Gootsy, a breath of cold, fresh air worked wonders, every time. Gootsy smiled as the cold air tickled his back and wondered whether he should call it 'fresh air therapy'.

Gootsy over many years had worked out what made people afraid, and what made them laugh. He was often tempted to combine the two therapies into one experience; after all, to Gootsy they were simply different examples of life therapy: fear and joy and everything in between. The point to Gootsy was that it made the participants feel alive.

As the silent cold air reached the centre of the room, each one of the group shivered in turn, not quite sure this time whether the cold air was part of the set up or not. Mandy by now was not so cock-sure. In fact a fear was beginning to grow inside Mandy's mind, a nagging troublesome fear. No one could hear Mandy's internal mantra – 'it's all bullshit, it's all bullshit' – but then everyone was going through a very different experience.

Gootsy had planned this one to precision: Candle goes out in twenty minutes, creaking doors, closing doors, sounds of horses, cold wind – this was all designed to whet the appetite of the group's imagination. Now the real fun could begin.

As the chilled air passed and the darkness and silence became ever more intense, Gootsy's absolute favourite sound started, slowly at first and then ever so gradually becoming louder and louder. There was something deeply unsettling about the sound of a baby crying; the sound betrayed no obvious distress, but the possibility that things might take a different turn very quickly was enough; it hit the nerves on so many levels, and then it stopped and a nauseating silence followed.

After a while the silence was broken by a very distinct sound. Each one of the group could now hear a deep male voice coughing, but unsure as to whether anyone else could hear the same sound which felt to everyone as too real and too close to be coming from the speakers. Gootsy was the only one with his eyes open, a firm believer that there was a lot to be seen in the dark, particularly when the red light on the remote control could be pointed towards the door, acting as a landing light for a barefoot visitor. Gootsy guided a foot past him and into the centre of the group.

"Now," shouted Gootsy, "come out now, now, reveal yourself, NOW!"

The lights in the Encounter Area suddenly burst into life to reveal – standing right in the centre of the group – the life form of a man, or perhaps a beast in a dark cloak, the sight of which caused the group to let out a collective, uninhibited and quite spectacular scream.

The black cloak dropped in theatrical fashion to reveal a man dressed distinctively in a white sequined stage suit wearing fighter pilot sunglasses, wearing a deep black coiffed wig, exaggerated sideburns and holding a microphone.

At the same moment the cloak hit the floor, the unseen speakers burst forth with the soundtrack to one of The King's best known songs with the words: *'uh uh, I'm all shook up, oh yeah'*.

Mark let out a sort of laughing scream that he hadn't heard from himself for many a year and clutched his stomach in the throes of giggles.

"Elvis, Elvis baby! Where have you been brother?" Mark started clapping and wiping the tears from his eyes.

Davy Crockett couldn't resist his favourite line. "Classic, brother, classic."

Toni was laughing hysterically, hugging Betty who was also crying but in a very ambiguous manner because it wasn't really clear whether the tears were of sorrow, fear, joy, shock or hysteria or a combination of every extreme emotion Betty had ever felt in her life.

The man that would be Elvis spoke into the microphone. "Why shucks, thank you, thank you all, thank you so much, I'll be here all week." And with that David took off the Elvis wig and took a bow, gave Gootsy a high five and walked out the door.

It wasn't until the pitch of the laughter had come down a few octaves before Gootsy noticed that Mandy was completely frozen; her eyes were wide open, but she was as still as a statue.

"Don't worry everyone. This is quite normal. Mandy is a very intuitive young lady. It happens. She'll be right as rain in a few moments, just getting over the excitement in her own good time."

Metti without instruction sat next to Mandy, placed an arm around her and held Mandy in a tight cuddle. "You'll be OK Mandy," said Metti.

19

Simon Hall's shark-like eyes focussed on Ralph Crossley with undisguised contempt. "You know why you'll never be the boss, Ralph? I mean the boss of anything. It's because you've got no balls. See, with people like me – not that you'd understand old boy – we understand that decisions have to be made. Hard, risky decisions. You see, we're different, Ralph. I was born to lead, I was made captain of the school cricket team when was I was thirteen, you know. Bet you've never played cricket in your whole life. I don't know why I'm wasting my breath, you just don't know what I'm talking about, do you?"

Ralph kept his eyes on the floor and shook his head.

"OK, let me share something with you. The powers that be in New York are very keen on the unholy Trinity, real keen. They seem very up-to-speed on this one. I guess they find the whole scenario kind of... you know... British. It tickles them, I reckon. And they know we can milk this for all it's worth. The point is this, there's a level of interest in this story that worries me, a bit. If it worries me, it needs to worry you even more Ralph because we have to get this right. But don't get me wrong, we're going to print this story come what may."

Simon paused and looked up to the ceiling as if he was about to spout some very important truth. "Thing about lawyers Ralph is that they're intellectual mercenaries. Pay them enough and they'll say what you want to hear."

Simon looked back at Ralph as if coming out of a mini-trance. "I know I don't own the *Sunday News* Ralph but I own this story – I'm going stick my neck out on this one, so get it right – do you understand me – if I get hit on this one you're going to break my fall – you get that, don't you?"

"Sure do, boss."

***

Helen, David and JC had convened for a very early meeting to assess the state of play.

"OK, where are we?" asked David. "Metti is sharing with Mandy, just for tonight, then she'll be off. Do you think Mandy will be OK, Helen? She looked completely fazed by the Gootsy special. I mean she seems to have retreated into herself. How long do you think that will last for?"

Helen looked, and sounded very serious. "I've seen this before David. Mandy's in a state of shock, that's all. We'll let her sleep for the morning and then see how she is. We might need Aaron to fix this one, I don't know. It depends on where her head is at when she surfaces."

Helen turned her attention to the other guests. "Betty will be thinking of leaving soon. Toni is really one only session away. I'm having a chat with Toni a bit later this morning to assess his progress and how he feels. I don't know if Mark will want to stay when Toni's left. Davy's got some distance to go, but his time is nearly up."

"Well," said David. "Look's like a busy week, one way or the other. We've got a major ego, sorry celeb, turning up later today or tomorrow. We're already on red alert for this one." David's mobile buzzed indicating a new arrival. "Shit, spoke too soon, she's here already. Action stations guys, this one's a hotty. We'll need to be real careful of the tabloids with this one. JC, your time to shine, son."

"Thanks, dad. Look while you're on my case – and talking of tabloids – do you think you can let me know how the impending doom is to be averted? We can't have more than a couple of days left before the *Sunday News* goes into print – it's going to be front page I guess this weekend. I mean how's that one going, dad, if I may ask?"

"JC, you do jump to conclusions son. I reckon we'll be alright, don't worry. I had another little chat with Simon and told him my Q.C. had said if they go to print then he and his boss would be arrested and be in jail within one hour. I told him my Q.C. had said new provisions of the Human Rights Act had come into force just recently and he better check the position, you know, for his own good."

JC did not look convinced. "When did you take advice from a Q.C.? Which Q.C.? What are these new laws you're talking about dad?"

"Listen, JC. Simon Hall is worried about something. I can sense his fear. Helen knows I've got quite a special skill in that respect. I can see what's happened here, maybe even more clearly than Simon sees. He's not to know I was being a bit – you know – creative. It's stalled him; he's got to think about this a bit more. Oh, by the way – I've changed our wireless password and upgraded the security on our systems, so all in all, no worries, JC. Anything else worrying you?"

JC sort of shook his head as if he couldn't quite believe what he was hearing. But David was his dad, and his dad had never – ever – let him down in the past, so JC reluctantly let it go "OK, dad. I know it's a trust thing. Jesus, how often do we say that to our guests."

"Quite," said Helen in her best matriarchal tone.

"Right," said JC. "I get it. Moving on – maybe it's as good a time as any to review our responsibilities here? I mean I understand that it's important for a whole load of reasons to keep things tight but I'm getting a bit pissed off with organising all the food, the shopping, the cooking even."

Helen and David looked at each other betraying a slight mutual feeling of guilt on that score.

"Yeah, we've been thinking the same thing, JC. Let's just get through the next couple of days and I promise we'll have a rethink about that side of things, OK?"

"Is that a promise, dad?" asked JC.

"Sure is son, I promise." No sooner had David stopped talking than a dishevelled bundle in female form was ushered into the room, accompanied by a young male, a manager-looking type, who asked Helen where he should put the new guest as if he was delivering a recorded package.

The young lady was placed carefully on the sofa while JC made a discreet exit before the brief introductions were completed.

"Is she OK, I mean are you sure about this?" David looked at the young lady who by any standards was a wreck.

The young man took a step back and looked at the almost unrecognisable form of Katie Windsor, the well-known American singer and actress.

"Hi, you must be David, and Helen, hi. I'm Steve, Katie's manager. Well, I look after her and stuff like that. Well, in Europe anyway. Thanks for this. Look it was a close call whether to call an ambulance or drop her off at the hospital. But I've seen this before. There's nothing wrong with Katie except she's exhausted and got a bit too wasted last night, and the night before, in fact ever since the premiere of

Lost Cause at Leicester Square last week. I've cleared her diary for a couple of days. Do you think that's enough? She's got a bundle of promotions to do over here before she's due back in New York at the end of the week."

Steve looked at Helen and David if they were car mechanics. Helen sat beside Katie and placed a hand on Katie's face, wiping away the straggly hair hiding the face of a very tired and hung over movie star.

Steve looked deeply into Katie's vacant, weary eyes. "Katie's whole image is built on the innocent girl-next-door thing. You can keep this under wraps, can't you David?"

"Steve, that's what we do. Leave Katie with us. Why don't you call in or phone a bit a later and we'll let you know how things are going. Can't guarantee a forty-eight hour turn around, Steve, but we'll see what we can do, OK?"

"OK, David. Thanks and you too, Helen. There's a lot riding on this, my job included. I've a thousand and one excuses to make so, I'll be off and I'll speak with you later."

Steve disappeared out of the door and left David and Helen alone with Katie Windsor, the starlet known to the public as the darling innocent face of one successful film after another.

"OK," said Helen, "now we've got Mandy and Metti sharing there's more than enough room for Katie to have her own space for at least one day. Let's get her to her room David, and I'll keep a close eye on her. We can chat through later."

***

"OK, Toni, tell me where you're at." Helen looked surprisingly composed considering the physical effort that was involved in getting Katie to bed only a few moments earlier, but Helen was a trouper, after all.

"Where am I at? Jeez, Helen, I've been here for a few days, and it feels like years. I mean in a good way. I've laughed, I've cried, I've shat myself – what more could I ask for?" Toni smiled a broad genuine smile from ear to ear.

"But how do you feel?" asked Helen.

"Well, it's funny you should ask, Helen. If I'm honest, I feel real horny. But in a good way if you know what I mean."

"I'm not sure that I do Toni. Go on."

Toni for once looked quite solemn, serious even. "Helen, it's like this. I didn't come here to be free from my urges. I'm sure you've heard that before. I can see that I'm like an alcoholic; it's not about being 'fixed', it's about accepting that you've got a problem and then dealing with it one day at a time. Sex is a bad habit, that's all. I've learnt a lot Helen and I guess as time moves on I'll learn more. This place is very real in its own way; I mean the encounters are bizarrely real. The people are real. The relationships are real. I guess it's about growing up. I certainly feel as if I've aged, Helen. I mean in a good way."

Helen studied Toni carefully. "That's about as much as you can expect to get from *The Place*, Toni. An understanding of yourself and a sort of new found maturity. Is that a fair way of looking at it?"

Toni knew what was coming and looked quite sad. "OK, Helen. I'm ahead of you. It's time for me to click my little red heels and head back to Kansas. There's no place like home, is there?"

"Toni, I'm glad you feel that way. I really am. But listen, it's not over yet."

Toni's eyes opened wide with the possibility of a new challenge.

"What I mean Toni, is that we'll organise a proper Graduation Ceremony for you. You deserve it, OK?"

"OK, Helen, thanks, for everything." Toni thought for a moment. "Can we do this tomorrow morning maybe? Mark and I are working on a new song; I reckon we'll crack it today."

"A new song, that's great. What's it called?"

"It's a work in progress, Helen. But the working title is 'Rehab Blues'."

"'Rehab Blues'? I like that Toni, sounds perfect."

"It will be Helen, I promise."

***

Helen, David and JC had convened for a quiet moment before Toni's leaving do started.

"Are we OK, with this? It feels a bit risqué." David looked uncomfortable.

"It'll be fine, David, stop fretting," said Helen.

David was still in a bit of a state of concern, although he was trying hard not to show it. "It's just that I didn't expect the whole band to appear. Katie's not ready and is staying in bed, as is Mandy, so I can't see any problem, really. We'll have Metti, Betty, Mark, Toni of course and Davy. Who's turned up to see Toni?"

"Just the drummer Zack what's-his-name and Sig, the lead guitarist," said JC.

David, Helen and JC approached the French windows that lead out to the patio area. Metti was having an impromptu training session in the garden, demonstrating a few material arts poses surrounded by Zack, Sig, Davy, Toni and Mark while Betty stood to the side, watching.

Helen stood on the steps and called for order, which took some time to prevail. In time everyone turned to face Helen and David, falling into an awkward silence that precedes an unwanted speech.

"Please, can I have your attention, thank you. As I always say on these occasions, it really is a great pleasure to reach this stage. Today is Toni's leaving day, his graduation. Toni has been a star pupil, he really has. Toni we've a couple of special guests to present you with your leaving present."

On cue Tim and Tamara stepped in front of Helen, Tamara holding a large present.

"Toni," said Tamara in an impressively loud voice, "is a very special person. He came here knowing he had issues to face up and has done so very… courageously. Tim and I are really, impressed, aren't we Tim?"

Tim nodded in clear approval while Tamara continued.

"We all had a think as to what you should take away with you from *The Place*, and after much deliberating we decided on this, although I must admit Mark did help out here." Tamara held out a present of some size and waited for Toni to step up and receive it. Without a moment's hesitation Toni carefully peeled off the wrapping paper to reveal – eventually – a beautiful, state-of-the-art electric guitar which could let loose any number of sounds, imitate any instrument and let rip with countless melodies at the touch of one of its many buttons; a stunning, glittering example of the modern age.

"Oh my word, that is absolutely fantastic. Thanks so much, really. Yeah, a new – space age – guitar, that's right on, it really is. Jeez doesn't even have any strings. Wow, what a *thing*. Look, I'm not a great one for speeches; I tend to do my talking so to speak with my guitar. I can only say I've had a weird, wonderful, exciting, enlightening time here. I'm ready to head out a new man and take care you all because I'm looking for a partner, someone to share things with, lot of things, not you know just one… er thing. I could stay here forever I guess, it would have been nice to see more – a lot more – of Wetti Mati, I mean Metti Wati." Toni knew he was almost done but had one final announcement to make.

"Before I leave I want my mate, my best mate, Mark to step up. We're going to give you a preview of our latest song – it's not quite the finished, polished deal yet, in fact it's a bit rough, but we're nearly there. Come on Mark, let's give them a send off to remember, let's hit them with 'Rehab Blues'."

Mark had no hesitation heading up to stand next to Toni. For a moment, Mark held Toni's stare with a playful on-stage look and shouted: "OK, one, two three…" and with a random press of a few buttons on Toni's new toy, something resembling a heavy beat filled the air and they were off on a rough ride through an early version of 'Rehab Blues.'

"Ain't got no smoke / ain't got no lady / ain't got no booze / ain't got no hang-over / ain't got no bruis-es…"

Toni found some inspirational solo guitar riffs and he was off, on a wild one, until he let Mark back in with some lyrics that bore some resemblance to what they had been practising all night and day as a rough duet:

All I got is… all I got is… all I got is…
All I got is hope / I got my… dig-nitty… / I got love / I got… feelings
I've got friends / I got… my pride / I got my soul… /

I got a book / to read… / I got a movie / to watch /
I got a mountain / to climb /
I got a connection / to make / I got an apology / to
offer / I got tears / to shed /
I got time / to live / I got a brother / to hug… /
I got nothing / nothing / but the Rehab Blues
brother.

20

"It's time we talked more about *The Place*, don't you think?" asked David casually of his son, JC and his partner Helen Pope. "I mean it all seems to be a bit random sometimes. I'm not sure what we're doing half the time, you know what I mean? Maybe we should – you know – pause and have a think about what this is all about? Maybe get a bit more structured, all round."

JC looked at his dad as if he had taken the wrong drugs or something.

"But, it's perfect," said Helen, "what do you want to change?" Helen was very sincere, but she was being deliberately mischievous.

"Perfect?" asked JC. "We're perfectly stuffed aren't we?"

"Now JC I've told you, I've got all that *Sunday News* stuff all under control. No worries. Let that one be, son. I want to know if you've got anything to say – constructively mind you – about how we run *The Place*, and what we do, you know – all of that sort of stuff. You know, like you've been saying all along."

JC's demeanour suddenly changed and he seemed quite pleased that everything seemed both under control and up for grabs. "I'll tell you what I think, I think I'm being made to do too much of the behind the scenes stuff. No wonder I'm so fit, heaving all the gear out of the hidden spaces and back again, I do all the food stuff which really pisses me off and costs us a fortune by the way especially during the 'I want a WagYu phase' and the demands – I mean did I ever tell you how long it took me to deal with Toni's socks freak out – we should have a socks session you know – we really do need to talk about the laundry bill at some point I mean why are socks my problem and..."

"Listen kid..." David interrupted his son with a rare, impatient edge.

"I thought we agreed that you wouldn't call me *kid*. I call you dad which is OK, OK? I don't call you 'old man'..."

"Yeah, yeah, sorry JC. OK? How many weetabix did you have for breakfast? *The Place* works as far as I'm concerned, but only up to a point. We live in this nice little annex, the guests' demands are met, the agents and lawyers and pr guys are dealt with. What I'm saying is that we perhaps need some focus on what services we're giving, be a bit more market orientated."

Helen looked at David. They were sitting comfortably round a small dinner table in a functional kitchen area of the self-contained two bedroom annex to *The Place*, the part of the small complex which the guests knew little about.

Helen looked at David with renewed intensity. "David, please enlighten your son and me, what are you going on about?"

"It's this. What are we offering these people? What's the deal?" David paused as if he had made his case out but Helen and JC were still unsure as to what the case was.

"Here's the deal," said JC viewing a real opportunity. "First of all, if we want to sell – forgive me – *sell* equilibrium, then we should be, you know, in a state of equilibrium. I mean isn't that right? It's not just about treating our guests like kids who need spanking."

David couldn't resist the open goal. "That that might be arranged – 'spanking therapy'. Sorry JC you were saying?"

JC continued, "OK, Helen, how many therapies have we got?"

"OK, JC, I'll tell you. At the last count, forty." Helen knew every one of them as most were her own creation, in one form or another.

"You see, that's what I mean, we're therapy orientated, not person orientated," said JC as if standing his ground for the first time. "I think we should start to think from the person out, not us imposing stuff from outside."

"OK, JC, be specific."

"OK, take Betty. I like Betty. But I don't like fat people. I just think they're lazy, end of story. They annoy me. But I like Betty and she's fat, so I guess I'm developing. I think we should get Metti to take a martial arts session, perhaps starting in the Encounter Area and then move into the garden. And the purpose of the session is really to make Betty feel great. That's what I'm saying, it's nothing to do with the therapies; it's simply about finding a way to make our guests leave here feeling great, that's all I'm saying."

Helen and David looked at each other, quite impressed with JC's outburst.

"OK," said Helen. "I get you JC, it's a fair point, let's go with it. It's about Betty. Martial arts session. Betty comes out feeling great – 'the winner', perhaps. Metti's taking the session. Got it. Now, why don't you, JC, take part in this session, you know as one of them, the guests."

JC paused for a minute as if a deal-closer had just been placed on the table. "Sounds good to me, Helen. I was going to suggest Metti, thanks."

David rubbed his hands as if a deal had just been struck.

"Well, I'm glad that's sorted. I've got a new one. You know, number forty-one on your list, Helen."

"And what might that be, David?" asked Helen.

"'CDT'," said David cryptically.

"And what is 'CDT'?" asked JC.

David leaned forward as if he was explaining something quite complex. "'CDT' is controlled drinking therapy. I'm sorry, but I'm tired of pretending I don't like to drink. I don't want to get drunk or out of control, but I think we should relax the drinking side of things and have a session which is about drinking with the message that 'hey you're allowed to have a drink, provided you know when to stop'. It's an old-fashioned 'moderation' message. I know we allow small amounts of alcohol on special occasions but I'd like to perhaps formalise it a bit."

Helen and JC tried not to look at each other with some concern. "Er, sounds interesting, dad. Maybe Helen and you can have a chat about that one." JC changed the subject, quickly. "But Helen you're right, I'll join in the Metti session, in the background so to speak."

"Great," said David, "that's progress, thanks, now, do you mind if I have a beer before you get another bright idea? I mean at this rate you'll be talking about spiritualism next."

JC looked at his dad in what he had now come to think of as the 'Doris Day' look and said, "Sometimes dad, I wonder, I really do."

"OK," said Helen, "I'm fine with the Metti session. David let's talk later about this CDT idea. In the meantime I'll check up on Katie Windsor. Hold on, is that your phone going off David?"

David took his phone out of his pocket and realised immediately that the caller was Simon Hall. In fact it wasn't a call; it was a buzz alerting David to a text message which David quickly accessed and it read: *'Hi, God, gonna roll with this nxt w/e, any probs call legal dept. luv SH.'*

"Oh shit," said David.

"I don't like 'oh shit' at any time dad, and not from you. Show me, come on."

David handed JC his mobile which JC read in about one second. "Oh shit," said JC.

***

As a martial arts squad the group didn't look too impressive, but as an eclectic gathering of celebrities it was quite spectacular.

Betty Grisse, Davy Crockett, Mandy Haddock, Mark Bolland, Katie Windsor and David Cooper were gathered in the Encounter Area all dressed in loose-fitting judo robes and barefoot waiting for Metti Wati to make an entrance and began some kind of martial arts session.

Mark, like an excited schoolboy, was throwing around some Karate moves.

"I'm there already with this one. Look. Wax on, wax off, wax on, wax off. Come on Metti."

Metti suddenly appeared looking like a samurai, dressed in a black half robe.

"I'm wearing, in case you're wondering, a Harkama, normally used for Aikido." Metti then performed a ritual series of movements which were as smooth and as complicated as any Bollywood dance.

"Right," said Metti, "this isn't going to be like the last time. No pile ups. No nonsense. I need you to give me everything you've got. Concentration. Focus. OK, copy me."

Metti jogged around the room swinging her arms around her head forwards and then backwards, occasionally touching the floor with one hand and then the next. The group looked rather the worse for wear after only a couple of minutes. Metti suddenly stopped and suggested they catch their breath.

Metti asked the group to form a line in front of her, facing the large mirrors behind her. Without any command Metti adopted a squat position and punched out with each arm in turn, shouting out what sounded like a battle cry each time her arms extended. The group needed no instruction to copy Metti's exercise, each one trying their best to emit some form of noise which sounded if not scary then at least a little bit loud.

Once the group seemed to get the hang of it Metti changed her shout to a number, starting with 'one hundred' and then counting down. At first the group looked quite relaxed; simply punching out their arms didn't seem too demanding.

Metti watched each of the group carefully. Without exception they all appeared obsessed with how the other members of the group were getting on, as if expecting someone to stop and give up.

It soon became apparent that this was a competition and a very, very tiring one at that. Mark was already sweating profusely by the time Metti had shouted 'eighty' and it looked as if the famous rock star would be the first to throw in the towel, but something seemed to keep him going, perhaps the fact that the ladies, Betty, Mandy and Katie seemed to have found a rhythm.

Unexpectedly to the group, but not to Metti, it was JC who stopped by the time Metti had shouted down to 'fifty'.

Then Davy, followed by Mark, until only Betty was still going by the time Metti had shouted down to 'one' and then 'stop'.

JC tried hard not to give Metti some form of signal that would have given the game away. Betty was not to know that Metti and JC had agreed with each of the group to let Betty complete on her own. They were all happy to do so, even more so when they saw the immediate transformation that seemed to overtake Betty once she had recovered. There was such a broad genuine smile, a sense of achievement and an obvious pride which was a joy to witness.

The group spontaneously rounded on Betty and gave her long lasting and heartfelt hugs.

"OK, well done Betty," said Metti, "that was a real achievement. Now, let's practice some real moves. Give me everything you've got; I need to leave after this."

Metti continued with her session, nothing too involved was needed to finish the session off; the main aim had been achieved, which was for Betty to feel like a winner.

Metti and JC exchanged glances as if to say 'well done' to each other. Within the briefest of moments the intended glance turned into an intense and hunger-filled stare, causing both of them to blush and turn away.

***

Helen, David and JC sat in silence in David's office pondering the 'Betty issue'.

"Did Betty have any idea that she was being – you know – set up yesterday?" David was keen to know whether the plan had worked; Betty's time was coming to an end and real progress needed to be made.

"I don't think so," said JC. "She was buzzing all day. Helen's idea of getting her to eat as many chocolate hobnobs as she could before she threw up was a stroke of genius, I have to say. She vowed never to touch another one, ever again."

Helen smiled. "It's a risky strategy but in this case worked very well. I think we just need one more heavy session and Betty will be ready to face the world in a more positive state of mind."

"One more 'heavy session' Helen, what have you got in mind?" David was genuinely curious.

"Later this afternoon, our friend Paul Jones is dropping by. They've all got their schedules planned out in their own minds, and a surprise rebirthing session is just what Betty needs."

David lowered his head, his stomach always turned over when he heard the name 'Paul Jones' – the rebirthing sessions made him feel sick with worry.

"Don't worry David. There's an added surprise. I took a call earlier from Huck. He wants to come back for the afternoon." Helen looked over at JC to see his reaction.

"I thought Huck had run out of cash, Helen," JC went straight to the point.

"Well, actually, JC, we're not charging him for this one. He's playing for us this time." Helen looked rather coy.

"How do you mean, Helen, 'playing for us'?" said JC looking rather put out.

"It's like this JC. Huck feels likes there's some unfinished business here. I mean as far the rebirthing is concerned. From what I heard, I think I agree. And he's got a surprise announcement to make, should be interesting. After today's over, Huck won't be back for some time, if ever."

It was JC's turn to lower his head, looking relieved but unconvinced. "OK dad, maybe there's fun to be had."

"Fun? When was rebirthing ever fun?" David couldn't hide his fears.

***

Helen looked around at the faces in front of her and smiled broadly. "OK, here we are in the Encounter Area. I know you're all expecting the 'Confrontation Therapy' but we'll pick that up later. This afternoon, we've a surprise for you."

On cue, in walked Huck looking mean and relaxed and immediately went over to hug Betty who seemed overjoyed to see him again.

"And," Helen continued, "I've another surprise." This time in walked Paul Jones who immediately approached Huck and gave him a manly bear hug.

"That's my part over; I leave you all to it. Have fun." Helen slipped out the door leaving the group in some confusion.

"OK," said Paul, "my name is Paul Jones. For those of you who don't know me, I'm a rebirthing specialist. Huck and Betty know the routine but I'll take it from the top for the rest of you. Mandy, Davy, and Katie had a collective look of very deep apprehension not knowing what to expect, at all. Mark Bolland by contrast looked quite ecstatic, like a young lad clinging for dear life before the roller coaster heads off up the steep track, shit-scared and enjoying every moment.

Huck quickly scanned the faces looking for Metti, but she was nowhere to be seen. Huck was not to know that JC had insisted that Huck and Metti should be kept as far apart as possible; Metti's time had already come and gone, for now at least.

Paul ran through his opening spiel, looking carefully at the reactions of the uninitiated, making his mind up as he talked as to where he would place each participant. There was no debate as to who was to be the centre of attention today; that had already been decided. It was Betty's day.

"OK I hope that all makes sense, so far." Paul had decided that it was time to get to it. "I'll just create a little ambiance, it does help."

Paul turned down the lights and pushed a button on the remote in his hand and the room was suddenly filled with the sounds of the beautiful, haunting, angelic voice of a female soloist.

Mark felt like a little school boy who knew the answer to a difficult question, the only problem being that no one had asked a question.

"Hayley Westernra, love her, love her to bits," said Mark smugly.

"Er thanks, Mark. Well spotted. Now Betty, if you will."

Betty seemed surprised, as if she was expecting Huck to adopt the foetal position. Betty had thought, wrongly, that the purpose of this exercise was to straighten out Huck; that's why she thought he was in the room.

With some hesitation Betty, as best she could, crouched on all fours and placed her head in her hands. Paul, tactfully, adjusted Betty's position to something which he felt would work better and didn't look so *wrong*.

Without saying a word, Paul indicated to Huck to place his hands around Betty's head, as had been previously discussed and agreed with Helen. This time Paul had decided that for a person of Betty's size the 'anchorman' needed to be skilled and experienced, which meant that he had to assume the challenging responsibility of holding this whole package together.

By the time the human womb was complete, with Davy Crockett and Mandy Haddock on one side of Betty, Mark Bolland and Katie Windsor on the other, Huck at one end and Paul at the other, they were ready to roll.

"OK," said Paul in a soft, confident voice. "Let's all breathe together, as one." Paul exaggerated his breathing, in and out, and the group followed.

"Now," said Paul raising his voice slightly, "GO, it's time to GO!"

Even by Paul's standards this was a tricky one. It was like, he said later, being a midwife to the birth of a baby elephant or maybe a water buffalo. Betty squirmed and shuffled; her cries of angst and loud sobbing caused Paul, perhaps for the first time in his career as a rebirther, to wonder whether he had bitten off more than he could chew.

The group as a whole swarmed around the room sometimes appearing to lose control completely. Huck held on manfully to Betty's small head with his big strong hands but this one went on and on and on.

After a full half hour a sort of battle pulse took over. Huge efforts were made by Betty to struggle free, resisted with all the strength of the group, followed by brief periods of calm where by Betty seemed to gather even more strength for another big heave-to.

Paul tried hard not to show his concern, he had seen this only once before when one of the group had shouted 'Jesus, this might need some intervention' but somehow he dug deep and carried on, confident that this would resolve itself, somehow and soon.

After what seemed like an eternity a strange smile came over Huck's face and he looked over to Paul. Huck instinctively it seemed knew that Betty was ready and so she was. Betty heaved and screamed and as Huck let her through his widening hands Betty appeared to come through a makeshift birth canal which was no more than Huck's strong arms. Betty collapsed into a heap and found herself eventually, weeping uncontrollably on Huck's broad shoulders.

Paul and the others spontaneously comforted Betty, stroking and patting her, all the while passing reassuring comments.

Mark Bolland was in a particular state. He hadn't even been present at the birth of any one of his own seven children and this was the closest he had experienced to the real thing. He felt even more emotionally and physically shattered than he had after a two hour concert in front of tens of thousands of hard core fans. Katie, Davy and Mandy were too exhausted to say much at all.

Paul was in no rush to spoil the moment which lasted for some time. Eventually Betty seemed to surface and looked deep into Huck's eyes with the unfocussed attention of a newborn baby.

"Huck, Huck. Thank you, thank you." Betty sniffled a bit and sat up slightly.

"My god, that was weird, I mean really, really weird. It was like it was really happening." Betty suddenly lapsed into further sobbing, but this time it was the tears of a grown woman who had experienced the trauma of childbirth, for real. "You know why I didn't want to come out Huck? Do you know why?"

Huck shook his head. If he hadn't been through a

similar experience he might not have been so empathetic, but he had and knew how real it felt.

Betty seemed to pull herself together and steadied herself as if what she was about to say was going to be ridiculed. But out it came. "I... I didn't want to come out because I thought no one wanted me. I was so afraid I'd come out and be... I don't know... thrown away... I wasn't sure anyone would want me. That's why I came here. I was beginning to feel that no-one really wanted me. Not even my daughter, Diane." That was about as much as Betty could muster before breaking down again but the group was with Betty on this one. Each one in turn without being asked or prompted looked into Betty's eyes and said comforting words. By this stage Davy was in tears, the likes of which he had never been through, sadder and more real than Snow White's death.

"Oh, Betty. Betty, we all want you girl. You're here with us, babe," said Davy with the quivering voice of a young boy.

Slowly the group sat away from each other and Paul discreetly turned up the lights. No one had noticed that the music had stopped some time ago. With the lights on the group resembled the survivors of a major catastrophe – a flood or an earthquake or some event from which they had all managed, just about, to survive and tell the tale.

No one heard Helen open the door and enter the room. The contrast between Helen's immaculate and hair-perfect persona and the group's post-apocalyptic appearance was striking.

"My," said Helen, "looks like that was some event, everything OK?"

Betty looked strangely different. There was a definite

gleam in her eyes and a colour in her cheeks. In fact by any standards Betty was positively shining with life.

"Everything is fine, Helen, thanks. I feel so great, it's difficult to explain." Betty gave Huck another hug and stroked in a thankful manner the rest of the group in turn.

"And, Huck, how do you feel?" Helen's presence suddenly came across as premeditated and her tone slightly rehearsed.

"Thank you, Helen, thank you." Huck looked at the group as if to make a confession. "Helen and I and Paul of course agreed that I could come back and help do – I mean rebirth – Betty. OK, for my sake as well as Betty's. I needed to go through this again but on the outside this time. It's straightened me out, it really has."

"And Huck, anything else?" Helen looked at Huck as if he had forgotten his lines.

"Oh, yes, yes, of course. Listen everyone. When I first came here I didn't really know why. All I could say was I needed to be here when I felt most 'at risk'. Hell, I wasn't really sure what I meant by that. What I wanted to say was that I wanted to be here when I felt most afraid. And, you know, I came to realise what it was that I was most afraid of."

The group stared at Huck; it was clear that a 'big announcement' was imminent.

"What I was most afraid of was accepting who I am. Who I really am, and I've decided. I'm having a sex change. Not like in one go, it takes time. But my mind is made up. I'm crossing over – for good. In a year's time it will be complete. Goodbye Huck, hello Dolly."

"Dolly?" asked Davy. "Dolly?"

Huck put on a deliberately deep voice and puffed out his chest, theatrically.

"Yeah, *Dolly*. You got a problem with that brother?"

"No, no I ain't got a problem with that er… brother. Just a bit of a shocker, I mean you wanna join the ladies – that's cool. Freedom, brother, freedom." Davy knew Huck was joking on one level but it still felt like the danger zone to Davy, Huck being a cage fighter and all that.

"Yeah, look, I now it's a bit of a shock but that's how it is." Huck looked over to Helen who was now holding the remote control.

Helen smiled at Huck and pressed the remote a couple of times. Out of the speakers came the undisputable sound of Barbara Streisand.

The group looked at each other in disbelief at first and then got the point. Within a few bars, everyone was joining in, led by Mark Bolland, the most famous rock star in the world, serenading Huck the micro-psycho.

"Well hello, Dolly, well hello Dolly, you're looking swell, Dolly, it's so nice to have you back where you belong…"

Helen took Huck's hand and they sashayed and swayed together in a little impromptu dance. Betty rose unsteadily to her feet and seemed to hold on for dear life to Davy Crockett who quickly found a rhythm of sorts with his new found dancing partner. After a few awkward moments they were swooning around like an old couple on a farewell cruise, without a single care in the world.

Katie Windsor was the only one who looked completely baffled and she turned to Paul and whispered: "Er, is it like this every day at *The Place*, Paul?"

Paul ignored the question, took the famous actress in his arms and gently waltzed Katie around the room. "Some days, Katie, it's even better."

For the first time ever Katie felt something inside, a

feeling of belonging, of camaraderie, looked round the room and smiled. "Really, Paul? Maybe I should stay here a bit longer."

21

Ralph Crossley looked intensely at Simon Hall trying to disguise the raw hate that filled every part of his weary heart.

"Well, what do you think, boss?"

Simon could not contain his pleasure as his finger whipped the images and text across the tablet he was studying. There, laid out in glorious detail, was an expose of the highest order.

"It's ok, old boy, very ok indeed. I'm tempted to give you a bonus – well a day off maybe – just for the main photo. How did you get that one?"

It was Ralph's turn to smile. The photo was good, almost too good to be true. It gave the impression that a group from *The Place* had agreed to participate in the article. There they were all television smiles, staring straight ahead, striking a light-hearted pose in front of Kenwood House, looking so happy, so stupid. It was perfect.

"Judas dressed up as a tourist with his girlfriend. Japanese style, I recall. They knew what was afoot so the girl stood in front of the house with the group behind her. They all saw the picture being taken and couldn't resist the attention."

"Fucking classic. Ralph. The powers that be in New York will be ecstatic with this one."

"I hope they are, Simon. I really do."

***

Helen had reconvened the 'Confrontation Therapy' session in the Encounter Area. This particular session always worked best early in the morning Helen had decided; the participants tended to be half asleep and their egos more manageable than they were later in the day. Helen liked to describe this session as 'deliciously dangerous', for reasons the group would soon discover.

"Well, I do want to thank you all for yesterday, from what I heard – and saw – it was quite a session. Betty, how are you feeling, today?"

Betty, it had to be said, did look different. Perhaps it was the way she had tidied up her hair or the fact that for some reason she no longer felt totally out sorts in a two-piece tracksuit. Her complexion, without a trace of make-up, looked healthy, and her eyes seemed especially clear and bright.

"I'm feeling so good, Helen. I'm so up for whatever this involves, I really am. I slept like a newborn baby. I really did." Betty looked and sounded ready for anything, which was more than could be said for the rest of the group.

"OK," said Helen. "Let me explain how this works. First of all before we start, I want to you to shake each other's hands – hug if you want to. Look into the other persons' eyes. I want genuine contact. No air kisses."

Helen sat back while Davy, Mark, Katie, Betty and Mandy went through the motions of shaking hands, hugging and getting straight into the spirit of what was already beginning to feel like a very warm and friendly session.

Davy Crockett seemed to make a meal of every mini-encounter, going on about '*spreading the lurve*' which Helen knew Davy was likely to regret, very shortly.

The group quickly sat back down on their little chairs and

looked to Helen for guidance.

"There are no props or gimmicks or distractions today. Only us. We're just a group of random people who happen, at this point in time, to be sharing each other's company. No two people ever come here for the same reasons. They may have similar problems, but their reasons for coming here are always different."

Helen stopped abruptly and looked around the intense-looking faces, each one eager to know where Helen was heading.

"Now, I do need to warn each of you that of all the sessions I conduct, this is the one where people get most frightened. I mean scarier than what Gootsy dishes up." Helen had suddenly adopted a very different, almost sinister tone. The group, as one, started to shuffle around feeling a collective sense of impending doom.

"So, this is how it goes. This session is in two parts. This is the first part. I'll get to the second part when I think it's time."

Helen paused to make sure she had everyone's complete attention.

"What we're going to do is to pretend we don't like each other. I want you to say whatever you want to any other member of this group. Be brave. There's no physical contact and you stay in your seats at all times. It's not about being rude, it's about saying what someone doesn't want to hear. Is that understood?"

Helen remained silent, as did the group following the same pattern, as always. Helen waited until the silence edged from slightly uncomfortable to quite embarrassing.

Helen knew how to get this party started. "You see one of the real problems each of you have – and you don't even know it – is that because you're so well-known, each for different reasons of course, you've become used to people saying what you want to hear. This is a special, a sort of protected space, during which you can say things which are not what you want to hear. It takes a lot of courage."

"OK, Helen, I get it. I get it." Davy looked at Katie and took a deep breath. "Katie baby, your last movie was crap. I mean it made no sense, and you looked as if you'd rather be somewhere else. No offence, but from what I read, it was more shit than hit."

Davy sat back looking rather pleased with himself, not noticing that the force of nature that was Katie Windsor had just been whipped into a storm and was now heading towards Davy Crockett.

Katie's persona changed with frightening immediacy. "Don't 'baby' *me* you halfwit. You can't sing, you can't dance. You can't even mime properly. You haven't had a hit in my whole lifetime and quite frankly you'd do well to take out your false teeth, shut that stupid, decrepit badger's arse that you call your mouth, and get on with getting through your bucket list before you keel over and die, if you're not dead already that is."

Helen tried not to smile; as an opening shot, that wasn't bad.

Davy looked stunned but sat back is if to say 'it's only a game' and then crossed his eyebrows in deep thought.

Mark Bolland, however, was having none of it, not from a fresh-faced starlet who probably couldn't even manage to drink a bottle of scotch without losing consciousness.

"Listen, Katie, Katie Windsor. Here's how it is. You're barely out of your nappies. You haven't really lived. You've done a bit of acting and won a piece of plastic to put on your daddy's mantelpiece. You think you're in the drinking game but in my world you wouldn't last five minutes. You're just a kid who's got lucky. Davy over here has been through it, lived it, survived it. Show some respect girl."

Betty knew she would have to jump in sooner rather than later and there was a part of her that was enjoying this immensely.

"Don't try and intimidate Katie just because she's smaller than you, Mark Bolland. Try picking on someone your own size. The thing is about your music – I mean your whole *repertoire* – is that it never was as good or original as *The Who*, or *The Beatles* or *The Rolling Stones*, it was sort of right for the time you know when people were drunk or stoned or both, but when everyone sobered up they realised your music was just you know, sort of average."

Betty leaned back feeling pretty hot but not quite prepared for the next scud missile which was coming her way.

"I don't need protecting by some beached whale who's past her sell by date, I can take care of myself, fatty. I know ten year olds who could do a better job presenting a braindead telly programme better than you. Why don't you stop eating like a pig and go for a jog?"

Davy and Mark made a spontaneous, synchronised 'oooh' sound as if to register that Katie had entered new and dangerous territory. If Katie was acting, it was clear she was a very talented actress.

Betty for a moment looked quite stunned, not by what had just been said but by the mouth it had come out of. Betty also realised that a few days ago she might have disintegrated into a big, blubbering heap if someone like Katie Windsor had said such a thing, no matter what the circumstances. However, all that Betty had been through seemed now to make sense and she felt a great surge of confidence, an inner power, and was up for it.

Betty placed her hands confidently on her knees and straightened up. "Listen girl, by the time I was your age I had been raped twice, had three abortions and seen my mother die of cancer before she was forty. Your problem is that you have only known success; you probably haven't been hungry – really hungry – for one day in your whole life. I guess you're here because you can't even handle a night out on the booze. You know what Katie, knowing what you've got to go through I wouldn't swap my life for yours, not for one minute. Your time in the spotlight will come and go in the blink of an eye and you'll spend the rest of your life wondering how it went so quickly. In ten years time you'll be shuffling around the bargain buckets in Asda, in your pyjamas, wondering whether the life you had was all a dream or not. And you know what Katie, no one will care because by the time you've sobered up everyone you know will have had enough of your crap, your parents will be dead and you won't be able to buy a kid, let alone have one."

Betty's outburst did set the bar a touch higher than was expected and for Katie it seemed a bit too real. She placed her perfect face in her dainty hands and sobbed like a little girl. It was as if Betty had caught Katie's hand grenade and managed to lob it back from whence it came.

No one, apart from Helen who was very astute at such matters, noticed Mandy's fists clenching tighter and tighter until the whites of her knuckles were disarmingly noticeable.

It was a truism to Helen that 'he who blows last, tends to blow loudest' as Mandy was about to demonstrate. At first it seemed as if Mandy was trying to say something but couldn't quite get the words out. But once the dam burst, she was off.

"Listen. All of you listen. We're playing a game. That's OK. I know how to play games; I play games all the time. Mark you're shit and you know you're shit. Betty you're fat and you know it. Davy you're tired brother, real tired. Katie you're lucky that's all and nothing wrong with that. Enjoy it while it lasts. But with me, I'm just so screwed up from start to finish I don't even know who I am half the time. So, I thought I'd save you all the bother of saying things to me I don't want to hear, I'll just talk to myself – whoever that it is. I'm a mess, a total mess inside and out."

Mandy's speech was met with a respectful pause, as if the group wasn't quite sure of the rules any more, as if in a dream and afraid to test out whether the dream was real, or not.

Davy felt sort of stoned but without any drugs involved; it was quite surreal.

"You're screwed up girl because that's where you're at. Is anyone here saying to you, 'hey you're screwed up'? That's the game here, let me give this to you right between your eyes. There ain't nothing wrong with you at all. You're OK. That's about the worst thing I can imagine you hearing. Everybody tells you that you're screwed up. But you ain't. Here's the truth girl, there ain't nothing wrong with you at all. You're a *fake*. Have some of that, honey."

Davy sat back looking quite content with himself and folded his arms as if to say 'I'm done'.

"OK," said Helen, "that's real – I mean real – progress. Honestly, you lot really astonish me. I've had sessions where it can take hours to reach this point; you are a very talented group."

Betty, Davy, Mandy, Katie and Mark looked at Helen as if she was a parent gate-crashing a teenage party and turning the lights on.

Mandy was first to challenge Helen. "I thought the idea was to be – you know – as rude to each other as we could be, to say things we wouldn't usually hear. But you're now being like nice to us. What's the game, Helen, I'm confused. We were just warming up."

"Yes, sorry for that. It is confusing. This game, as I said at the beginning, is in two parts. The first part is over; the second part, which has already started, is for each of you to say nice things to each other. As nice as you can. Then you'll realise how false this nonsense is that you hear day in day out. You're all beautiful, talented, caring people. See, I've already started."

22

Helen, David and JC were in David's office sitting with Betty as they had the first day she had arrived. "Well, Betty, your last day, you look great." Helen felt quite attached to Betty and the affection was obvious.

"You're not just saying that, are you? I mean this isn't a game, like yesterday?"

"Betty, you would know if it was, because I would tell you. It's not a game, well not the same game, if you know what I mean. You've been through quite a lot since you arrived, Betty."

Betty sighed. "That's an understatement, Helen. I mean what with the episode over the ponds – jeez that was a hoot. The sessions with Gootsy – those I'll never forget; what a riot."

"And what was your favourite session?" asked David.

Betty took her time. "Hmm, tough one, David. It's got to be a toss up between the Gootsy laughing session – the one where he freaked out Huck – and the rebirthing, you know my rebirthing. That was something else."

JC was keen to let Betty know that he too had grown since Betty's arrival. "Betty, I guess I owe you an apology. When you first arrived I had in mind that your issue was simply about more exercise and less eating."

Betty interrupted JC before he could go any further. "And so it is, JC."

"Yeah, but I remember you saying when you first arrived that you decided to come here because you'd heard that *The Place* gets inside your head. Was that the expression you used?"

"JC, I remember it well, and yes that's true as well. Time will tell. This time I'm more confident about myself, I feel I understand myself a lot better and I want to shock you all in a few weeks and show you the new Betty – you wait."

Helen looked a little sombre. "Betty, there is something I want to tell you, it takes a bit of courage from my side. But please don't be angry or upset."

Betty looked at Helen and smiled. "Helen, I think I know what you're going to say. I'll make it easy for you. I know what happened in the Metti session. It was a set up. I'll tell you something. It was Mark who told me. It's OK. I understand that you wanted me to feel like a winner at something, and you know what, it did work."

Betty stood up and gave Helen a big hug and they held on to each for what seemed like a long time.

"OK," said Helen, "are you ready, Betty?"

"Sure am, Helen," said Betty knowing from experience that her leaving do would be something special.

As Betty left, David closed the door and spoke in a solemn voice.

"OK, this might be a good time to update you on the *Sunday News* front. We've all read through the material, several times. It's pretty sensational stuff. It's highly damaging, completely libellous and unfortunately absolutely true, very accurate I have to say. I guess what I'm saying is that we're kinda played out. You know when you see the Tsunami coming, you either run or face up to it. I suggest we sit tight and roll with the blows."

"So, as I said all along dad, we're stuffed." JC didn't look too impressed. He had thought that no matter what, his dad would come up with something.

"Well, I think it's a bit of publicity. They had to concede that Helen's qualifications are kosher – I mean I think they were quite disappointed when they realised that Tallinn University was for real. OK, there's the bit about Helen's indiscretions when she was a lot younger and of course my time out at Her Majesty's Pleasure, but I reckon we'll be OK."

JC looked as if he'd just been whacked around the head. "You reckon we'll be OK? I reckon we'll be screwed, shut down, arrested and…"

"Listen, JC," said Helen firmly, "your dad once said to me if a man pulls a gun on you there's no need to show fear. You're either going to die or you're not. Either way, what's the point in showing any fear? In fact, if I remember correctly David, you said such moments are to be relished. Wasn't that what you said – 'relished'?"

"Yep, Helen, that's what I said. Relished. Listen JC, I know it may seem bad right now, but you're simply worried about what *may* happen, that's all. I mean it's what we tell our guests all the time isn't it?" David smiled. "You know the line JC. 'Don't worry, be happy.'"

JC tried to raise a smile. "OK, dad, I get it. I think."

***

"Listen, everyone please." Helen collected the attention of the small group – Betty, Davy, Mandy, Katie, Mark, David and JC who were waiting patiently in the garden of *The Place* knowing that Betty's 'Graduation Ceremony' was imminent.

"Betty has been a star pupil here at *The Place*. She has been through more than most and has stayed the course. I've had confirmed that in the few days – and it has only been a few days you know – Betty has lost over ten pounds in weight."

The small group managed to make quite a racket, whooping and cheering.

"But," continued Helen, "it's not about what Betty has lost, but what she has gained. In that respect Betty has gained so much; it's really incredible. I've seen it with my own eyes. It's about confidence, inner strength, self-restraint... it's about a whole new perspective of herself. You are a very special lady, Betty. Thank you for coming here and sharing with us, it's been a pleasure, it really has. Now before Betty says a few words – if she wants to of course – I've another special person who has come here to present Betty with our leaving present."

Helen turned round to introduce Diane, a very young-looking girl who couldn't have been more than fifteen or sixteen years old.

Betty placed her hands around her mouth and screamed with obvious delight.

"This young lady, Diane, is Betty's daughter. Isn't she beautiful?"

Young Diane blushed and held out a large, carefully wrapped present towards her mum, Betty.

"I'm so proud of you mum, this is for you." Diane sounded as sweet as she looked; there was no doubt about that. Betty stepped up and hugged her daughter as they wiped away each others' tears and laughed, nervously.

"I can't tell you how happy, really happy, I am. It's just so great to have Diane here." Betty and Diane hugged again but

Diane was keen for Betty to reveal her present, which Betty ceremoniously did.

Inside the box was a very small package indeed. Betty unwrapped it carefully to reveal a stunning, designer, glossy black, Lycra bathing suit. Betty read out the note that was attached to it.

"*Size 12 or thereabouts. For the real Betty, when she's ready.*"

Betty looked at the group and belted out an uninhibited laugh.

"When I'm ready? Sure enough, I will be. Helen, that's a wonderful idea and a great present. I will wear it soon. In fact I think I better get on with it, otherwise Huck – I mean Dolly – will be after it. Thank you, thank all of you."

"We're not finished, yet," said Helen as she wrapped around Betty's head a red, white and blue striped ribbon, attached to a glittering, gold-looking medal.

"This medal says, Betty, that you're a winner. I'm awarding it to you because you really are a winner, and always will be. Good luck." Helen stood back and applauded Betty as did the others, a long and genuine applause.

Betty studied the heavy object and turned the medal over to read the words '*Betty: A Winner*', and held back the tears. Betty turned towards her daughter who was staring at the small group trying to figure out why the faces looked sort of familiar as it was only Katie and Mandy who Diane could put a name to.

"Diane, I can't tell you how much it means to me for you to come here. Friends?"

23

"I'm so glad you agreed to let me share with you, Katie. I wasn't sure whether you would agree to, or not. Thanks." Mandy wasn't a great fan of Katie Windsor the actress, but was grateful for the company. Besides, Mandy wasn't that much older than Katie and felt quite safe in her company.

"I'm glad you asked, Mandy. It's good to have company. I'm still a bit – you know – shaky. It's good not to have all that pressure and chill a bit. Well, not that I can see much chilling going on in here. I mean, I thought rehab was supposed to be all about self-analysis and stuff like that. Where does the rebirthing come in?"

"That's nothing Katie. Wait till you get a load of the Gootsy guy." Mandy wasn't sure how much to give away.

"Gootsy? What does he do?" Katie asked innocently.

"What does he *do*? This guy looks like something out of *The Rocky Horror Show*. I swear he's as mad as a hatter."

Katie was feeling a bit confused. "Yeah, OK Mandy, but what does he do? I mean what sort of stuff is he into?" Katie was beginning to worry whether it was just too weird or something for Mandy to be able to describe.

"Gootsy's thing, Katie is… well… I guess it's shock laughter therapy or maybe laughter shock therapy, whatever. But that's nothing compared to the Aaron guy, he's into regression therapy. Don't ask. I shared with Annie Young – you know the singer – OK maybe not, the one the papers call 'Botox Annie', but anyway after one session with Aaron she thinks she's the reincarnation of a Greek Goddess or something."

Katie's eyes lit up. "Regression Therapy, I read a book about that once. I'm really into all of that, actually. Have you done it, Mandy?"

"Have I done it? The creep – I mean the Aaron creep not the Gootsy creep – had me thinking I was Joan of Arc for goodness sake."

"Joan of Arc? Could have been worse, you know like Anne Boleyn or Florence Nightingale or… OK come to think of it Joan of Arc is pretty much up there with the worst of it." Katie looked over at Mandy and asked in a very sincere tone.

"Mandy, tell me, why are you here? I mean I was kinda thrown in here to sober up and get my act together, that's it really. Funny thing is they want me out to promote the new film which is rightly called *Lost Cause* but I'm happy to stay for a bit longer. But anyway, what happened to you? You play a soap opera character, don't you? I mean that's what you do, isn't it?"

Mandy took her time in answering, obviously not sure as to how truthful to be.

"Katie, it's like this. I don't know how much you know or think you know about me. I seem to be in the tabloids too often for all the wrong reasons. I get a bit mixed up with the character I play who's a sort of bad 'un always getting into trouble, fighting, drinking, stealing, lying, scheming, bitching…"

"I get the idea, Mandy…"

"Well, anyway every time I get the script I end up getting into the part so much it sort of takes over my life. I ended up shoplifting – not once Katie but like a habit – and sure enough I got caught and the judge put off the sentencing for reports and suggested I got some treatment which my agent took to mean rehab. I'm on a suspended sentence for the same thing, Katie. I might, you know – actually for real – go to jail."

"You don't seem that bothered, Mandy."

"Well, I don't know if I am. It's like I'm a character in a play and whatever the writer comes up with, that's my lot. I haven't got much choice about it, really. 'Que sera, sera' and all that. The point is that I'm here because my agent and lawyer thought that if I get a sort of 'good report' from here, then I might not go to prison. I'm on my best behaviour. I can't wait to get out, really."

"That's pretty real, Mandy. But you know what, every actor, I mean every really good actor I know goes through the same thing. I mean not to the extremes you go through, but it's a common problem with really good actors and actresses. Mandy, listen to me, what you need to keep sane is to have the right people around you."

Mandy thought for a moment; there was a knock on the door and in walked Helen.

"Hi, Mandy, hi Katie. Look I know it's late but if you're not too tired there's an opportunity to experience a real natural phenomenon over the Heath."

Katie and Mandy looked at each other suspiciously.

"You mean like right now – it must be gone midnight, Helen." Katie really wasn't sure what to say but Helen, as always, looked so serene and professional both Katie and Mandy were willing to rely on Helen's judgment.

"I mean, right now ladies. David will drop off some warm clothes in a minute or two. You're going as a group;

there'll be David, Davy, Mark and you two. I think the time is right for some *Nature Bonding Therapy*."

"Nature Bonding Therapy? What does that involve, Helen? I mean are we going to have Gootsy jump out of the bushes in a Halloween mask waving a chainsaw or something like that?" Mandy clearly needed to know.

"Mandy, funny you should ask." Helen smiled serenely. "Nothing that like, quite the opposite really. I mean the intention is for nothing to happen, just for you to enjoy yourselves. It will be fun, I promise."

***

"Are you sure we're allowed to do this?" JC was surprised that Mark was the one who raised concerns over the small fire around which Mandy, Mark, David, Katie and Davy were huddled in the middle of a small group of young fir trees, deep inside Hampstead Heath. It was a bit cold but each member of the group had been given a warm blanket to wrap around themselves; the light pine-scented breeze was quite refreshing.

"No worries on that score, Mark. I know who to speak with, and they've been er... spoken with, so please relax, we're OK." David leaned backwards and pulled out a few cans of beer from his bag.

"I've been speaking with Helen, about her drinking policy and we've decided that a total ban is not what we're about. It's about learning to drink in moderation, not swinging from one extreme to the other, so a couple of beers are in order, I reckon." David passed the beers around.

"This is cool, brother. I'll just fire up, if that's OK David. Same goes for the smoke, I guess." Davy pulled out one of the harmless joints Helen had been providing for Davy not noticing the smirk on David's half lit face.

"So, is this it, David? Sitting round a camp fire in the middle of the night, what kind of therapy do you call that?" Mark sounded almost disappointed that there wasn't something more exciting in the offing.

David looked at Mark, having anticipated every move that the group was likely to make. Helen was quite clear on that score.

"Well, Mark," said David taking a long slug from the can of beer, "for some reason, out in the open, away from the stresses and strains of every day life, perhaps just breathing in fresh air, people tend to open up a bit more than they would usually do. If it's therapy to have an open and honest chat around a camp fire then yes, this is therapy."

"It's funny you should say that David, it does seem to feel – I don't know – safer in some way." Mandy was enjoying herself; that much was obvious. "You know I've never – I mean never ever – sat round an open fire in the dark before. It feels a bit weird but fun. And I can't believe I'm sitting with Mark Bolland – not that I'm not a great fan of you or Davy or you Katie but you know what I mean." Mandy stopped, abruptly realising that she might dig herself into an even bigger hole than the one she found herself in.

"No worries sugar I feel the same." Davy laughed and passed the joint discreetly to Mark who took a small puff.

"What is this shit? You been drying out horse shit, brother?" Mark was a connoisseur of many things, shit being one of them.

Davy took back the joint and looked at it quizzically and took another puff. "Really? Works for me brother, I'm cool."

The group seemed to lose themselves in the small flames

of the fire and were content to say nothing for some time.

David decided to up the stakes, as gently as he could. "It's a funny thing about *The Place*. You know we're very careful about who we take in – and for how long. We don't pretend we're in the business of curing people. We prefer not to rely on drugs – well, you know what I mean – medication. It never ceases to amaze us what can be achieved through personal encounters of one kind or another."

"Hey, brother," said Davy "there's no need for the sale's pitch; I mean we're here already. Works for me, I'm feeling great."

"And how about you, Mandy? Are you feeling great?" Mandy was staring deep into the fire with unnerving intensity, as if in a trance.

"Sorry, David you were saying? I was so lost in the fire, it's strange. I guess people used to live like this all the time."

"No, sister, the animals lived like this all the time. The human lot were in caves, making more humans. At least the white ones were. I mean they can be seen too easily in the dark, you know what I mean, brother." Davy couldn't help get in a dig, but the group took the comment in the friendly spirit in which it was intended.

Mark seemed to pick up that David had some kind of agenda and wanted to test a theory, just out of curiosity.

"Yeah, it's about honesty, I guess. Mandy, do you have a problem with being honest?" Mark knew he was jumping the gun, but couldn't help himself.

Mandy continued to stare into the fire. "I've not got a problem with being honest, it's just that whenever I've been honest I've ended up in deep shit, that's all."

Katie could sense some fun here. "But why is that, Mandy? If you're not doing anything wrong, then why should telling the truth be an issue? I can't see the problem."

"You want to tell your mother you've shagged her boyfriend? Is that what you mean?" Mandy's response caused Mark to spit out his beer.

Katie was surprisingly quick. "No, Mandy, I mean it's about not shagging your mother's boyfriend in the first place."

Mandy's mini-confession seemed to shock the group into silence, just for a while.

"I'll tell you a secret." Mark took a long glug from his beer and braced himself. He wasn't going to be outdone by Mandy, not with a little shocker like screwing her mother's boyfriend. Mark was way further up the scales, in fact Mark was in a different league all round.

"OK, here it is. I've had my way with… royalty. In a private loo in Buckingham Palace. Beat that." Mark sat back as if he just laid down four aces.

"No shitting, Mark," Davy was impressed.

Katie and Mandy were just curious. "OK, then," said Katie. "It would of course be totally wrong for you to let slip a name. But maybe if we just speculated and if during our speculation you might, I don't know, cough or something, we could draw our own conclusions." Katie looked intensely at Mark to see if he was willing to play.

"Hey, Katie *Windsor*, I might cough, sneeze or whatever, but I ain't telling," Mark smiled and the group as one realised it was game on.

Davy was first. "Princess Anne?"

Mandy jumped in. "Fergie, bet it was Fergie. No, OK, Princess Margaret."

"Which Princess Margaret?" Katie laughed out loud but no one seemed to get her joke. "This is fun, it's like I shagged with my little eye." This time Katie was rewarded with a little group titter.

Davy, Katie and Mandy mumbled away collectively as if racking their brains for an obvious name. Out of the blue Davy burst into hysterical laughter, rolling in contortions on the ground and just managed to splutter out: "Say it ain't' so, Joe, say it ain't so."

Katie and Mandy looked at each other. This was above their heads, whatever it was, because there was an evil-looking smile broadening across Mark's face and Davy's hysterics continued.

"I got you, brother, I got you. Listen ladies, you don't get it. The man here said he'd screwed royalty. The man didn't say whether the vibe was like AC or DC." That was all Davy could come out with before the contortions of laughter took over again.

Mandy held her hand over her mouth. "You mean…"

"Yeah, baby I mean Mr Mark ended up having some batty boy, some royal batty." And with that line Davy was reduced to further uncontrollable contortions which even David found infectious.

"Really, Mark. Is that right?" Katie was hooked.

Mark tried to look serious. "OK, game's over. Look, I'll tell you something. I'm with Mandy on this one. I mean yeah for sure if you do the right thing then OK the truth is going to be your friend and ally. But you know not everyone has the same idea as to what's wrong and what's right. Sometimes – not all the time – Mandy's right and the truth can land you in some deep shit. It's like coming through customs and being asked: 'Anything to Declare?'"

David picked up that Mark had taken this as far as he felt comfortable and decided to shift the spotlight on to Katie.

"OK, Mark er, thanks for sharing that with us. I'm OK with leaving the rest of the story to my imagination, well maybe not. Anyway, Katie. Do you think Mark and Mandy are right when they say that sometimes the truth can get you into trouble, I mean what do you think?"

Katie suddenly looked very serious, sad almost. "I'll tell you what I think, honestly. I feel like a fraud in this company. I like you Mandy I do, but I can't get my head around having sex with your mother's boyfriend. I mean apart from the fact that it's simply weird, what a thing to do to your mother. Mark, good for you, if anyone should get away with sticking it up royalty, I reckon that should be you. As a life metaphor, that's up there Mark. Davy, get stoned and drunk if you want to, it's got nothing to do with me."

Katie paused as if steeling herself for the big confession. "Listen, guys, I'm no use at this sort of stuff. I get drunk – out of it drunk – on two beers and one shot of vodka. Here's my truth – I hate drinking. It makes me feel sick, I look twenty years older the next day, my head aches, my mouth smells vile, my hair is sticky for god's sake, I can't do anything, I just want a power shower and to make myself look attractive. Am I the only one here who thinks that's cool? My problem is that I am and always have been naturally straight. I like to jog at dawn, go to bed feeling physically tired but good and wake up feeling great. I like reading books, preferably in a hot bath surrounded by scented candles. I'd rather go and watch a fringe play than get drunk. It's other people that's my problem, I'm OK actually. Tell me why I'm the odd one out here? The idea of inhaling whatever you're inhaling Davy turns my stomach. It really does smell like shit. And I'm not going to have sex until I fall in love. I just think you're all stupid really. There, I've said it.

Sorry, but there's my truth and I guess I'm now the one in deep shit. Oh god what I've just said? I'm sorry."

Katie placed her head in her hand and sobbed quietly.

No one noticed David smile with relief. It was as if Helen had not only foreseen the direction this session was going to take but was in control of the weather. On cue there was a clap of thunder and rain, monsoon-like, that appeared out of nowhere.

"Someone's decided to piss on our parade, time to head back to the ranch." David didn't need to encourage the group to up themselves and make a quick dash back through the Heath in the darkness aided only by the light from David's mobile phone which made a pretty good impression of a torch, when needed.

24

David tried not to wake Helen as he crept into their little bedroom in the annex to *The Place*, but he was never going to be successful on that score as Helen was already awake.

"Pity about that. I heard the rain and thought of you lot and then tried to get back to sleep. It must be very late, David. Was it a good one?"

David wasn't entirely sure. "I guess so. It was like you said it would be. But you know it wasn't Mandy who burst open but Katie. I think she's ready to head back to the real world."

Helen sat up not willing to let such a comment go unanswered. "You mean to her real world. This is our real world, remember?"

"Yeah, yeah. You know what I mean."

"And oh yes. We've two newcomers coming later today. We'll screen them this afternoon. There's a lot at stake with both of them."

"How's that?"

"You heard of Charlie McQueen?"

"Jeez, big fish, better keep this one quiet. How many Oscars has he won? Charlie's an absolute legend, I'm impressed."

"Not so fast, it's not Charlie McQueen who's on his way here right now but Charlie's daughter, Sarah-Jane."

"Sarah-Jane McQueen? Better do some crash research on this one, it doesn't ring any bells at all, Helen."

"That's the whole point. Sarah-Jane, from what I've been told has been forged in the classic mould of invisible off-spring of famous parents. High aspirations, low on talent. Her mother, Charlie's second wife, committed suicide a long time ago when Sarah-Jane was very young. Charlie quickly remarried and there was absolute venom between Sarah-Jane and the step-mother from day one. If you wanted to produce a screwed up kid, I guess this is how you would do it. Sarah-Jane's had some sort of meltdown – I mean like meltdown number whatever – and Charlie wants to keep her out of the LA scene, completely. Seems we've been recommended, highly recommended."

"And, Helen. I feel there's an 'and' coming on."

"You're right there. And we've a fallout from that new reality television programme *Britain's Got Issues.*"

"What's that about?" David asked innocently. "I don't watch television much, as you know."

"Britain's Got Issues is sort of like a combination of *Embarrassing Bodies* and *The Hunger Games.* You don't get it, do you? OK, each contestant stays in a house and the public get to know their issues in detail and then they vote to keep in their favourite until it's last man standing. It's quite simple. In BGI each *contestant* has an issue; a physical or mental issue and the winner gets to have the best treatment in the world to sort the 'issue' out. There's someone with hair problems, we've got the boob job that's gone wrong, there's a really weird but talented OCD guy in there, a young girl who thinks she's got deformed flabia – she'll make the final, that's for sure. And then there's our very own Sean Beanie who's about to become a guest at *The Place,* paid for by the way by an anonymous sponsor. It's a great game."

David waited for the punch line but Helen was having fun.

"Yeah, Helen – but what is Sean Beanie's *issue?*"

"Sean Beanie is the most handsome young man you've ever seen. He's also a very talented singer, dancer, actor, you know – *entertainer.* But here it is – he's chronically shy and gets crushing stage fright every time he has to perform." Helen smiled. "Not only that, the other housemates have sort of ganged up on Sean and he's had a bit of nervous meltdown. The producers want him to spend a few days at *The Place* not because they've any expectation we'll sort him out – that's for the next series – we're just supposed to get him back on his feet, you know, back in the ring. We've three days otherwise he's out of the competition. Might be a full breakdown but I guess Sean's just exhausted and needs some TLC."

David sighed. "How young is Sean?"

"Seventeen. I know, we'll need to talk to our insurers about this one. But, he does need *The Place*, David, he really needs it, well, according to the producers of *BGI*. To them, *The Place* is like some sort of mental health farm, a place of peace and tranquillity, a sort of urban paradise."

"Funny that… I mean if you work in paradise, where do you go on holiday?"

"I think you need what we tell all our guests they need."

"That'll be a few beers, a long holiday and Gootsy up my arse, Helen?"

"No, David. That'll be no beers at all and a good night's sleep. You're tired. Get some rest and I'll wake you later, a lot later."

"You're right, thanks. You seem always to take other people's problems on board without it having any impact on you Helen. Sometimes their pain sort of spills onto me, you know what I mean?"

Helen looked closely into David's tired eyes. "You know it took you a long time to feel empathy. I guess that only began when you became a father. It's good that you share the pain. Maybe I'm just a tough old bird underneath it all."

"You may be a tough old bird but you've got a heart of gold. 'Night, Helen, I'm pooped."

Helen tucked David into bed like a nurse with a patient. "Night, David, I'll join you in a minute."

"By the way. If I told you Mark Bolland had sex with a male member of the House of Windsor, in a private toilet in Buckingham Palace, who do you think it would be?"

Helen stopped brushing her hair, stared into the dressing table mirror and paused, momentarily. "Hmmm, tough one. Get some sleep. You'll need all the sleep you can get. Isn't the *Sunday News* running with the story this weekend?"

David lifted his tired head. "Oh yes, I had almost forgotten about that little challenge. Que sera, sera, as Doris Day would say."

***

"My Katie, you're up bright and early."

"Well, Helen I just thought I'd take my chances and see if you were around. Here you are. This is David's office isn't it?"

"Sure is. Sit down, Katie, what's the matter?"

"I'm ready to leave, Helen. Listen there's nothing wrong. I should have left by now, really. It's nothing to do with the texts I've been getting and I know you've been getting from Steve; it's just that I'm ready. I've had a great time. I don't want a leaving party thing – you know the whole Graduation Ceremony number, well, not right now. I do want that Helen – I do – but not now, not today. Sometime later. I'm sure you understand, Helen. I've already said goodbye to Mandy."

Helen had seen this coming and in her own way was relieved to hear the words from Katie, who was ready to leave, that much was obvious. Helen had seen it so many times before.

"Katie, Katie Windsor. Let me tell you Katie that you are a truly talented actress. I admire you, I really do. Don't get sidetracked by other people, Katie. Show them how strong you are."

Katie gave Helen a hug and held on to her for some time. "I know I am, Helen, thank you. Sometimes I just need someone to remind me."

***

"OK, David, JC, are we up for this?" Helen made it sound as if the unholy Trinity was about to set sail round the world or charge into battle. "We've back to back screenings with two very live wires. We need to be 'specially careful with Sean Beanie on account of his age. Sarah-Jane McQueen is going to be a real handful, so let's be very alert."

David's mobile buzzed and soon enough a sheepish knock was heard on the door of David's office.

JC was quite taken aback at to how young Sean Beanie looked, or perhaps JC was a bit too used to being the youngest person in the room.

Helen immediately went over to embrace the talented singer and dancer who by all accounts had cracked up with the pressure of impending new found fame and had a serious meltdown.

"Sean, please sit down, let us introduce ourselves." Helen could see that Sean had no pretentions or airs or graces; in fact he had the appearance of a school boy who had been invited into the teachers' room.

As the four of them settled in to their well established places it was obvious Sean was having trouble even keeping his hands steady.

"Now, Sean. The first thing is that we're on your side; we're not here to cure you of anything or to change you. You understand that?"

Sean looked at the floor and spoke softly. "Yes, doctor, I understand."

"Sean, Sean look at me. Call me Helen, please. This is not a hospital. Some people call us a rehab place but that's just a modern sort of reference for a place where you can feel free to learn about yourself, grow more confident, maybe just understand yourself a bit better. Does that make sense?"

Sean tried hard to look Helen in the eyes but could only manage a brief fleeting glance before his eyes rested on the floor. "I think so, Helen."

Helen and David looked towards JC for the next move.

"Hi, Sean. I've seen a couple of clips of you on YouTube. You're quite a talent, Sean. Better than *Glee*." JC had been doing some research on this kid.

Sean smiled. "You're into *Glee*? Cool."

"I'm their biggest fan, Sean. They sing, they dance, they act – it's something else. I get it, Sean, I love it." JC was beginning to convince himself.

JC leaned towards Sean and tried hard to make eye contact. "Sean, I've heard from the management what happened. Please believe me – we've seen this before, it's OK. The reason why you've been asked to come here is because we don't pile you full of drugs of any kind, that's the last thing we'd do. What happens here – and I know it's going to sound a bit weird – is that we encourage you to experience life, other people, 'encounters' as we call it. But look, I guess we just wanted to say 'hi' and introduce ourselves. I'm going to show you around *The Place*, introduce you to the other guests, show you your room, just settle you in and then we'll be meeting up for a session later." JC looked at David and Helen who nodded in approval.

"Session? What do you mean?" Sean sounded very apprehensive.

"I'll explain as we're walking around. In fact, Sean our first 'session' is going to be a long walk around Hampstead Heath. There are so many celebs strolling around this time in the morning no one will bat an eye, I promise." JC placed his arm around Sean's small shoulders as they left David's office.

"He's coming along mighty fine, don't you think Helen?" David was obviously very proud of his son.

"He sure is, David. He's a natural. The idea of a long walk around the Heath was inspired. OK, next up is Sarah-Jane, looks like we'll do her screening on our own, David."

"Now, David, while we're waiting for Sarah-Jane, let's have a little chat about Mandy. She's nearly ready to leave, don't you think?"

***

Despite the number of times David had been through the experience, every time his mobile buzzed indicating the arrival of a new guest, his heart seemed to miss a beat with excitement. Perhaps it was because so much could go wrong. Or perhaps it was just the nervous excitement of it all.

This time there was no knock on the door; Sarah-Jane McQueen just breezed in. The contrast with Sean's entrance was quite marked.

"Hi, you all. God this place is so cool. I've heard all about it, I can't wait." Sarah-Jane McQueen was not quite what David and Helen were expecting. Sarah-Jane was, according to her dad, twenty-nine, but she looked older, not that much older but you wouldn't guess the attractive young lady was in her twenties.

"Sit down Sarah-Jane on the sofa. Do you want anything? I'm Helen by the way and this is David. You'll have heard of us, I guess."

"I'm OK, thanks. I've heard all about you, and David. Where's JC? I can't wait to meet JC." Sarah-Jane was disarmingly bright and breezy; there was a confidence about her which Helen knew was superficial. Sarah-Jane epitomised a phrase Helen had once heard which described Americans as 'deeply shallow', an impression reinforced by Sarah-Jane's 1950's style of dress'

Helen knew it was an unfair judgment to make, but it was Helen's first impression and Helen was pretty good with first impressions.

"Tell me Sarah-Jane, I'm just curious, but what is your expectation of *The Place*? I mean what are you hoping to get out of this experience?"

Sarah-Jane looked all primed up and ready to roll, as if she couldn't wait.

"Well, I've been to a few rehab places in LA and to tell you the truth they're all much the same. My theory is that the weather's to blame. Always the same, always perfect. It's as if nothing changes. This is the first time I've been outside the States, you know. I've been doing some research on this place, I mean England, and you seem to get like all four seasons in one day. That's what everyone tells me."

As if to emphasise Sarah-Jane's point there was a loud crack of thunder.

"Wow, thunder – and lightning – in the middle of spring. That means it'll be sunny and warm later. I love this place already. Do you get rainbows over here?" Sarah-Jane was already beside herself with excitement.

Helen had already made her mind up about Sarah-Jane McQueen. "You know you're absolutely right Sarah-Jane, that's very observant of you. *The Place* is like just like weather – you know – as you say, you can have all four seasons in just one day. We do get rainbows, Sarah-Jane, but not every day, only when it's sunny and rainy at the same time."

Helen looked over at David, discreetly. "I'll show you around Sarah-Jane. I'll talk you through your schedule a bit later. You can either have a room of your own or share with one of our other guests – if that's what they want. Any preferences?"

Sarah-Jane looked up and had a think as if she was being asked to choose between two different coloured pairs of shoes. To Helen and David it looked as if she wanted to have both, but couldn't.

"That's tricky, Helen. I'll tell you what. How about I spend tonight on my own, get to know the other guests and then see how we all feel tomorrow."

"That's a very wise approach, Sarah-Jane. I'm

impressed. Now we need to go through some boring paperwork and then I can settle you in. We've a session later which I know you'll enjoy."

Sarah-Jane clapped her hands together like an excited cheerleader. "Oh, I can't wait, sounds perfect, Helen."

25

"OK, Gootsy, we need to talk through what you have in mind for this evening." David, at JC's request, had insisted that Gootsy shared some detail about his next session.

"You know, Gootsy, that we've great admiration for your work, it's always different and often quite spectacular."

"But," said Gootsy, defensively.

David continued. "But, this time we're not sure whether it's going to be too heavy for all our guests, in particular Sean Beanie. Sean's a seventeen year old, and a very fragile one at that, which is why he's here."

David was being a bit too diplomatic for JC. "Gootsy, dad is absolutely right about this. I'm a great admirer of your work but sometimes I wonder if we – well you – might try and think more of what the guests might specifically benefit from, rather than – you know – put them through a session because it works for you. Don't take what I'm saying as a criticism Gootsy, please."

Gootsy sat back on the sofa looking a bit concerned. "And you, Helen? What do you think?"

Helen took her time as if to emphasise the delicacy of the situation. "The real point Gootsy is that what you do is very effective, but there's a risk it might be too effective. There was that time with Mandy when I thought she had retreated into what some might call a catatonic stupor. Mandy had the strength to pull herself out of that one –

with some skilful intervention from Metti I should add – but it was close and in some ways we were lucky. I don't think Sean would cope with that type of extreme encounter. Sean needs to have his confidence built up, in stages."

Gootsy stroked his chin, deep in thought.

"Let me think about this boy Sean. JC you're very wise, for your age. Yes, I see the problem. I have always said that my work involves complete trust. That trust needs to be put to the test, I think."

David, JC and Helen looked at each other not entirely convinced but the air had been cleared and it was obvious that a decision had to be made. David was tempted to suggest that the easy solution was simply for Sean not to take part in any Gootsy session but he felt that option was simply a cop out.

"OK, Gootsy. We trust you. Perhaps JC can talk to you a bit more about Sean's background and give you some further insight into what his problems are. Is that OK?"

"Sure, Helen, that's OK." Gootsy smiled. "I will talk with JC about the boy. Perhaps it's best if JC joins in the encounter?"

***

"Good evening, good evening, good evening one and all." Gootsy seemed particularly excited as he addressed young Sean, Sarah-Jane, Davy, Mandy, Mark and JC. The Encounter Area seemed unusually bare, devoid of any props apart from an exercise mat in the centre of the room, a couple of benches against one of the walls, and a small holdall at Gootsy's feet.

"I'm thrilled to have you all here and we should make a

special welcome to JC who will also be participating today. Now, JC, does everyone know each other or are some introductions in order?"

JC looked slightly embarrassed as he didn't really know the answer to that one, and decided to play safe. "Perhaps everyone should say hello to each other and introduce themselves anyway Gootsy."

"Yes, yes, quite, thank you," said Gootsy as each guest awkwardly shook hands, embraced and said hello. Even Davy and Mark went through an exaggerated exchange as if they'd never met, just for the fun of it.

JC was keeping a close eye on Sean who showed no sign of recognising any of the other guests, not even Mandy, which was of some comfort to JC.

"Now," said Gootsy with a gleam in his eye. "Today is a special day. A very special day. There are two benches over there, please bring them to the centre of the room and place them on either side of the mat."

Gootsy watched closely as Davy and Mark immediately paired up and took one end each of a bench whilst JC and Sean brought over the other.

"Very good, thank you." Gootsy slightly rearranged the benches so they were exactly in the centre of the room and parallel to each other. The group watched transfixed as Gootsy placed the benches at what seemed a very precise distance apart until eventually he was clearly satisfied that the positioning was exactly right.

Gootsy reached into his holdall and took out the remote control, pushed a couple of buttons and the room darkened causing Mandy to mutter a touch too loudly, "oh shit, here we go again."

"Oh, no Mandy. Not 'here we go again'. I never 'go

again'; it would not be possible to do the same thing twice."
Gootsy sounded a bit put out, as if someone had criticised
his art.

"Now, let's sit down. But before we do so, I need a volunteer." Gootsy looked at Mark who felt complimented at
the signal.

"OK, Mr Gootsy. Mark Bolland at your service, sir. How
can I be of assistance?"

"You are a star, Mr Bolland, thank you." Gootsy smiled
as if they were old friends. "All I want you to do is lie down
and die. Right there on the mat. Please just lie down as if you
are dead, no more, gone. You have the easy part to play. You
are the dead man."

Mark Bolland looked slightly taken aback but shrugged
his shoulders, lay down on the mat, as still as he could make
himself, and closed his eyes not noticing the lights dimming
again.

The group silently took their seats on the bench, Gootsy,
Sean and Sarah-Jane on one side of the mat on which Mark
was laid out and Davy, JC and Mandy on the other.

Gootsy reached into his holdall and produced seven red
roses, like a conjurer pulling a rabbit out of his theatrical hat,
and handed each member of the group one rose, keeping
one for himself.

Without further explanation, Gootsy sounded off like a
sodden old vicar winging it front of six or seven people
who, to get out of the rain, had wandered into a service for
a person with no friends or known history: "We are gathered
here today to celebrate the life of Mark Bolland, sadly no
longer with us. Let us pray in silence, in our own thoughts
and remember the life – *the force of nature* – that was Mark
Bolland." Gootsy held out his hands as if in prayer, holding

his rose between his thumbs.

The group quickly got the idea and each one copied Gootsy.

Gootsy opened his eyes and stared down at Mark who was doing fine and, judging by the broad smile on his face, was enjoying himself. Gootsy spoke in a whisper, as if in a church speaking quietly on his own to a corpse. "I didn't know you very well Mark Bolland. I heard about your music which I didn't like much. Too loud and 'bang-y' for my sensitive little ears. Nothing personal old boy, just not my scene."

Mark's smile disappeared from his otherwise still body. Gootsy continued. "In fact, I preferred the other lot. Can't remember their name now but you would know who I mean. You had a great talent but you could have done better. Yes, I'll give you a seven out of ten for the contribution you made to this world."

Gootsy then placed the rose onto Mark's chest and sat back and looked to his left where Sean was sitting and looked at Sean's rose as if to signal to Sean to say or do something.

"Er... I thought your music was great. Can't believe you're dead. Bye." It was all Sean could manage but it was enough for him to feel his bit was over as he clumsily placed the rose onto Mark's body.

Gootsy looked at Sean as if there was something more to be said.

"Oh yes, I'll give you nine out of ten, thanks." Sean smiled knowing he was now finished.

Sarah-Jane needed no encouragement; whether it was her turn or not, she was ready to play.

"Mark Bolland. The real Mark Bolland. Wow. I met you

two minutes ago and now you're gone. What a bummer. Had you been alive long enough I would have told you that my dad thought you were the best."

Mark's smile returned to his otherwise still body. Sarah-Jane continued as if she had played this game before. "Personally, I think you suck." Sarah-Jane placed her rose on Mark's groin and Mark's smile disappeared again. Sarah-Jane hadn't quite finished. "I'll give you six out of ten."

JC decided it was his turn. "You were a great man, who made a great contribution. You inspired a whole generation. Your music will live forever. You're a ten out of ten in my book." JC carefully positioned his rose on Mark's chest, careful not to disturb the other roses.

Mandy made a heavy sigh. "Oh, Mark. Can't believe you're gone. What a shame. I liked your music, er sometimes. You deserve at least eight out of ten. Goodbye, Mark."

There was a long pause before Davy spoke. The lights were a little too dimmed for the tears in his eyes to be noticed, but the quiver in his voice betrayed his emotion.

"Oh, man. This is a sad, sad day, brother. You were one of the all time greats, no doubt about it." Davy placed his rose on Mark's body with some care. "Just wish you'd told me more about the royal batty boy. But nine out ten I guess is fair." Davy paused to wipe a tear from his eye. "Hey man I would have given you ten if you'd let us be your supporting act all those years ago. I didn't want to dig that one up brother but now you're all kind of like *dead*, I couldn't help myself. But you know, cool runnings brother."

Gootsy let a silence grow before addressing the group as a whole. "OK, let's take a vote. All those in favour of the resurrection of Mark, please raise your hands."

In turn each guest looked at the others, smiled and raised

their hands. Gootsy surveyed the group approvingly, pressed a button on his remote and the lights brightened. Gootsy then spoke in a loud theatrical voice. "Arise, Mark Bolland, the group has spoken, you live."

Mark however did not move. The group leaned over, a growing sense of concern quickly developed. Sean was the first to make a very close inspection, placing his ear near Mark's face and bursting out in laughter. "He's fast asleep. Would you believe it? Couldn't stay awake for his own funeral service."

Gootsy pressed another button and out of the speakers came the distinctive sound of one of Mark's most famous songs, causing Mark to awake with a start.

"What the hell? What?" Mark looked around the amused faces and rubbed his face as if to wake up a bit quicker.

"Oh, shit. I'm still alive."

Suddenly the music changed to the tune of a song which everyone recognised from the Monty Python film *Life of Brian.*

"OK," Gootsy shouted. "All together now: '*Always look on the bright side of life, always look on the bright side of life*'…"

***

"OK, Mandy. How do you feel?" David had decided in his own mind that Mandy was ready to leave but he wasn't sure if Mandy agreed.

"You mean, am I ready to leave? That's what you're really asking me, isn't it, David?"

Helen smiled knowing where this was going. "Well, do you, you know, feel ready to leave, Mandy?" Helen had her own views and didn't want to be seen to be influencing Mandy's decision.

Mandy looked and sounded worried. "OK, I've learnt something while I've been here and that's the reward for being honest. So, being honest I'm not really sure what all of this means to me right now. I guess over time I will. I'm here because the court wanted an assessment of me before I go back to be sentenced. A negative report will probably send me to Holloway. So, the honest answer is I'm ready to leave if you think I've made progress. I mean the type of progress which would sway a judge. That's my honest answer."

Helen looked at Mandy with her headmistress stare. "Mandy when you first came here I wasn't sure. You've got a truckload of problems to deal with. We can only help you up to a point, but there comes a stage when you're on your own. My feeling is that you're on the right road. It will take courage, but I think I've seen enough to know that you've, let's say, got the point. I hope that answers your question; if not I'll spell it out. If the judge decides to send you to prison it won't be because of our report. You've got a lot to offer, but you've also got to accept that *your* life is in *your* hands, not in the hands of a committee of scriptwriters putting your character through the mill for the sake of viewer ratings."

"Helen," said Mandy thoughtfully. "I'm ahead of you on that one."

"How do you mean?" asked David sounding quite intrigued.

"Well," said Mandy. "I worked out I've got a choice. God that sounds pathetic. It's like this. I was kind of expecting some form of personal analysis here and then at some point as if by magic I'd find out why I have this urge to play out my character. But I can see it's not like that. I'm not mad; I'm just shit-scared of what life might dump on me. What I'm going to do is write and produce my own scripts, and boy am I going to give myself something to look forward to. You know, like *Shirley Valentine*."

Mandy looked at Helen and smiled as if sharing a private joke. "That's a wonderful idea – very clever. Let's have a celebration later, Mandy, after your court appearance, and we can celebrate your freedom, and your new life."

Mandy stood up and hugged in turn David and then Helen.

"Promise, Helen?" For the first time Helen saw tears in Mandy's eyes that were not of outrage or fear or self-pity but of hope and joy.

"I promise, Mandy."

26

Helen, David and JC had asked for another chat with Gootsy in David's office but the few minutes they had on their own soon focussed on the impending expose by the *Sunday News*, now only three days away.

"I suppose they've already gone to print on the story, dad. I mean it's Friday so they print today don't they?"

"I guess so, JC."

"Why aren't you bricking yourself dad? I've tried that 'be happy stuff' and it works for about three seconds then I'm shitting myself. Is there something you know that I don't or what?"

David looked at his son with a sort of bored, nonchalant look. "It's not that I know something you don't JC. It's that I don't feel something you do. Maybe it's just an age thing, son. Talking about age, that must be Gootsy. I'd recognise that shuffle in my sleep."

Gootsy made a solemn entrance and sat down where he knew he was supposed to sit.

"So, how did you know the funny bit would be when Mark fell asleep, Gootsy?" David sounded a tad concerned, but Gootsy was feeling – and looking – very comfortable, smugly confident and deeply secure.

"I didn't; it was always going to end in laughter, the way it ended was just one way out of countless ways, but it went well, don't you think, David?"

Helen decided to intervene. "Look, Gootsy from what I heard it was a great session. What I want to know is can you go to another level without freaking anyone out completely?"

"How do you mean, Helen, 'another level'?" Gootsy gave a great impression of looking dumb, if need be.

JC was equally inquisitive. "Yes, Helen, how do you mean 'another level'?" he asked, deliberately echoing Gootsy.

Helen smiled. "OK, let me put my cards on the table. I've read through Sarah-Jane's file and I've also had an opportunity to make my own judgment. I've also just received a long email from her dad. I'd say Sarah-Jane is the biggest challenge we've ever had here at *The Place*. She's been in and out of institutions of one kind or another since she was quite young; in fact from the day of her mother's suicide Sarah-Jane was a 'case' and that was when she was seven years old. I doubt if there's been one day in her life since then that she hasn't been on one type of medication or another in therapy of some kind. Sarah-Jane has had every treatment listed in most psychiatric textbooks of the western world. She's a living memorial to that psychiatric textbook 'DSM', I mean every edition. That's why the dad emailed me, to make sure she's taking her meds. This is the list that the dad thinks she's on: levothyroxine, olanzapine, priadel, propranolo and simvastatin."

David looked concerned and sighed. "That's quite a cocktail. Do you think we're maybe out of our depth with this one Helen? I mean maybe Sarah-Jane needs a 'slug 'em, drug 'em, easy does 'em' psychiatrist of the old school. We know plenty of them. I mean if she flips out can we really deal with her without phoning for an ambulance? Do we need that?"

JC had his own view. "Maybe the dad knows the whole lifestyle hasn't really helped. Maybe the dad's ahead of us and wants Sarah-Jane to experience something a bit more real, outside her usual med-filled life. Isn't that why she's here? I mean when I looked into her eyes there's life there – just about – but in the midst of thick fog."

Gootsy stroked his chin. "Yes, JC I saw it too. Listen, I have an idea."

"Really, Gootsy? Let's hear it." said David.

"There is something missing from this lady's life. I can see a sort of 'absence', in a way. Yes, I know what might help. I think we need some divine intervention, as Helen suggests – another level."

JC wasn't going to be convinced that easily. "Er, not sure what you mean, Gootsy. 'Divine intervention' sounds scary. You gonna conjure up some religious figure or something? I mean I don't mind a bit of hamming it up every now and then just for laughs but taking a religious turn is something else."

"No, not religious, just… spiritual. Maybe Sarah-Jane has a friend, an angel…" Gootsy looked deep in thought.

Helen looked surprisingly pleased, as if Gootsy had got her point about 'another level.' "You got it, Gootsy, some quality 'Angel Therapy', that'll do for starters; it will be a long haul this one. I prefer 'divine inspiration' to 'divine intervention', but I'm sure Gootsy won't disappoint us."

Gootsy smiled. "And you Helen, David, or maybe you JC, would you like to attend?"

"I'll pass on that one," said JC, quickly. "I'll think I'll go for a jog over the Heath. Thanks, anyway, Gootsy."

"I'll think I'll join you, son, if that's OK with you." David looked relieved for a quick get out from 'Angel Therapy', the very thought of which made him shiver.

"Sounds great, dad, you're on," said JC immediately thinking of how fast he might set the pace.

"And what about you, Helen, would you like to attend?" asked Gootsy.

"I'll think about it, Gootsy. I'm a positive maybe." There are times to hedge your bets, thought Helen, and this was one of them. "In the meantime I think we'll need to pull out all the stops with Sarah-Jane, I'll start with a one-to-one session. We need to also keep a close eye on Sean. JC, why don't you take Sean out for a jog before you and your dad wear each other out, and I'll take Sarah-Jane through a Kaleidoscope Review. David maybe you can check up on Mark and Davy? How does that sound? OK, let's get to work."

***

"Thanks for seeing me Sarah-Jane. How are you finding Highgate?"

Sarah-Jane seemed somewhat distracted, as if her mind was elsewhere. Helen waited a few moments and tried again.

"It must be quite a culture shock in comparison to LA. How was the session with Gootsy?"

Sarah-Jane again failed to respond. Helen looked deep into Sarah-Jane's eyes, trying to detect signs of life.

Sarah-Jane's eyes suddenly lit up, as if a loose connection in her brain had miraculously been fixed. "It's great here, really, Helen. That Gootsy guy is something else. Bit mad, but then again…" Sarah-Jane trailed off realising that she was on dodgy ground.

"Well, you'll be seeing more of Gootsy later. In the

meantime can we try something which I've found can be very useful, in certain circumstances." Helen said.

"In 'certain circumstances', Helen. How do you mean?"

Sarah Jane was clearly a little worried about what Helen had in store, especially as she was beginning to understand that there was a certain unpredictability about *The Place*.'

Helen placed on the table the same type of device she had used with Richard Beckett, one of several she had bought some time back knowing instinctively that it would be a useful tool to bring focus to a person's life.

Helen knew well the sequence in which to push the little buttons, and as she did so she asked Sarah-Jane a loaded question in a quiet voice.

"Now Sarah-Jane, I should know this but I'd like to hear from you. What age will you be on your next birthday?"

Sarah-Jane looked at Helen as if she was being asked a trick question.

"Er, twenty-nine, I think, Helen." Sarah-Jane sounded far from convincing.

"OK, Sarah-Jane, I think we can do better than that, don't you?" Helen had anticipated that starting this session was going to be a challenge. "You must remember what year you were born?"

Sarah-Jane looked genuinely confused. "Er, I know it sounds a bit odd, but never been sure of that one, Helen."

Helen gave Sarah-Jane a stern but friendly look. "OK, Sarah-Jane how about we take the date from your passport. When you arrived we put some of your things in a security box. I had a look at the date on your passport. Hope you don't mind. As I recall you'll be thirty-three on your next birthday. Does that sound right?"

Sarah-Jane placed a hand on her mouth in mild shock.

"I'm thirty-two years old? Really?"

Helen, despite her years of experience, wasn't totally sure whether Sarah-Jane was sincere or simply lying. It didn't matter, they could start now.

"OK, Sarah-Jane. Look at this little clock thing. It's quite cute isn't it? I'm going to set a number – you see the number thirty-two? That number you see on the screen represents your thirty-second birthday – your last birthday. When I press a button that number will start to count down, you know from thirty-two down to zero." Helen paused to make sure that Sarah-Jane was following.

"That's neat, Helen. And what do I do?"

"What you do, Sarah-Jane, is think of your birthdays. You know, maybe where you were, who you were with, any special presents or fun moments, anything really that you remember about a particular birthday. We can start at thirty-two and work backwards or maybe there's one particular special birthday you'd like to start with?"

"Sounds like a good game Helen. But I'm not sure that I can remember any of my birthdays. Not one. Not right now anyway. Can we play this game later? I'm feeling kind of tired."

Helen felt quite taken aback that she could have mis-judged a guest so badly. Sarah-Jane was nowhere near ready for this one and Helen accepted immediately that this would take time.

"Sure, Sarah-Jane. I'll tell you what. I'm going to give you a piece of paper, a blank piece of paper. When you've got a quiet moment could you write down any birthday you remember or even a birthday you'd like to remember – and we can sort of try and fill in the blanks, you know, over time."

"Yeah, that sounds OK, Helen. I'll try that."

"Good girl Sarah-Jane. OK maybe you'd like to have a little sleep before the next Gootsy session, you look a bit tired."

"Thanks, Helen." Sarah-Jane yawned. "Yep, you're right; I do feel a bit tired. The air's kind of different over here, it's like I'm on another planet."

27

JC and Sean paused for breath; they must have been jogging for a full twenty minutes and had covered quite a lot of ground.

"You're pretty fit Sean. It helps being young too, I guess." JC wasn't used to being outrun by his jogging partners; it was normally JC who set the pace, but Sean was clearly the fitter of the two.

"I do a lot of dancing and stretching. I guess that helps, JC. OK, you ready for another circuit? Can't be more than five kilometres."

JC struggled to his feet. "No bother Sean, let's do it."

***

"How you doing, guys? Hope I'm not disturbing you. You look busy. You writing some new songs?"

"Hell no, David," said Davy. "We're writing a book. Would you believe it? It's called *The World According to Davy Crockett and Mark Bolland.*"

Mark wasn't having that one. "It's actually called *The World According to Mark Bolland and Davy Crockett.*"

David smiled; they would have to work this one out on their own.

"What's it about?" David asked innocently.

"What's it about?" Davy asked, looking at Mark. "That's

what we're arguing about. I mean discussing. That's what you do with books, you know, *discuss*."

"OK," said David trying a different approach. "Who's the book intended for, I mean what's your market?"

"What's our market? The market is the whole world, young and old, straight and not-so-straight, men, women, and everything in between. It's for people who can read, that's our market."

David thought of Huck and then snapped out of it. "Well, sounds like you've covered all the bases."

"Well, it's a work in progress David. It's sort of *Aesop on Acid*, do you get it?" Davy knew he was trying his luck with David.

"*Aesop on Acid*? Sounds er… interesting, Davy," said David.

"Yeah, it is interesting, 'cause it was my idea, that's why it's *The World According to Davy Crockett and Mark Bolland* and not *The World According to Mark Bolland and Davy Crockett*. We're talking about stories of life for today's savvy kids. It's what Aesop would have written if he was kicking it in today's world maybe living in Tottenham – he was a black dude brother – you know with the internet, and all the gadgets and all the distractions. We're putting together little stories which bring home the important things in life. So far we've got 'The Drummer and the Singer', a story about a drummer and a singer. The drummer is the talented one who gets the boot from the band by the singer. Once the drummer's gone the singer realises he hasn't got any material to sing. Mark and I are sort of role playing the parts. Do you get it?"

"Sounds great Davy. What else you got?" asked David out of curiosity.

"I'll tell you," said Mark slightly put out. "We've got *'The Guy Who Can't Shut Up'*, you know about a guy who can't shut up," said Mark staring at Davy.

"I'll tell you what guys, I think you two need some quality space to work on this. I'll catch you later, before the Gootsy session."

"Yeah, that's another story," said Davy.

***

Inside the Encounter Area Davy, Mark, Sean and Sarah-Jane huddled together as if they were about to be told some bad news.

Gootsy bounded in looking fresh and mischievous.

"My, doesn't the room look just great?" exclaimed Gootsy looking towards the rear wall, which was exposed to reveal a huge expanse of mirrors, like a dance studio.

Gootsy lined everyone up in front of the mirrors and challenged each member of the small group to pull a funny face. Eager to reduce the tension and get the game going, they all tried their gurney best but it sparked no collective reaction. The exercise appeared to fall flat and an embarrassing silence descended. The group, now distracted, collectively failed to notice what Gootsy was up to.

He held in his hand a remote control, and was discreetly pushing some pre-programmed commands into the device.

A few discrete projectors situated on the ceiling, which shed images on the mirrors, created the effect of a high definition plasma screen, larger than some multiplex cinemas; the result was so dramatic that each one of the group yelped in utter shock and fear.

As the lights went out and the simple sound of a healthy

human heartbeat pounded out of the speakers. The group looked at the wall-sized screen and felt as if they were in a deep blue sea, swimming menacingly with a shoal of killer sharks ready to attack an unseen prey in a pre-frenzy ritual.

The sounds became subtly more complex; first there was the sound of an underwater swish of a shark's tail, the frenzied ripping of some unidentified carcass. The scene changed dramatically to outer space as if the viewer was gliding across vast swathes of galactic wilderness between planets at a ferocious speed.

A voice came out of the speakers, Gootsy's voice.

"We're on a journey, through life. So intense, so brief, so sad." The voyage through space continued round planets, through time itself. The images continued until it was apparent that the scene was now millions and millions of tadpoles, all heading towards a huge planet-like dome, each tadpole trying to burrow through the outer shell.

Gootsy's voice came out clear and loud from the unseen speakers. "We're one of millions. Our creation is a miracle, a flicker of life that comes and goes in the blink of an eye."

The images suddenly changed in rapid succession from a smiling foetus to a young child crying in a corner holding a teddy bear, then a beautiful male teenager emerging from the sea to a man and woman holding a newborn baby; an old couple walking along an isolated beach against the backdrop of a perfect sunset, followed by the scene of a burial service being watched from above.

Suddenly the lights came back on and the images on the screen disappeared, and everything was as it was. The group was still staring at the mirrors, now only seeing themselves, speechless and stunned. Each one felt as if they had been born and died and been reborn in the space of a few minutes.

Gootsy stood in front of the group. "That was an experience wasn't it? Now we're all going to sit down and have a little chat, now that I've got you in the mood to reflect on life."

The group slowly sat down as best they could on the floor, in a small circle. "Now, my friends, I want to share something with you, something very, very special. Since I was a little boy, I've had a friend. You know the sort of thing, a special friend. But I'm not stupid you know. I knew that no one would believe me, they would all think I'm crazy. Could you imagine that, me – crazy? This friend has been with me all my life. It's not a ghost, I don't like ghosts. You know what this friend is?"

The group collectively shook their heads.

"It's an angel," said Gootsy, "my very own angel. It's not male or female; it's not young or old. It's not sent from a Christian God, it's my own special friend, my angel who looks after me. It's not like a person, it's more like a spirit, a presence – not a ghost, I told you, don't like ghosts. What I do know is that my angel watches over me, guides me, loves me." Gootsy paused. "You know I think each of us has an angel who is with us at all times, especially when we think they're not there. Do you think I'm mad?"

Gootsy looked around the group waiting for an answer.

Mark had no worries on this score. "You ain't mad Gootsy, you're blessed. I've got an angel – well sort of – I reckon it's my gran – my mum's mum. Don't worry Gootsy, I know what you mean, I'm not talking about a ghost, just, I don't know, a presence. When she died I was very little but we were real close, I kind of felt she never left me; she's not around all the time, only when I've needed her. I don't ever see her but I have caught her fragrance if you know what I mean. You know in those days it wasn't Channel Number Five it was just some common soap I guess. It would have been pretty cheap in those days but it's the type of stuff you now only find in the best sort of natural beauty shops. Funny that." Mark seemed to drift off, his nose sniffing the air.

Davy looked a bit taken aback. "You're spooking me out brother. I mean when you're gone, you're gone. I ain't denying your truth but hell I'm on own – always have been. My papa left us soon as he couldn't mount my mama no more on account of me taking up his space, well, that's the story my mama told me. That's what she always said to me 'we're on our own, kid.' Never seen him since, I don't even know what he looks like." Davy seemed suddenly very sad.

Gootsy looked at Sean and Sarah-Jane. "And you two, do you have an angel?"

Sean shook his head as if he was embarrassed not to be able to share with the group. "I haven't had anyone close to me die yet. Maybe that's it."

"Maybe it is, Sean, maybe you're right." Gootsy and the group tried not to look at Sarah-Jane but it was hard not to, given it was clearly her turn to have a say.

Sarah-Jane stared into space and without warning broke down into a flood of tears; even by the standards of *The Place* this was a torrential downpour.

Slowly Sarah-Jane seemed to pull herself together. "That's so sad, so sad. You know what made me cry – I don't often cry you know – but you know what it is, it's not that I don't believe in angels, I do. It's just that they don't believe in me. I'm not worth it, I guess." The tears flowed again and the group spontaneously surrounded Sarah-Jane and hugged her, tightly.

Mark lifted Sarah-Jane's quivering chin with a finger and looked into her eyes.

"Do you know what, Sarah-Jane? You can share my angel if you want. I know she'd like you, how about that?"

Sarah-Jane hugged Mark and cried on his shoulder. "Oh, Mark, that's the sweetest thing I've ever heard. Can I? Thank you. That's so nice. She won't mind will she?"

"No she won't mind. Her name's Doris by the way."

"Doris. I like that." Sarah-Jane seemed so genuinely happy, even Sean was wiping away the tears.

Davy looked quite touched but couldn't help himself thinking ahead and tried, discreetly to whisper in Mark's ear. "'The Singer and his Angel', I like that one Mark, I mean that's got to be good. I could write a whole chapter about that one. Do we have to stick with Doris, you know maybe we could change it to Dorian or maybe Darius? OK, I get the vibes, brother, later."

28

David and Helen were in bed together, it was quite early in the morning, and they both knew the other was awake.

"You know it's great when it's kind of quiet; it's just how I like it, really." David was in a great mood and it showed. "I mean we've only got four full-time guests but it feels just right. What we got in store for today? Remind me. It's Saturday, isn't it? I love Saturdays."

"You better get your skates on David or your swimming kit more like it. We're off to the mixed bathing pond. The water won't be too cold, there's hardly anyone around early in the morning, should be great."

"It will be great. Who you taking?"

"Well, Sarah-Jane for sure. She doesn't know it yet, but I'm telling you, she's coming. Mark and Davy and Sean – everyone, I hope."

"Not sure Davy will come, he's like a cat when it comes to water. I mean he just can't see the point of getting cold and wet."

"Can you try and persuade him? It's good if we can get them all doing something together."

"OK, I'll try. Just please don't say 'what can go wrong'; it's too much like tempting fate, I'm hoping for a nice, quiet, enjoyable day and to share a quiet Movie Therapy experience with Mark Bolland and Davy Crockett, with maybe one or two light beers. Just a perfect day."

***

"But it will be fun, Sarah-Jane, I promise you." Helen was surprised at the level of resistance Sarah-Jane was putting up to the idea of a quick dip in the mixed bathing pond on Hampstead Heath, but wasn't going to give up easily.

"I don't know. Everyone thinks we spend half our lives around swimming pools in LA, but it's not my sort of thing, Helen, to be honest."

"Listen Sarah-Jane, it's a beautiful day. Hardly anyone will be there, I promise you. I'll be there, and so will JC, Mark, Davy and Sean. Why don't you just come with us, take a costume and see how you feel when you get there?"

"JC's going?" Sarah-Jane's eyes brightened.

"Why, of course JC's going. He doesn't spend all day jogging around the Heath, you know."

"Well, OK, but no promises."

Helen had a flashback to the time when Tracy Howler jumped in the men's pond without being able to swim and a thought crossed her mind.

"That's great Sarah-Jane, thank you. Come on, let's get ready."

***

"Well at least Mark had a great time. I mean considering his age and what he's put his body through over the last half century, he's amazingly fit and agile. He reminds me of that Iggy Pop guy. Strange isn't it how some people can abuse their bodies for years and years and seem almost to come out stronger for it while others just, you know, fade away or er… drop dead. I wish I knew the secret to that one."

JC was sounding a bit too smug for Helen. "JC, to tell you the truth I'm more concerned about Sarah-Jane. Tell me again, what actually happened?"

"OK Helen, I'm not sure if it was a big deal or not. You remember, we get there and before we know it Mark is leaping off the diving board like a little kid, goading Davy to join in."

"Yes, JC of course I remember that bit, but what happened between you and Sarah-Jane?"

"Nothing *happened* Helen, as such. I went back in the open changing area and to nip to the loo and Sarah-Jane was sitting on her own. She looked a bit frightened more than spaced out, so I sat down and we had a little chat."

"What exactly did she say, JC?" Helen obviously felt that JC was leaving something out and was determined to get the whole story. JC paused as if he was trying to remember the precise words used by Sarah-Jane. "I sat beside her and asked if everything was OK, that's all. All she said to me was 'I'm not ready', that was it. She wasn't crying or anything, that was it – '*I'm not ready*'."

Helen looked sternly at JC as if she wasn't totally convinced but then seemed to change her mind. "OK, JC, thanks. Look, I'm sorry if I came across as if I didn't believe you, I do. It's just that I feel I'm at a very delicate stage with Sarah-Jane and what she said is very important."

"That's OK. You seem very worried about her Helen."

"I am, JC. You know I shouldn't really look at Sarah-Jane this way but she is a real challenge to me – in fact a challenge to everything I believe in."

"And," added JC, "there's the dad, Charlie McQueen in the background, I guess that's added pressure you don't need. The point is Helen, as you always say, it's about what we're going to do next; that's all."

Helen took a deep, heartfelt sigh. "You're right, JC. You know I think we need to lighten things up a bit for Sarah-Jane. Let's have an impromptu Movie Therapy night. I can sit through with Sarah-Jane, you can talk with Sean and I'm sure David will enjoy having a couple of beers with Tweedledee and Tweedledum."

"Now that's sounds like a good idea, Helen. What you got in mind? I think Davy and Mark could do with *The Defiant Ones* – you remember Tony Curtis and Sidney Poitier on a chain gang escape story, handcuffed together on the run, being chased by the dogs and everything."

"JC, those two are already playing out the sequel to that one. I think we should be a bit more creative than *The Defiant Ones*. I mean that would be like giving you and Sean *Loneliness of a Long Distance Runner*. I know what they need. It's not about Davy, but Davy's mother." A broad mischievous smile came over Helen's face. "And I've got an idea for you and Sean."

"OK, Helen. I got the point. I trust you to come up with something. And what about you and Sarah-Jane? I guess *Bambi* would be too heavy for her, now there's an irony for you."

Helen wanted to be cross with JC but couldn't hide a little smile. "You're right on that score, JC. I've got an hour or so to work that one out, we'll see over breakfast whether I was right or not. And remember we've got David's Tai Chi Master arriving early, he'll be joining us for breakfast and then taking a session."

"Oh, yes, I'd forgotten about Sagi, Sagi No Sun. Dad said whatever you so, don't call him saggy, apparently from what dad told me, he doesn't like being called saggy, not with his pedigree."

***

"I do like these breakfast sessions, perhaps we should do them more often," said Helen. The makeshift breakfast table was covered with an array of fresh fruit, pastries and chilled drinks, coffee and tea; the guests slowly began to fill their plates and settle down to a discussion of the films they watched the night before.

"OK, before we… tuck in. David and JC are busy right now and won't be joining us, but let me introduce Sagi No Sun." Helen didn't need to point out which one was Sagi No Sun as there was only one bald-headed, saggy-eyed, martial artist-looking guy dressed in a white tracksuit sitting around the table.

Sagi No Sun placed his hands together in front of his shining face and bowed his head to each guest in turn. Mark, Davy, Sarah-Jane and Sean in return awkwardly said 'hi' in their own way and carried on concentrating on the food.

"So, Davy, what did you make of the film you watched? Helen had been up for some time and was keen to have a good debate.

"Not what I was expecting? After the last time I guessed it would be a surprise package, Helen. But man that film was something else. *Madame Butterfly*, what a choice. Yeah, if you wanna know if it got me, yeah it got me. Can't say I under-stood all of it. But there's that bit where the lady is singing about how her man is gonna come back – and like we know he ain't coming. Man, it was so sad. I guess I'll need to dig into his stuff a bit more, but those melodies, how can I have missed Puccini all my life? How can you know someone's music but not know the guy? Jeez, it makes me think of what else I don't know." Davy looked into space as if he had been through some form of dramatic experience.

"Kept him off the book project for an evening, Helen, thanks for that. I guessed *City of Angels* would be too obvious, but *Madame Butterfly* was inspired. You'd be surprised how many of our songs come from Puccini." Mark looked and sounded far more alert than the others expected.

Sarah-Jane looked puzzled. It just didn't seem right to be having a healthy breakfast with a rock star talking about Puccini. "I can't believe what you just said. Your music comes from Puccini? I wouldn't have guessed that, Mark Bolland. Like which songs?"

Mark looked at Sarah-Jane with an unnerving stare. "Sarah-Jane. Where does any of our stuff come from? We sit down and we jam around and we joke and the rest. At some point a line or a riff sort of takes over, some lyrics get thrown in, we know that we're on to something and we roll with it. We just you know sort of tune in, the same way Puccini must have done. It's just like opening your mind to the cosmos and letting the vibes flow through you, and you pick it up as best you can." Mark trailed off not sure whether he was being taken seriously or not.

"I'm with you brother, I get it." Davy was convinced. "That's what it was like when we laid down 'Boogie Yer Woogie' in ten minutes; classic it was and is and will be, 'Boogie Yer Woogie'."

Sarah-Jane wasn't going to get sidetracked by 'Boogie Yer Woogie' and ignored Davy completely. "Yeah, well OK, Mark. But I don't get the Puccini bit, that's all." Sarah-Jane sounded as if she was backtracking, realising who was talking to.

"I guess you never will, Sarah-Jane," said Mark sadly.

Helen thought the conversation was going rather well.

"And, Sean. You're very quiet. Come on, what did you and JC watch?" Helen knew that Sean would say nothing at all if he could get away with it.

"Er, we saw that *300* movie. I'd seen it before Helen but it was even better the second time," said Sean.

"You got to see one of the best ass-kicking films ever and we was watching *Madame Butterfly*?" Davy said trying badly to feign jealousy.

"What did it say to you, Sean?" asked Helen.

"What did it say to me, Helen? Not sure what you mean. It's about death and honour I guess."

Sagi No Sun smiled the tiniest of smiles, which didn't go unnoticed.

"Death, honour and fearlessness, Sean, don't you think? Didn't it strike you that the Spartans looked forward to a glorious death and that there was never a sign of fear?" Helen wasn't going to let Sean off easily this morning.

"I suppose so Helen," said Sean confidently. "But maybe they had nothing to live for except a good death, I mean that was their life."

"Yeah, brother you got it, that's it. You're there Sean. And I didn't see no black dudes among them Spartans. They would have taken one look at me said 'Hey this brother's been in the oven too long' and thrown me away into the reject pile and asked a few questions of the mama, you know what I'm saying?"

Sarah-Jane had a thought. "It's funny you should say that Davy. I was thinking, if your dad left you before you were born, and you've never met him or even seen him, how do you know he's black? I mean maybe your dad is a white guy."

Davy spat out his mini-croissant, almost hitting Sagi No Sun square in the face. But true to expectations, he moved ever so slightly to his left and the offending half-chewed pastry flew past him.

Mark couldn't help howl with laughter and Sean went bright red as if he was going to burst trying to stop himself lapsing into a serious attack of the giggles.

"How do I know my papa ain't white?" Davy stood up and stared at Sarah-Jane with a real menace in his voice, but a moment or two later sat down and seemed to visibly control himself. "Like one minute ago we're having a talk about music and Puccini and then all of a sudden we're talking about my papa being a white dude. Hey lady, you're gifted, that's what I think. But you know what, just for you lady, I'll have a little think about that one and I'll let you know, like later, about my papa. So I'll let that one go 'cause I know you ain't well and…"

Helen decided some diplomatic intervention was in order. "Can we get back to the movies? Sarah-Jane, tell them about our movie."

Sarah-Jane was happy for Helen to change the subject and looked all romantic. "Oh we watched *Breakfast at Tiffany's,* now there's a sad movie for you." As if simply to emphasize her point Sarah-Jane started to sing ever so softly and sweetly the opening lines of 'Moon River', which the group respectfully listened to until Sarah-Jane ran out of lyrics and began sobbing gently.

Helen was quite relaxed about Sarah-Jane's crying which, by the standards of *The Place,* was at the milder end of the fairly routine breakfast breakdowns but Mark couldn't ignore her distress.

"See what you've done Davy, you've only gone and upset the lady."

Davy realised that he was going to come out the worst of

this and decided it was his turn to change the subject. "I don't want to upset you girl, I'm not that type of brother Sarah-Jane. Listen, let me tell you about this book Mark and I are putting together."

Mark buried his head in his hands and looked sternly at Davy, "Not now brother. Might not be the right time."

Helen was keen to hear Davy out. "No, go on Davy, tell us how the book's coming along."

Davy's eyes sparkled and he was off. "We're doing great; we've got a few stories going now. The new story is the 'The Dog and the Bitch' about a dog and a bitch. The bitch loves the dog and wants to stay together forever and ever but the dog keeps sneaking round the corner with other bitches, so the bitch has a go at the dog and demands like exclusivity, I mean *fidelity*, and the dog refuses and storms off and leaves the bitch for a night of freedom and dies that very night in a stupid bar brawl. It's a short and sweet *fable*, man, Aesop would be proud. And you know what caused the fight? A bone. Ain't that a classic?"

Sarah-Jane looked confused. "How does a dog end up in a bar?"

"It's a story, Sarah-Jane; like a fable." Davy hadn't thought about how a dog might end up in a bar.

"OK, I get it, I think." Sarah-Jane tried to sound interested. "Like you two role play and sort of brainstorm these ideas?"

"Yeah, that's the way we do it; it works for us." Davy sounded very pleased with himself.

"So, like which one plays the dog and which one plays the bitch?" Sarah-Jane had a smirky grin and Sean tried to pretend to cough but in truth he was stifling another attack of the giggles.

"Man, you are up for it this morning girl." Davy felt he was being pushed and had to try hard to keep his cool.

"Listen, Davy. I'm here because I've got more problems than you lot put together. I'm not trying to upset or annoy you. I guess it's my way of playing. I'm sorry."

Sarah-Jane got out of her seat and went over and gave Davy a little hug and kissed him on the cheek. "I'm a pain in the ass, Davy, sorry."

Sarah-Jane went back to her seat and poured herself a fresh glass of orange juice. "I've got a little story for you Davy. I remember Aesop's Fables. OK, here's one for you and Mark. It's like this: it's about a little rich white girl and a slave, a black slave, that's it 'The White Girl and the Slave'. The white girl is a spoiled brat and gets everything she wants, except love and friendship. She's not allowed any friends because she's always unwell. So, the only person she has to talk to is the slave and he treats her like a real friend but she treats him real bad because he's a slave. One day the little girl breaks one of her daddy's favourite things – a real expensive vase – and the girl blames the slave and the master beats the slave to death and then the girl has no friends at all."

Davy looked as if he was deep in thought and then pronounced judgment. "That's real nice, Sarah-Jane. I like that." Davy raised his little glass towards Sarah-Jane to thank her and looked over at Mark who seemed to be reading Davy's mind.

"Don't worry Davy, I'll role play the slave," said Mark, relived that he could now laugh out loud, and on cue Sean started to laugh openly.

"Well, I'm glad we've sorted all that lot out. Come let's finish up and then Sagi No Sun can take us all through some well-deserved Tai Chi, yes?"

Sagi No Sun looked over towards Helen.

"It'll be my pleasure," said Sagi No Sun in a clear north London accent. "Maybe in the garden or even over the Heath, what would you all prefer? You can call me Edmund by the way, I'm from Finchley. I don't really like being called Sagi. Don't ask; it's a long story."

29

"I don't understand it, dad. I was up at five this morning looking for places that sell newspapers. I waited at King's Cross station for the first editions of all the papers, searching for spoilers on the net. At 5.30 this morning I get this copy of the *Sunday News*. We're not in it. Nothing. I thought today was our D-Day. But there's nothing, I don't understand. You been pulling tricks dad? I'm so relieved, I can't tell you. Do you think they're just holding off to get more dirt for next week or what? I mean has the storm passed, blown out or is it about to hit us next week – or the week after? I mean what's your take on this dad?"

David smiled as if he knew all along that there was nothing to worry about.

"I told you JC, there was nothing to worry about. Would daddy lie to you?"

JC made an exaggerated 'phew' sound and sat back as if he had just been given the best news ever. "Oh god, I'm so relieved. Can this day get any better?"

"This seems to be as good a time as any I think," said Helen cryptically.

"As good a time as any for what, Helen?" asked David; the same thought was in JC's mind.

Helen continued confidently, as if she had been thinking about this for some time. "It's time to really take stock, you know, seriously appraise *The Place,* think about what we do –

and what we don't do – who we let in and don't let in; what we charge, the therapists we use – I mean remind us David how we brought in 'Edmund from Finchley' – what activities we use – and why – what doesn't work, whether we need more staff, eating arrangements, sleeping arrangements, I mean everything."

David and JC, a bit taken aback, looked at each other with some concern.

David decided to cut to the chase. "OK, I put my hands up to the Sagi No Sun cock-up, or should I say misunderstanding? Edmund, from Finchley. I thought from his website he had trained as a monk from birth at the Shaolin Temple – you know the sort of centre of the universe for all the real Kung Fu stuff going back hundreds of years, near the Pagoda Forest in China. I should have read his website a bit more closely. I really expected something more… authentic, that's all. When he said he's a frequent visitor to the Pagoda Forest I think he must be talking about the Chinese take-away in Golder's Green. I thought his real name was Sagi No Sun. Turns out his students used to call him saggy, and he'd say 'saggy', wave a finger, and say 'no son' which he then decided, as a name, was pretty cool. That's what Henry told me anyway. No harm done; I guess the tai chi session went alright, didn't it?" Helen and JC tried not to smirk; it didn't seem fair.

"Anyway," said David, quickly checking that it was OK to move on, "maybe what we really need is a holiday. Somewhere real special, away from *The Place*, you know just for a few days and mull things over. What do you think?"

"OK, David. Maybe you're right, I'll have a think. But that's the point you see. Because it's really just the three of us who run *The Place* there's no opportunity for us to relax –

I mean really we're all on duty twenty-four seven. It's wonderfully balanced right now – there's only Davy, Mark, Sean and Sarah-Jane here, but as we know that can all change in the blink of an eye."

David took the opportunity to change the subject. "And what about Sarah-Jane? I can see that Mark, Davy – even Sean – are all about ready to leave, but I can't see the end in sight for Sarah-Jane, can you Helen?"

"Hmm. It's a balancing act, David. The problem is that Sarah-Jane is still suffering from the trauma of her mother's death. For nearly thirty years she's been medicated and treated with kid gloves to avoid dealing with all the issues: the pain, the guilt, the horror of it all – it's a high risk strategy to let the volcano go off but by the same token what's the point of her being here if we don't try to engage with her on some sort of real level."

"OK," said JC, still on a high from the relief of not seeing a hatchet job on the unholy Trinity on the front page of the *Sunday News*, "so what's the problem?"

"The problem JC is that if we screw this one up I'm not sure we'll recover. All that stuff with the *Sunday News* was mild in comparison to what could happen with Sarah-Jane. I'm not sure you understand how disturbed Sarah-Jane really is. I mean all I'd have to do is take her meds away for one day – I mean one day – and you'd see a very different creature emerge. We always say that we're not about curing people and that's very much the case with Sarah-Jane. We can't cure her any more than we can change her past."

"But," said David, "we can make her emotionally stronger, let her understand herself better, give her experiences that provoke strong emotions, make her feel more alive. You know, what we do all the time."

"David, I'm saying that Sarah-Jane is different. Mark is incredibly talented, successful – balanced even. He's here for the ride, for the fun of it and that's fine, why not? Davy, well I think Davy's getting the point – whether he sees it or not – that he's got more energy than he's had for a long time, that's what his book is all about. He knows there'll come a point soon when he feels ready to get back on the road, and the timing is to a large extent out of our hands. Sean's just a kid whose confidence needs building up and that process is happening by the hour. I'm not sure he'll be staying for more than another day or two and then he'll be as ready as he'll ever be to get back into the fray. With Sarah-Jane it's all different, as I said."

"So," said JC, "what are you suggesting we do with her?"

Helen looked as serious as she had ever looked. "First of all I need to talk to the dad, Charlie. I'm going to explain it as I see it. I want to do with Sarah-Jane what we've done with Davy and substitute a placebo – here and there – for the cocktail of drugs she's taking. But I feel – if I'm really honest – a bit out of my depth here. I need to get a detailed opinion from Sarah-Jane's doctor what these drugs are really doing to Sarah-Jane and what's going to happen when we start a withdrawal process. This isn't routine cold turkey."

"Sounds good, Helen. What's the problem?" David knew that there were some wild waters to navigate and to David that was simply a challenge to be overcome. "I'll stay close to her Helen, she'll be OK, I promise. In the meantime I guess it's business as usual.

***

"What's the longest distance you've ever run, Sean?" JC

thought he was prepared for the answer and was thinking in terms of maybe eight kilometres or thereabouts.

"I couldn't tell you exactly, JC. I used to jog all the time when I was fourteen or fifteen, sometimes for hours at a time. It was never about the distance, it was about the length of time I could keep going."

"And you Davy and Mark? What about you two?"

"Man, I don't know. I've never seen the point of running on my own, it was never my thing." Davy clearly wasn't going to commit himself to a figure.

"I took part in a charity event once," said Mark. "I think it was ten kilometres but I flaked out about half way round. I'd like to do the marathon one day, just to show people I've got it in me."

JC looked at Sarah-Jane who among them all looked not quite right in her pastel coloured track suit.

"I used to do some cheerleading which I know like doesn't really count, JC, but we'd train for hours and keep going for long stretches. What have you got in mind?"

JC didn't have much in mind, really. He had agreed with Helen and his dad that he would take Davy, Mark, Sean and Sarah-Jane over Hampstead Heath at the crack of dawn and see how far he could push them, to the point of complete and utter exhaustion without killing them. That was the plan, to push them to their limits.

"OK, what we're going to do is this. We're going to keep with the slowest member of the group," said JC looking at Davy. "We're going to walk, jog and sprint. But the whole point is that we don't stop. If you get really tired, then we walk but we keep going. It's not about distance; it's about the length of time we can keep going. Is that clear? OK, let's go." JC had no idea how long this little jaunt this would last for.

***

"Well, how long did it go on for, JC?" Helen couldn't quite believe it, nor could David.

"Roughly," said JC proudly "all day. I thought Sarah-Jane would drop out quite quickly but she just kept going. I mean it was an art to balance out the walking with the jogging and to keep the sprints to a minimum but, all day, really. No food at all, only water and some energy drinks taken along the way."

"No wonder they're so quiet, reckon they haven't slept so soundly for years. I mean all of them." David was impressed.

"Listen JC, well done I really mean that, this is perfect. You know I spoke at length with Sarah-Jane's doctor and he said if you're going to mess around with her meds you'd better have a plan to substitute the effects of the drugs. He thought he was being cute when he said 'you'd need to keep her exercising for hours, and I mean hours'. This is a big step forward, JC, thank you."

"My pleasure, Helen. I like Sarah-Jane you know. Sometimes I feel as if she knows exactly what her problems are, but what's heart-breaking is that they're so deep rooted, like some unspeakable truth."

Helen looked as if it was all going to plan. "OK, we let them sleep for as long as they want. We take a healthy breakfast to their rooms and then straight into a Gootsy finale.

30

"Good evening one and all, welcome, welcome." Gootsy shook the hands of Sarah-Jane, Sean, Mark and Davy one by one as if he was letting them know that this was their last session with him.

The Encounter Area looked ominous. In the centre of the room were placed a number of armless white cushioned seats which fitted together to form a semicircle facing the mirrors. Gootsy signalled to the group to sit, which they did reluctantly not knowing what to expect next.

"Today, my friends, no props, no tricks, just us." Gootsy sounded very sad and bowed his head.

Without warning the lights went out and Gootsy's face appeared on the mirrors. "Fooled ya," said the image and the lights came back on as if nothing had happened. But no one was laughing, least of all Gootsy.

"Today I don't want you to trust me, not for one moment. I may lie to you, in fact I already have, and I will lie again. Today is the end day, the day when you can say what you want, it doesn't matter. Anything you want, you understand, it doesn't matter."

The group tried not to sneak a look at each other as if to reassure themselves it was alright but they had a feeling it wasn't alright. Gootsy looked down at the floor, his legs crossed and twiddled his foot round and round as if he was expecting something to happen and then looked up at the group.

"Why are you looking at me? Have you nothing to say for yourselves? Is it my job to put words into your mouths?"

Davy, Sarah-Jane, Sean and Mark began to fidget collectively.

"You know what I want to talk about my friends?" said Gootsy. "What I want to talk about is life and death, but not in that order. First of all, I want to talk about death. Is that OK? I mean does anybody mind? Perhaps someone thinks death has got nothing to do with them. Sean, do you think about death, or are you too young for such matters? Maybe you think you'll live forever and ever, happily ever after in a castle maybe with a beautiful princess who will bear you lots of nice little princes and princesses. Is that what you think?"

Perhaps it was because of his marathon expedition the day before or the magnificent sleep that followed or maybe it was the King's breakfast earlier in the day, but the fact was that Sean felt great.

"I'm nearly an adult, Gootsy. You remind me of one of my uncles – the one who died of cancer when he was forty. This type of crap doesn't freak me out; I've been more scared on a roller coaster or in a house of horrors in Great Yarmouth. Sure I think of death. Like I think, I better get out there and do my stuff before one day, soon, I won't have a choice because you know I'll be like dead."

Sarah-Jane was quick off the mark. "Hey, Sean, well hello to you. I thought you said that no one close to you had died." Sarah-Jane's tone was slightly sarcastic, as if she was trying to catch Sean out.

"Yeah, I did, Sarah-Jane. My uncle died before I was born, I never even knew him. My dad showed me a picture of him and he kinda looked like Gootsy, you know when he was dying after the treatment, all slap head-like and everything."

"Tell it like it is, brother." Davy seemed quite happy for Sarah-Jane to be put in her place.

"Let me tell you something my friends," said Gootsy solemnly. "I too have cancer, prostate cancer, inoperable. My days are numbered, but I am happy, really quite joyous – do you understand that?"

The group went silent.

"Oh, man that's really sad, Gootsy, I'm sorry to hear that, really, I am," said Davy.

"I don't know what to say, Gootsy," said Sarah-Jane, "that's really awful. Can't the doctors do anything?"

Gootsy smiled. "Do anything, Sarah-Jane? Maybe I can buy immortality? Death is a certainty; we can influence the timing, for what it's worth, but in the end it makes no difference. We come, we go. An eternity of silence interrupted briefly by a few tears and some smelly bits."

Suddenly the mirrors came to life and there on the big screen was what looked like a home movie from many years ago. The images were of a young boy building a sand castle on a beach somewhere. It was such a beautifully crafted castle, with a moat and turrets and a little flag flying from the castle wall. The boy stood back admiring his work, turned to the camera and then fell backwards, arms spread out wide with a big smile on his face, little spade in hand and fell full on the castle, flattening it.

Gootsy laughed out loud. "Yes, that's me. I still remember that moment as if it were yesterday. My parents always thought I was a bit odd – I always had this peculiar sense of humour. I remember thinking that the castle was so good, so perfect, that it wouldn't last. I knew someone bigger than me would come along and stamp all over it, or the wind would come and blow it down, or the sea would come in and swallow it up. I thought 'I built it, it's mine, I created it, so I want the pleasure of flattening it.'"

The images disappeared as quickly as they had appeared. "I'm sorry, my friends. This should be about you, not me." Gootsy seemed genuinely apologetic and started to sob gently. "I may seem sad my friends, but I'm very happy inside," said Gootsy as he continued to sob.

Sarah-Jane moved over to Gootsy and gave him a big hug. "Jeez, Gootsy. What can I say?"

Gootsy snuggled closer to Sarah-Jane and took his time before responding.

"What can you say? I'll tell you what you can say, Sarah-Jane. You can promise me you'll make a decision. Decide whether to live or die. Is that too much?"

Gootsy looked deep into Sarah-Jane's eyes. "Tell me Sarah-Jane, really, in your heart of hearts, do you want to live or die?"

Sarah-Jane stared into Gootsy's sad, old eyes. "I'll tell you what, Gootsy. I want to live, I really do."

There followed no theatrics or effects or surprises of any kind. A group hug just sort of happened, even young Sean clinging on to the others as if in a little boat lost in the midst of a wide ocean and there they remained in silence for what seemed like a very long time.

31

Helen took a long, hard look at Sean. "So, Sean, you're ready to leave. Are you sure you're ready to throw yourself back into the snake pit? What have you got left? Is it four or five days before the live final? Do you have any routines you need to learn?"

Sean looked at Helen, David and JC. To David, Sean almost looked like a different person to the one who had been brought to *The Place* only a few days previously.

"I'm OK. I haven't been rehearsing anything but when I've been running with JC I've been going over some lines of a song I'm going to do at the right moment. That's what goes through my head. I've been getting texts from my mentor and I reckon I've got my head sorted, you know enough to get back in there and not fall apart. I really feel as if I've been rehearsing a game plan, if you know what I mean."

"I think we know what you mean, Sean," said Helen maternally. "You remember what you were like when you first arrived? I'm sure I speak for all of us Sean when I say you've changed so much over such a short period of time, it's really impressive. We're really very proud of you Sean."

"Helen, JC and David, listen, thank you. It's funny you know. I do feel different. I guess I'll tell people I had a swim, went for a couple of runs, watched a movie, slept well, ate well, did a bit of Tai Chi, met some funny old geezer, just like any old holiday really. But I know it was a lot more than that. Maybe the difference was the people I've met – they seem so much more real than those I'm used to dealing with. Maybe that's it. Anyway, I'm feeling great, thank you. I don't know what to say really."

"Sean," said Helen "you've said it all."

There was a little knock on the door of David's office, which wasn't expected.

"Hold on Sean, I can guess who that might be." Helen had a feeling what was about to happen.

Helen opened to door and standing outside like two naughty school boys were Davy and Mark.

"Er, hope we haven't like disrupted anything," said Davy sheepishly.

"No, no it's OK," said Helen. "Sean is leaving and we're just saying our goodbyes."

Davy and Mark stepped into the office and Mark stepped forward as if he had prepared some speech.

"Can I speak with Sean here? I mean is that OK?" Mark looked around the room, uncertain as to whether what he was doing was OK or not.

"Sure, why don't you sit down on the sofa, with Sean." The sofa was just about big enough for the three of them to shuffle up comfortably.

"OK, this is cosy. What's the story guys?" asked Helen.

Mark and Davy looked at each other and exchanged a brief set of nods as if they hadn't quite agreed who was to say what, so Davy took the initiative.

"Helen, it's like this. My brother Mark and I are like ready to move on. It's not that I'm bursting to leave here, it's more like I'm bursting to prepare to hit the road. We wanted to do this right. So, we wanted to lay it down and tell you straight that we've both had a real experience here."

Mark decided he should get a word in. "Like the man says, Helen. It's been the best, it really has. But I guess the whole thing about being here is knowing when you're ready to move on and we're ready to move on. Like Davy says it's great being here, but it's made me feel ready to get back out there and you know – do *my thing*."

David stood up and placed out his hand for a handshake, but Davy wasn't having any of it. "You think brother I've been through what I've been through to give you a handshake? Man, come here and let me give you some love, brother."

Davy approached David and wrapped his arms around David in the tightest bear hug David had ever been privy to. "I love you brother," said Davy with tears in his eyes before he finally let go and headed towards Helen. "Man there's so much love in this room I can hardly breathe." And so the hugging and kissing went on until everyone was satisfied there was no more hugging to be done.

"OK," said Helen wiping a tear from her eye. "There's not going to be time to set up any Graduation Ceremony, I feel like I've let you all down."

Davy was having none of it. "Let us down? How can you say that, Helen? This *is* the Graduation Ceremony, like right here, right now. Hell we might all be struck down by er… lightning or something you know, this is the moment of joy. Man, I feel so happy I have to just share with you."

Out the blue Davy launched into his personal favourite, his band's classic 'Boogie Yer Woogie'. Sean and Mark seemed familiar with the beat and lyrics and the three of them were off, causing David and JC to break out into a little disco shuffle. Helen quite spontaneously let her hair out of its little bun and threw off her shoes.

"You think the old lady doesn't know how to boogie her woogie? Let me show, let me show you the way to go…" Helen let caution go to the wind and danced without inhibition and a party atmosphere took over.

Sean took Helen's hand and started to bump against Helen in an old-fashioned disco sort of way.

"I'm telling you guys, this is better than *Glee*," cried Sean as the other chapped and cheered as Davy carried 'Boogie Yer Boogie' to its very end.

After a while the energy seemed to leave the group and they all sat down wiping away tears of laughter.

Davy suddenly turned quite serious. "Oh, man that was great. Just one thing. What about Sarah-Jane? I mean I feel a bit worried leaving her all alone. Will she be alright, Helen?"

Helen composed herself and deftly placed her hair back in its little tidy bun with a hair band and put her shoes back on.

"That's sweet of you to think of Sarah-Jane, Davy. She'll be alright, I promise you. In fact, her dad is on his way over here right now. I expect she'll be leaving soon, too. Please do make sure you say goodbye before you go. I mean all of you."

David and JC looked at each other with some surprise.

"Really? I didn't know that. Charlie Macqueen is on his way here, like right now?" asked David.

"Sure is, David. Says he's got something for us that might help."

"Something that might help? Can't wait," asked JC with obvious concern.

"Hey brothers, as long as it's not a writ you'll be OK. I

guess you all know of Charlie Macqueen's legal victories, he's a legend all right, even in my world." Davy smiled and laughed.

"That's not funny, Davy," said David.

Davy straightened up. "Hey brother, this place has given me back my sense of humour. You know where I'm coming from."

Helen for one knew Davy was only joking. "I think I know what the dad's up to, it will be fine. Now before you go Davy, I just need to have a word with you, on your own if you don't mind. I need to tell you something, something that really is funny."

"Oh shit, sounds heavy, Helen."

"Not at all, Davy, quite the opposite." Helen smiled, confident that in a few moments Davy would get the joke; he had been off dope for longer than he had been since he was probably twelve years old and hadn't even noticed.

32

"My, Charlie Macqueen, this is a real pleasure, an honour even, you look great, if I may say so. Welcome to *The Place*. May I introduce David, our Group Operational Director, and his son, JC." Charlie shook hands firmly with each of the unholy Trinity and beamed his famous Hollywood smile.

Helen wasn't often impressed – *really* impressed – with another person's physical appearance but Charlie Macqueen looked every inch the Hollywood legend turned successful business man that he had become. Helen gestured for Charlie to sit in the spot usually reserved for guests and made a conscious effort not to outstare the Hollywood movie star.

"Can I get you anything, Charlie?" Helen quite often deliberately avoided asking that question but was willing to make an exception for Charlie Macqueen.

"No, no I'm fine. Let's get to it. We know why I'm here. I don't plan to stay too long; I've got some scores to settle at the ranch so to speak and a lifetime of family troubles to face up to today, so let's make the most of this."

David tried not let on how awe struck he was, but it was certainly surreal to be in the presence of someone so well known even by the high standards of *The Place*.

Helen was keen to demonstrate some authority. "Before we do so Charlie, I take it Sarah-Jane doesn't actually know you're here, I mean right at this very moment. Anyway, she's fast asleep; it's pretty late in the morning but Sarah-Jane's been through quite a lot and we're happy to let her sleep for as long as she wants; it's part of the process, if that makes sense."

"That's fine, Helen. Sarah-Jane and I text each other, so you're right, she knows I'll be here when she wakes up. Sarah-Jane speaks very highly of you all, and the other guests. How are the other guests by the way?"

"Well, funny you should mention that Charlie," said David. "As it happens, might even be the first time since day one that we've got one guest – and that's Sarah-Jane. Suits us, and I don't think Sarah-Jane will mind. We're fully focussed on Sarah-Jane for as long as its takes."

Charlie shuffled around a bit and undid the button of his exquisitely tailored suit. "That's interesting, I mean interesting in a good way."

An uneasy silence followed as if no one was quite prepared for the next move, nor really knew what the next move was going to be.

Charlie looked at JC "So you're JC. Sarah-Jane has taken a shine to you. I can see why." Charlie turned his attention towards David. "Your boy's a mighty fine young man, David, real fine."

JC blushed as David muttered "thank you".

"OK, Helen," Charlie was obviously gearing himself for the big statement. "First off, thanks for all you've done and are doing for Sarah-Jane. It's been heartbreak for me. Over twenty years of heartbreak. You know ever since that day, it's not been right. I've tried everything. I must know more about medications than a lot of doctors. I heard about *The Place* and did some research, I decided you three would deliver something different, something that might help… progress Sarah-Jane."

Charlie dropped his head but quickly composed himself as if he had decided to come out fighting. "Sometimes I wish I could have the luxury of falling apart myself you know. Maybe it's just not my style. I've got a bit of reputation for taking no prisoners, I'm sure you know all about that side of me. I reached the heights as an actor but being a newspaper owner is just so much more *fun*. Nearest I'll get to playing god, I suppose." Charlie looked at David and smiled.

"But you know I'm a businessman at heart and business is business and I'll be damned if anyone's going to screw me over." Charlie paused for a moment as if he knew that he was veering off course. "Anyway, point is that I feel I've come to a crossroads with Sarah-Jane, you know shit or bust." Charlie let his tough words hang in the air as if to set the tone of the meeting.

"That's all good to hear, Charlie." David felt the need to engage with Charlie on a serious level. "You said you did some research Charlie, I'm glad that put your mind at rest."

David was about to find out why Charlie was a Hollywood legend, for more reason than just his good fine looks and acting skill. Charlie Macqueen was a *player*.

"Yeah, David. You see when I say research, I don't mean tapping your name into Google. I mean research as in deep research. I mean CIA level. I've been tight with every president since Nixon. You don't think I'd entrust you with the person closest to my heart, the most important thing in the world to me, my only daughter, if I didn't feel that I knew the three of you probably better than you know yourselves or those you consider to be your best friends."

"Really," said Helen. "CIA level? We're flattered. Go on, Charlie."

"Helen I know all about you. I know more about you than those journey men at the *Sunday News*. I know what school you went to, I know what qualifications you have, from where. A doctorate in psychology from the University of Tallinn, capital of Estonia, very impressive, Dr. Pope. You've done pretty well for a rebellious teenager called Halina Putsep. I know also – forgive me Helen – all about the divorces and the money, about your psychologist dad who abandoned you, I know how you earned your pocket money as a teenager, I know how you funded *The Place* and I know how you operate."

Charlie looked at David with a mafia-type stare. "And I know all about you too David. I mean everything, including your personal battle with alcoholism. I've even met the governor of the prison where you stayed – how do you say over here – at *Her Majesty's Pleasure*."

Charlie turned his glaze back towards Helen. "I love the bit about how you two met, after you talked your way into a job as a prison psychologist, Helen, I thought that was genuinely romantic, even by Hollywood standards. Let me tell you the best bit. Do you know I've got a personal controlling interest in the *Sunday News*? Do you know it was me who set the dogs on you in the first place? When I read the first draft of the *Sunday News* piece I had to correct at least ten factual inaccuracies. They didn't even pick up on the joke between you that Helen's original surname – Putsep – is Estonian for *cooper*."

This time it was David's turn to blush and his head sunk.

"OK, Charlie. Why don't you come out with it? What is it you want from us?"

"David, I ain't finished yet." Charlie took a long look at JC. "JC, I know about your mom. I know how she died."

JC had to use all his will power not to burst into tears, a fact that didn't go unnoticed by David or Helen.

"OK, Charlie. Put your cards on the table. JC doesn't need this. His mother – my wife – died in a car accident. I was driving, JC knows all about it. He was in the car at the time. Why do you want to bring this up?"

Charlie looked around as if he had taken complete control. "I'm bringing this up to let you know that when I started to dig into *The Place,* the more I came to like you all. I just wanted to see how you'd react to a little pressure, that's all. Hope you didn't mind. I mean I needed to know if you were going to panic and do something stupid and I needed to know that before I sent Sarah-Jane over to you. Just a little test if you like. And hey, here's the good news: You passed. David, you're my kinda guy."

Charlie sat back looking very pleased with himself, and continued before JC, David or Helen could think of anything to say.

"You see Sarah-Jane already feels bonded with JC. I needed an emotional hook to persuade Sarah-Jane to go along with this, and that hook was JC's story. OK, it was different with JC's mother, her death was an accident, that was clear from the reports at the time but I told Sarah-Jane enough for her to feel connected to you, JC. As for you David – as a dad in prison – that must have been real tough. I thought if you three have survived all of that stuff – and got your act together to hold this place together – then believe me, you're on my team. That's where I'm coming from."

Helen, David and JC still weren't sure where this was heading.

"And you've travelled half way round the world to tell us

this, Charlie?" asked David.

"David, I've travelled half way round to world to meet you guys. Don't get me wrong. I'm not here to make any threats or demands. I'm here to make you an offer. I like you guys, I really do. What really gets me about *The Place* is that Helen over there is sitting on enough dough from the second divorce settlement alone to hang around a beach for the rest of her life and not worry for one second about money. But instead Helen, and you David, and you JC, slave away all hours working out ways to sort people out. And boy do you three have ways of sorting people out. I'll need to talk to you guys about security issues, by the way. And David, you'll need to pick your friends a bit more carefully – Henry Stallard has been very helpful to me. Let me tell you David, that guy's a cheap bastard in more ways than one. Now that one got you, didn't it?"

David tried to conceal his emotions but could not prevent himself biting his top lip and wiping away an ever-so-small tear from his eye whilst shaking his head in disbelief, as the betrayal of his best mate sunk in.

Charlie smiled as his best self-satisfied smile and continued. "You see I know that Helen hasn't worked all this out by reading some textbook or studying all her life. She suffered terrible emotional torture at the hands of her father and as a consequence spent years with her therapist, that Gootsy guy. Therefore she understands shock therapy, laughter therapy, inspirational therapy and all the rest better than anyone.

I mean there ain't one therapy that you use here that Helen hasn't tried and tested herself, ain't that right Helen?"

Helen look a bit shocked, but was composed and dignified. "OK, Charlie. You got it. That's right. I've been through it all and had to find a way out. I guess if you want to screw someone up, there are two ways that are almost bound to succeed."

Charlie's perfect Hollywood smile appeared in all its glory. "Two ways, Helen. Remind me."

"First off would be to have a father who is – publicly – a caring family psychiatrist but in reality is an emotional bastard to his family. The second would be to have a beautiful and successful mother who is so self-absorbed and depressed that she ends up taking her own life. Like Sarah-Jane's mother did. And if I wanted to make doubly sure that the kid had virtually no chance of a normal life I'd have the mother committing suicide on her kid's birthday, preferably when the kid is very young but old enough for it to hit home. Maybe the kid's sixth birthday. You know, like Sarah-Jane."

This time Charlie's head sunk and for one moment David looked around for a box of tissues. But Charlie was made of sterner stuff.

"Helen, you're my kind of lady. You've got a physical beauty and presence matched only by your inner strength. And you understand people. You'd make a great politician."

"Thanks for that, Charlie. But shall we, as you said, get back to business?"

Charlie rubbed his eyes as if he had to wipe away invisible tears.

"OK, Helen. Business. First, there's Sarah-Jane. I've brought something with me." Charlie took out from the inside of his pocket a little memory stick. "You see this little usb stick? On it in the very best format available anywhere in the world is a digitised home movie, taken at Sarah-Jane's sixth birthday party. I shot the film. It features a lot of

Sarah-Jane and some footage of Sarah-Jane's mother. Sarah-Jane has never seen this before. I've brought it over because I want you to show this to her if you think it will help." Charlie handed over the small device as if it was the most precious thing in the world.

"Thank you Charlie. Yes, I would like to show this to Sarah-Jane. The room downstairs is already set up for this type of 'activity'."

Helen looked over to JC who nodded to confirm that the arrangements were still in place as they had been for Gootsy's last session.

"I'll tell you what, we'll do this later today Charlie. I want to see it on my own first. I also want to decide whether you should be present, or not. How do you feel about that?"

Charlie looked slightly taken aback. "Helen, I'm not sure I could take it, really."

"And why do you think Sarah-Jane could 'take it' but you can't?"

Charlie looked uncomfortable for the first time since coming into the room. "I guess maybe Sarah-Jane's been prepared for this moment. I'm, you know, just off the plane, still skating on ice. Got other things on my mind, you know business issues," said Charlie unconvincingly.

"OK, Charlie. The point is that it won't do Sarah-Jane any good if you're there but don't want to be there. So, let's leave that one to the side and see how you feel a bit later. You're going to stay here tonight aren't you? I mean not as a guest in a formal way but as a guest in the sense that you're our guest. Make sense? Yes? We've plenty of room, Charlie."

"You're a mighty fine operator Helen. You know what, I'll think about the invitation. I'm actually booked in at The Savoy. I've got work to do; people to hire, people to fire.

There's only room for one silverback gorilla in my world, and that'll be me."

Charlie paused for dramatic effect as if to signal some dramatic move he had decided to make. "That's later. For now, maybe JC could show me around and then I'll freshen up a bit, thanks."

Charlie's little talk had sharpened Helen up. "We could do better than that, Charlie. Let's get you into something more appropriate and JC can take you for a little jog round Hampstead Heath. Don't worry about being recognised. I mean, it's not that someone won't recognise you Charlie, it's just that round here they don't give a damn."

"I'm beginning to see why Sarah-Jane likes this place, Helen." Charlie looked towards JC. "Hope you can keep up with me son, I'm a lot fitter than I look. I played Hercules one time you know."

"Well, that takes care of a lot of things," said Helen as if all everything was simply tickety-boo.

"Before you head off with JC, Charlie, I need to get one thing straight. You said you've come here to make 'an offer'. Care to elaborate?"

"Why David, that's a fine point to make. I'll tell you what, now that things have developed so nicely for us all I think I'll be able to be clearer as to the offer I have in mind. But first off, I'm going to have a little jog with JC while Helen and Sarah-Jane have a look at the home movie and then we'll have a little chat. How does that sound, David?"

"Sounds OK to me Charlie Macqueen, I look forward to it." David was not the best negotiator in the world.

33

JC and Charlie took the private and discreet path from the back of the garden of *The Place* to the edge of Hampstead Heath and paused for some warm-up exercises, keeping a close eye on each other. JC knew that if Charlie was as stiff as he looked the chances of him jogging round one circuit of the Heath would be minimal. Judging by Charlie's extended waistline, which could not be disguised despite the slightly oversized tracksuit top, Charlie wasn't used to regular exercise. Not of the type that JC had in mind.

Charlie lifted a leg onto a railing which was no more than waist height and tried to stretch forward with his arms without displaying too much effort or pain while JC crossed his legs and effortlessly touched his toes with the palms of his hands trying not to make it too obvious that he was all the while keeping a close eye on Charlie Macqueen.

Charlie stood up and placed his hands on his hips and pushed out his groin. "I'm not as young as I once was, JC."

"That's true for everyone, I guess," said JC trying not to sound too smug at Charlie's obvious limitations. "Maybe we should take it easy for the first circuit, Charlie."

Charlie continued his exaggerated stretches, trying hard to keep up with JC. "A circuit, JC? How long is that?"

"About five kilometres, Charlie. But the Heath is basically an almost-tamed woodland with streams, ponds and very steep hills, so it feels like a lot longer. It's more of cross country course than a track run out. You get used to it."

"Five kilometres, JC. What's that in old money?"

"In terms of miles, Charlie? About three miles, a bit longer. Shouldn't take us more than twenty minutes. You can complete this circuit at a decent walking pace in less than half an hour."

"Really? Well, I'll tell you what, why don't we walk the circuit at a decent walking pace as our warm up and then do a second circuit at a comfortable jog and see how we feel?"

"OK, Charlie, whatever you feel comfortable with."

"And, JC, I guess with all these joggers and dog walkers around there's got to be some sort of café or restaurant some-where?" Charlie asked, almost sheepishly.

"Well, there's a great café at Kenwood House which is in that direction." JC knew where this was heading.

"Do they do decaf espresso, JC?"

"I'm not sure, Charlie, only one way to find out, I guess."

***

"This feels a bit spooky, Helen. I feel really scared for some reason. Is my dad here yet?"

Helen and Sarah-Jane sat together on the comfortable white leather cushioned seats facing the mirrors in the Encounter Area.

"You dad is here, Sarah-Jane, but you were asleep when he arrived. JC took him for a little jog over the Heath and I guess he's flaked out for a bit with the jet lag and everything. You'll see him shortly. He is here, Sarah-Jane, everything's OK, I promise." Helen put her arms around Sarah-Jane and gave her a reassuring hug. It seemed as if by the moment, in front of Helen's eyes, that Sarah-Jane was becoming more and more childlike.

"OK, Sarah-Jane, this is a big day, I mean a really big day. Your dad brought with him something very special. It's a film of when you were a lot younger. I've plugged it into our system and when I press this button here the lights will automatically dim and the film will come up on the mirrors. Is that OK, Sarah-Jane? I mean are you ready, now, for this?"

Sarah-Jane closed her eyes and sort of mumbled to herself and took a deep breath. "If I'm not ready at this moment Helen, I know I'll never, ever, be ready. Can I press the button, Helen, is that OK?"

"Sure, Sarah-Jane of course." Helen handed Sarah-Jane the remote. "Just press that button there, that's all you have to do."

"OK, I get it." Sarah-Jane took the remote and pressed the button, the lights dimmed and on the full wall-wide screen appeared the film.

As a home movie it was nothing out of the ordinary. The film was following the antics of a young girl in a bright red swimming costume all smiles and giggles, splashing around in the outdoor pool of a fabulously rich home amidst a busy birthday party for the young carefree princess. The camera focussed in to capture the arrival of the birthday cake, which had six candles on it. The little girl and her friends clambered excitedly out of the pool and rushed towards the cake being carried to a large table by a gorgeous, glamorous-looking lady. From every corner adults and kids rushed around the cake and started to sing happy birthday as the camera focussed on the wide-eyed young girl who blew out the six little candles and clapped her hands in uninhibited joy.

Sarah-Jane held her hand to her mouth and started to cry. "Oh god, that's me and my mom. Isn't she beautiful?"

Helen placed her arm around Sarah-Jane and held her tightly. "It's OK, Sarah-Jane, it's OK."

Sarah-Jane pressed the button on the remote and the film froze on the screen. "Can we stop it there, Helen? Just for a moment. I think that's all I can take right now. Honestly, Helen, I'll need to take this in little – you know – baby steps."

Sarah-Jane and Helen heard the distinctive sound of a grown man crying and simultaneously looked over their shoulders. Standing at the door was Charlie, wiping tears from his eyes.

Sarah-Jane jumped up and ran over to her dad. "Oh, dad, dad. Why haven't you let me see this before?" Charlie held open his arms and embraced his daughter tightly.

"Oh baby. I couldn't. I wanted to so many times. But you know what happened later in the day – that was the day your mother…" Charlie couldn't go on, and wept.

Helen stood up and approached Charlie and Sarah-Jane. "Listen, you two have got a lot to talk about. I'm going to come back later. Why don't you both sit down here, and I'll come back in a while. I think that's best, don't you?"

Charlie led Sarah-Jane towards the seat and tried to say 'thank you' but couldn't quite get the words out.

Helen opened the door and stole a brief look before leaving the room. Sarah-Jane and her dad were sitting together in an embrace known only to fathers and daughters, both quietly sobbing on each other's shoulders.

34

Ralph Crossly had been with the *Sunday News* for thirty-two years and had never felt so happy. In fact he was so over-joyed he could hardly speak. But, as fate would have it, he had a speech to make and this was to be his finest, most glorious moment in an otherwise faltering, frustrated career.

"OK, OK, can I have your attention, please?" Ralph paused as he remembered reading somewhere that being the boss meant never having to say 'I'm the boss'. It took a nanosecond for Ralph to feel the adrenalin kick in, big time. Smiling, he mumbled a quiet "sod that" to himself as he panned the eyes of the staff on the *Sunday News* nervously standing in front of him, waiting for some drama.

The seventy-odd staff on duty at that point had been emailed to expect an important announcement at 3.35 p.m. sharp. Ralph suddenly stepped on top of a work station desk and let rip: "Listen, you half-wits. I'm the Daddy now so shut the fuck up, all of you, right now."

A shocked silence followed the outburst; this wasn't the old dog Ralph Crossley the staff had been treating with barely disguised apathy for as long as they could all remember. Not sure whether the 'new' Ralph was on the wrong drugs or to be taken seriously, the group, as one, erred on the side of caution and did as Ralph commanded.

"Why, thank you so much my esteemed and lucky colleagues. I say lucky because you're all still in work – today at least – unlike your boss Simon. That youthful bundle of energy, that great shining beacon of skill and outside-the-box-thinking, the one and only Simon Hall is, I must announce with no regret whatsoever, no more the boss. If the penny hasn't already dropped here it is – our puppet masters have seen the light. Yes, the day of reckoning has come, and yes, Ralph Crossley, is now *the man*."

Ralph Crossley stood as upright and proud as he ever had in life and surveyed the wide-eyed, frightened-looking, completely mute audience. Then something happened. Maybe initially out of fear or shock or because no one really knew what to do a round of applause started which grew into a crescendo of whoops, cheers and whistles.

Ralph smiled broadly and gestured for the noise to abate.

"Simon Hall was told by our esteemed owners across the pond to leave the building and join us at precisely 3.45 which is right now. Right on cue, I see Simon has graced us with his presence. Simon, thanks for coming. This is your leaving do, so enjoy, please. I know I will. Simon, you must have been informed by now that the reason you're here, right now, is to be told, in person by me that you are hereby formally and irrevocably sacked. Let me tell you one of the reasons why. Simon, you lied. You lied to your bosses and to me. You manipulated and distorted the legal position of what we were doing and jeopardized everyone's future here at the *Sunday News*. You can give your side to the jury when you face the charges of interfering with computers in court. I'll say no more about that on legal advice. I've been told I'm allowed to say: 'May justice prevail'. Anyway, you're due a package, Simon. Here it is."

Ralph pulled out from inside his trousers what looked

like a small bone, rubbed it against his groin like a cricket player and bowled it in Simon's general direction without any intended accuracy.

"Tucked inside that bone – which is hollow plastic not the real thing – *such poignancy ladies and gentlemen* – is your leaving package. Go fetch. If you don't want to go fetch then I'll email your lawyer the basic legal package instead which is not so… generous. There's a choice for you, you lying, scheming, over-rated, arrogant dick-head. It's been a pleasure, now pick up your bone and in the words I've been asked to convey on behalf of our esteemed owners: 'go fuck yourself'."

***

"Well, this is a lot better. About time." David peered through his sunglasses and took a long satisfying look at the crystal clear emerald coloured sea in front of him. "I'm glad we agreed on Greece; the sea is warm, the breeze is heavenly. Happy days, Helen, happy days."

David looked over his shoulder in Helen's direction. The joy it gave him to cast his eyes on Helen Pope in all her bikini-clad glory, cocktail in hand could not be expressed in mere words.

"Well, I thought it best if we took some time out to think about things. The timing seemed right."

David took another sip from his cold beer and stared up to the gloriously blue sky through his designer sunglasses and lifted his state-of-the-art tablet into view.

"Wow. This looks interesting. News just in; let me read you a bit. 'Ralph Crossley has been appointed the acting chief executive of the *Sunday News*, taking over from his former boss, Simon Hall who is to be charged with computer hacking.'"

"Really?" Helen pretended not to be interested. "Is that it?"

"There's more. Listen to this: 'Apparently the dismissal by veteran reporter Ralph Crossly of his former boss Simon Hall was one of the most brutal corporate sackings ever known throughout the history of The Street of Shame. Unconfirmed reports allege Simon Hall was thrown a bone – I mean literally a bone – and told to leave without notice in front of the whole staff.' Had it coming, I suppose."

Helen sighed a weary sigh, took another sip from her early morning cocktail and let the moment pass without comment. "I guess that's what Charlie meant when he said there's room for only one silverback in his jungle."

"OK," said David, "I'm sure we'll see a full replay on YouTube, but getting back to our world, we've a lot to think about. Have you actually read Charlie Macqueen's offer? It must be over a hundred pages long. I don't even understand it."

"Paperwork never was your strong point, David. American lawyers will always use three words when one will do. I can't say I understand it all either. But I get the gist of it."

David turned over to take the heat off his bright red stomach. "OK, give me, you know, the gist of it."

"In a nutshell, Charlie wants to become a shareholder in our business. He wants a stake, twenty-two and half per cent to be exact."

"That's a very precise number."

"Tax advisers tend to be very precise."

"OK, he wants a cut of the business. What else?" David,

for some reason, was already bored with the detail.

"Well, you know all the legal stuff that comes from being a shareholder."

"You've lost me already. Did I recall seeing a figure somewhere, a large figure?" David smiled in anticipation of enjoying the next round.

"Yes, there is a figure in there. It's… now let me think… oh yes, 'ten point five'."

"'Ten point five what?'"

It was Helen's turn to take another sip from the cocktail placed on the table next to her heavily padded sun bed. "That will be ten point five million dollars, roughly."

"Ten and a half million dollars for a twenty-two and a half per cent stake in our business. Hmm, that's some offer."

"It's some business."

David sort of dozed off for a few moments and came back to life with a start and sat up.

"Ten and a half million dollars? Really?"

"Really."

"So, we're going to accept this offer?"

"I'm not sure."

"You're not sure? I'm not sure what you're not sure about."

Helen took off her sun glasses and sat up facing David.

"*The Place* is all about balance, equilibrium. I mean just because it says that on our website doesn't mean it isn't true." Helen suddenly realised why she didn't like alcohol. "We don't need the money, we need each other. And I think we've found the answers to a lot of the questions JC has been raising about who does what, the food and the chores, even the martial arts activities…"

"I can't believe you can be talking about ten and a half

million dollars one moment and frigging chores the next."

"Look over there. Go on, look down the beach."

David peered through his sunglasses and caught sight of a carefree, young, happy and clearly besotted couple, sitting next to each other on the otherwise deserted golden sand as the gentle waves lapped their feet.

"Have you ever seen JC so happy? And look at Metti, doesn't she look so in love? I'm so glad we agreed to bring her with us, that was such a smart call."

David took another look and had to accept that the sight of young Metti was quite glorious. "I have to confess I didn't see that one coming."

"I did. A woman can always tell, you know. You're a lovely, lovely man David but emotional intuition is not your strength, in fairness."

"OK, I get it. It would solve quite few issues if Metti moved in. She's very well read, you know. But I'm a bit worried about Charlie. I mean he's probably not used to the 'no' word. Might he – you know – turn on us? Have you thought about that?"

Helen smiled as if she had already thought about that one.

"I don't think so. Not now that Sarah-Jane is training to be a therapist and is moving out on her own for the first time in her life. He's got what he really wanted – a relationship with his independent daughter. No, he's not going to wreck us because he knows that would wreck his relationship with Sarah-Jane. Sarah-Jane and I – as they say over there – are *real tight*. And she's got over her little infatuation with JC – I mean thank God for that. What I'm going to do is visit Charlie and Sarah-Jane in LA before we get back to work at *The Place*. I'm sure we can do business together in some way David, which is what he really wants. Maybe a little franchise arrangement. We can think about that one; no rush from our side. Anyway, point is, I reckon we've got four days left before we'll be as busy as we've ever been."

David sat up again, slightly worried. "Is there something you know that I don't?"

"Sure is. I wanted you to have a little break before I told you but you've kind of forced my hand on that one. You remember Mandy, Mandy Haddock."

"Of course I do. Go on."

"Well, Mandy went back on the set and made all sorts of demands. From what I've heard she's a different person. The upshot is that the producers faced a near riot from all the other actors. It's all got very messy, complicated and just so stressful for them all."

"And what has this got to do with us?"

"In four days the whole cast – well just the core cast of six and one of the producers – are all turning up for some good old-fashioned group therapy as a sort of make or break weekend. We've been highly recommended. And there's premium money on offer for a kind of exclusive zone just for them. Gootsy will have a field day with that lot, bless him. Let's hope we have no mishaps with this lot."

David let out a deep sigh and took a gulp of beer. "I think we'll be all right." David took another look at JC and Metti who were holding hands and walking along the beach towards them. "All we need is some serene equilibrium, and I think I see that right in front of me."